HOME *With* YOU

SHIRLEE McCOY

ZEBRA BOOKS
KENSINGTON PUBLISHING CORP.
http://www.kensingtonbooks.com

ZEBRA BOOKS are published by

Kensington Publishing Corp.
119 West 40th Street
New York, NY 10018

First Printing: March 2018
ISBN-13: 978-1-4201-4522-9
ISBN-10: 1-4201-4522-3

eISBN-13: 978-1-4201-4523-6
eISBN-10: 1-4201-4523-1

10 9 8 7 6 5 4 3 2 1

Printed in the United States of America

HOME IN HIS ARMS

She took another step back and bumped into a swing that hung from a thick branch.

Not a tire swing.

No. That would have made things too easy.

This was a long plank of wood that hit at thigh level. She stumbled, fell backward and probably would have done the least graceful flip in the history of mankind if Sullivan hadn't grabbed her by the waist.

He pulled her upright, his hands resting just above her hip bones, his fingers splayed along her lower spine. Her heart did that thing again. The one where it just kind of stopped and then started beating so fast she thought it might jump right out of her chest.

"Thanks," she murmured, and he nodded, but he didn't release her.

She didn't want him to.

Which was stupid and dangerous and asking for trouble.

But, she couldn't make herself move away, and she couldn't make herself tell him to let her go. . . .

Books by Shirlee McCoy

The Apple Valley Series
THE HOUSE ON MAIN STREET
THE COTTAGE ON THE CORNER
THE ORCHARD AT THE EDGE OF TOWN

The Home Sweet Home Series
SWEET HAVEN
SWEET SURPRISES
BITTERSWEET

The Bradford Brothers
HOME WITH YOU

THE MOST WONDERFUL TIME
(with Fern Michaels, Stacy Finz, and Susan Fox)

Published by Kensington Publishing Corporation

Chapter One

Here's how it all went down:

She'd been sitting at the kitchen table, minding her own business, trying to eat breakfast. She'd had the newspaper in just the right position to block her view of Lu and the little glass cup that held Lu's false teeth. Nearly two months living back on the homestead, and she knew the routine. No Internet. No TV. Five a.m. breakfast followed by mucking out the stalls and feeding all twelve of Lu's therapy horses.

So, yeah . . .

She'd been trying to eat breakfast before she mucked the stalls. Multitasking, munching on toast and searching the help-wanted section of the local paper for a job.

God knew, she had to have one of those.

Lu needed money, and Rumer was going to make sure she had it. She'd already emptied out her savings and cashed in her 401(k), but there were still medical bills to pay. She'd be able to go back to teaching in Seattle once Lu recovered enough, but right now her only option for making money was finding a job somewhere local. Until she managed to do that, finances were tight.

That made Lu worry.

Worry wasn't good for someone who'd had triple bypass surgery. That being the case, Rumer had decided to get a job or two and put every dime she made into paying off Lu's remaining medical bills. When she went back to Seattle at the beginning of the next school year, she wanted to know that Lu was going to be okay both physically and financially.

And, *that's* why she'd been sitting at the tiny kitchen table in Lu's tiny house ignoring the false teeth and looking for work. If things had played out the way they had for the past couple of weeks, she'd have seen nothing in the help-wanted section, dumped the remainder of her toast in the scrap bucket, and headed out to do the chores. But, in one of those cosmic twists of fate or moments of divine intervention, Lu had shoved another paper across the table and directly in front of Rumer.

"Rumer Truehart," she'd said, tapping the page. "Take a look at that."

That had been the gossipy little newspaper that was published in the next town over: the *Benevolence Times*. Lu had been having the paper delivered for as long as Rumer could remember.

"What is it you want me to see?" she'd asked, glancing at the black print but not interested in reading the byline. She wasn't much for gossip. Probably because she'd so often been fodder for it.

"The county fair is two weeks from now." Lu had jabbed at the announcement. "Bet they'll have some horses and ponies."

"You already have twelve," Rumer had pointed out reasonably. She hadn't wanted to start an argument. She hadn't wanted to remind Lu of the medical bills or the cost of feed for the horses. She'd just wanted to get on with her morning.

"So? What's that got to do with the price of tea in China?" Lu had huffed. True to form, she hadn't taken kindly to having her plans questioned.

"Twelve is a lot." *Especially for someone who had a heart attack and nearly died.* Rumer hadn't added the rest of what she was thinking. Lu knew the truth.

She just hadn't wanted to admit it.

"If we train one more horse, I can accept three more children into the program." She'd folded her arms across her narrow chest, her black eyes blazing in her tanned and wrinkled face. She'd looked like what she'd always been—a hardworking, no-nonsense fighter who was used to doing things her way.

"I can't stay to train horses, Lu."

"Who said anything about you doing the training?"

"You said *we.*"

"Figure of speech," Lu had insisted. They'd both known she was lying. "I am perfectly capable of training my own dang horses, and if you say any different it will piss me off." Lu had shuffled over to the counter and poured herself a cup of coffee. Decaf because Rumer had done the shopping.

"I don't want to piss you off. I want to make you see reason."

"What's reasonable about sitting in this house day after day? I've been cooped up for too long. I'm getting antsy."

She was always antsy, always moving, always doing.

Rumer could have pointed that out, but she'd sworn six ways to Sunday that she wasn't going to argue with her grandmother. So, instead of pointing out the obvious, she'd grabbed the *Benevolence Times* and skimmed the article. That was when she'd noticed the ad. Right there on the bottom left.

Help wanted. Pleasant Valley Organic Farm. Full-time housekeeper / gardener / cook. Experience with children a plus. Live in or live out. Call Sullivan to set up an interview.

Pleasant Valley Organic Farm had sounded like a new-age hippie commune: Men with scraggly beards and bare feet. Women in long skirts and tank tops. Kids running around with dirty faces. Not her ideal job opportunity, but beggars couldn't be choosers, so Rumer had decided to check it out.

She'd waited until a decent time and called. When the phone had gone unanswered, she'd decided to find the farm and apply in person. She'd climbed into Lu's old pickup and headed for Benevolence, Washington, humming along to the oldies station as she drove. Ten miles outside of the little town, she'd found the sign for Pleasant Valley Organic Farm and had headed up the long, windy road that seemed to lead to it. She'd been able to see the farmhouse in the distance—a two-story traditional-style that someone had painted buttercup yellow.

Yellow!

She'd taken a quick peek at the slacks she'd borrowed from Aunt Minnie. Yellow polyester. Bell-bottom. Probably from the seventies. Minnie never got rid of anything. She had an entire lifetime of stuff shoved into the double-wide trailer she lived in. It sat on the eastern edge of the homestead, a small hothouse and huge garden right behind it.

Rumer had been thinking that maybe the yellow slacks and yellow house were a sign, a portent, a hint from God that the job was hers. That after six weeks of near hell, things were finally going to get better.

And, then she'd looked up at the road again . . .

She'd looked up, and the girl was right there!

Wandering out from between overgrown field grass, skin glowing rich brown in the midmorning light. Pink tutu shimmering. Ivory tank top hanging loose. Boots clomping. A bouquet of fall flowers clutched in her hand.

Rumer had had about three seconds to take it all in, and then she'd swerved, bouncing off the road and straight into a rain culvert. Nose down, steam spilling out of the hood.

She'd scrambled out of the truck, her purse hooked over her shoulder, and the girl had still been there. Standing right in the middle of the road, gawking at the wrecked truck.

And *that's* how Rumer had ended up here.

On a dirt road.

With a strange kid who was dressed in nothing but a tutu, a thin-strapped tank, a tiara, and bright green rain boots.

"Hello," she said, because what else would she do? She sure wasn't going to let the kid wander back to wherever she'd come from. Half naked and alone. It was chilly, for God's sake. Early fall in eastern Washington, and winter was gaining the upper hand.

The little girl cocked her head to the side, eyeing Rumer with a look that was both suspicious and mutinous.

"Who are you?" she finally replied, every word enunciated and precise. Surprising, because she didn't look older than three.

"Rumer Truehart. How about you? What's your name?" She crouched so that they were eye level, offering a smile.

She got a scowl in response.

"I'm not supposed to talk to strangers," the girl said, her eyes so dark Rumer could barely see the pupils. "Not even if they offer me candy. Do you have candy?"

"No, I don't. I do have a jacket, though. And, it's cold. How about I let you wear it?" She shrugged out of the yellow jacket that matched the slacks. Minnie had insisted she wear both. A job interview was important, and Rumer couldn't go in the jeans and T-shirts she'd brought from home.

Rumer could have and would have.

But . . . again: She'd promised not to argue with her grandmother and that meant she also couldn't argue with Minnie in front of her. So, she'd put on the pantsuit and the pretty white eyelet blouse that went with it.

She held out the jacket, and the little girl snatched it from her hand.

"I'm not cold," she declared as she struggled to get her arms into the sleeves with the bouquet still in her hand. Pink and purple petals floated to the ground as her hand and the flowers popped out through the armhole. "But, thank you very much for this."

She had a lisp.

Which would have been totally adorable if they'd been anywhere but on that road with not another adult in sight. The kid had parents somewhere. Parents who obviously were not doing their job.

"You're very welcome. I bet your mom will be happy that you've got a jacket," she said, hoping to break the

ice and get a little more information about the girl and
her family.

One minute, the girl was looking at the jacket's
daisy-shaped buttons, the next she was crying. Not loud
sobs. Just silent tears sliding down her cheeks.

"Mommy is at the hothpital," the girl said, the lisp
suddenly more pronounced.

"Are you trying to get to her?" Rumer guessed, because why else would the child be wandering around
carrying a wilted bouquet of flowers?

"I'm making her medicine." She sniffed back more
tears and waved the flowers in front of Rumer's face.

"Medicine?"

"Yep! Heavenly read me a book about a boy who
climbed a mountain to pick a flower that would make
his best friend better. One flower is good. Ten flowers
is better." She waved the bouquet again.

"Who is Heavenly?" she asked.

"My sister. She's twelve. I'm six."

"You're—" *Tiny* was on the tip of her tongue.

She didn't say it.

Six-year-olds didn't often want to be told they were
little.

"Is she taking care of you today?" she said instead.

"Nope. She's making cake for Twila. It's her birthday."

"Is Twila also your sister?"

"Yes, she is," the girl said emphatically. "And no one
better say she's not! Markie Winston tried it, and I
popped him right in the nose. He was bleeding and
everything." She swung her free hand in a wide-arcing
left hook. "Now I can't go back to school until Wednesday. The man is not happy about it."

"The man?"

"Yeah." She dropped her fist and leaned close. They were nearly nose to nose, and Rumer could see the trail of drying tears on her cheeks and a thin pale scar near her hairline. There was another one right beside her lip.

"He's not so good at kids," the girl whispered. "Heavenly says that's what happens when you get old without ever having children."

"Who is he?" Certainly not the girls' father. Maybe a relative who'd been called in to help while their mother was in the hospital?

"My uncle. Daddy's brother. Daddy is dead, so he had to come and help out while Mommy is in the hospital." The whisper had gotten softer, and Rumer almost didn't hear the last part.

She saw the tears, though.

They were rolling down the girl's face again.

"Oh, honey," she said, giving her a gentle hug. "I'm so sorry about that."

"Me too," the girl wailed, her skinny arms wrapping around Rumer's waist, the flowers rustling as they smashed against her back.

The sun was warm and bright and high, the sky blue, the air crisp. The dirt road stretched toward the yellow house and the horizon, tall grass and trees dotting the landscape. All of it picturesque and perfect. Except for the little girl standing brokenhearted in the middle of all of it. Alone except for the stranger who'd found her.

It was just so . . . *wrong!*

As soon as Rumer got the little girl calmed down, she was going to find the uncle and give him a piece of her mind. She didn't care if he was ancient as days. He should still have more sense than to let a six-year-old out of his sight. Sure, this area was rural. Sure, most people were pleasant, kind, and helpful, but there were predators everywhere. Not to mention the river, the woods, the roads that crisscrossed the land.

She brushed her palms down the girl's cheeks, wiping the tears away.

"How about I take you home? You can put your flowers in a vase and bring them to your mother the next time you go to the hospital," she suggested.

"I'm not bringing her flowers." The girl's chin quivered, but she'd stopped crying. "I told you: I'm making medicine. I'm going to bake it into magic cookies, and Mommy will eat them and wake up."

It would be hard for someone who was asleep to eat, but Rumer wasn't going to point out the flaw in logic.

"How about we go do that, then?" she asked. "Do you know how to get home?"

"Why wouldn't I? Mrs. Bridget says I'm just about the smartest first-grader she's ever met."

"She's your teacher?"

"Yes. She lets me read the second-grade books. She also sent me to the office when I punched Markie."

"Violence is never the answer."

"Maybe not, but it still felt good!" the girl responded, skipping ahead, her tiara glinting in the sun.

Rumer had to jog to keep up. Not easy to do in her borrowed shoes. Two-inch cream-colored pumps that Minnie had insisted she wear, because the slacks were too long, and not one woman in the Truehart family could fix that. They could muck stalls, train horses, teach kids. They could cook, clean, and organize. They could even run a very well-respected nonprofit, milk goats and cows, make cheese, plant and harvest a garden. What they could not do—had never in the history of Truehart women been able to do—was find a good man or sew a straight hem.

So, yeah, she was tottering on the heels, trying to not fall face-first into the wheatgrass. She didn't notice that they'd taken a sharp turn through the field until she jogged onto a gravel path that cut across a fenced cow pasture. Her foot slipped on loose pebbles, and she went down. Legs one way. Arms the other.

She landed with a solid thump that knocked the wind out of her.

She must have closed her eyes on impact, because she opened them and was looking straight up at the bright blue sky.

"You okay, Rumer Truehart?" the little girl said, suddenly at her side and peering into her face.

"Fine. I'm just not used to wearing heels."

"Mommy says they take practice. Maybe you should practice more." She offered her hand, and it was as tiny as the rest of her.

"That's a good idea, poppet," Rumer said as she got to her feet and brushed dirt off her slacks.

"Poppet?" She giggled, the sound like a creek bubbling over smooth stones. "Is that the same as puppet?"

"No. It's—"

"Moisey!" a man called from somewhere to their left. "Moisey Bethlehem Bradshaw! You'd better get your butt moving and get back home."

The girl froze, her dark eyes widening.

"That's the man!" she said. "And, he said *butt*!"

"Moisey!" someone else called. Female and young from the sound of it. "You're not going to get even one teeny tiny piece of cake if you don't hurry up home!"

"Coming!" the little girl yelled, and took off running, her scrawny legs churning beneath layers of pink tulle.

Rumer followed, abandoning her heels so she could keep up, racing across rough gravel and then onto soft grass.

The house was straight in front of her, maybe a quarter of a mile away, the clapboard siding well cared for, the whitewashed front porch railings sturdy and practical-looking.

Moisey was beelining it across the yard. No time wasted now. She was a girl on a mission, her tutu swishing, her rain boots gleaming in the sunlight.

Must have been the threat of no cake.

"Moisey?!" the man called again, and this time Rumer saw him coming around the side of the house.

He had to be the girl's uncle. She'd expected gnarled, stooped, old. She'd expected a cane or a walker, gray hair, chewing tobacco, a spittoon.

She sure as heck had not expected Mr. *GQ* cover model. Mr. Frilly-pink-aprons-make-me-seem-even-more-masculine.

She didn't expect him to be carrying a chubby baby, but there was that, too. A girl was jogging along beside him, dark blond hair in cornrows, big blue eyes filled with anxiety. She was a hot mess: too-short shirt showing three inches of skin, too-tight jeans clinging to bony hips. Red lipstick smeared across her mouth.

And her eyeshadow . . .

Rumer wouldn't even go there.

"Moisey!" the girl cried, running over to Moisey and grabbing her arm. "Where have you been! If Sunday were here she'd shi—"

"Don't," the man cut her off.

"What?" she snapped, whirling on him like they were mortal enemies about to go to war.

"Use foul language in front of your siblings. I've

already been called to the school three times because your brothers are repeating you."

"Don't blame me for the dweebs' problems," the girl said. "They've been brats since the day I got here."

"They are not brats!" Moisey yelled, pulling back her foot in preparation for what Rumer thought would be a well-aimed kick.

Time to put a stop to things.

She stepped forward, lifted Moisey off her feet, and set her down about a yard away from her target.

"Violence," she said, looking into Moisey's angry face, "is never the answer."

"It'd sure feel good," she fumed.

"Not when I kicked you back," the girl retorted.

"Enough, Heavenly. Nobody is kicking anybody," the man said.

Heavenly. The twelve-year-old sister. Only she looked sixteen, and she had trouble written all over her. Rumer recognized it. She'd seen it every time she'd looked at her teenage self in the mirror. Thank God time had tamed some of the wild out of her. Otherwise, she might have ended up like her mother—a burned-out druggy living on the streets.

"So," she murmured. "You're Heavenly."

"And?" the girl responded, giving her a scathing look.

"Heavenly Light," the man said wearily. "Be polite."

Heavenly snorted but kept her mouth shut.

The man's gaze settled on Rumer, his eyes tracking a path from the top of her head to the tip of her toes. She resisted the urge to smooth her hair, straighten her shirt, or brush dirt from her pants. After all, *she* wasn't the one who'd lost a kid. She had nothing to feel defensive about.

"You should keep a better eye on your niece," she suggested. "It only takes a second for children to find trouble. Or for trouble to find them."

He raised a raven-black brow, his jaw tightening.

There were probably a lot of things he wanted to say. It was never fun to have a stranger point out one's mistakes, and he would have been within his rights to tell her off.

Instead, his gaze shifted to Moisey. "I've been made very aware of that these past couple of weeks."

"Being made aware of a situation and doing something about it are two different things."

"I'm aware of that, as well," he responded, a hint of amusement in his eyes. "What I'm not sure about is who you are and what you're doing here."

"Rumer Trueheart." She extended her hand, realizing her mistake the second his palm touched hers. He had warm rough skin that made her think of things she was better off forgetting. He also had an easy smile that he turned on and off so quickly she would have missed it if she hadn't been staring straight into his way-too-handsome face.

"Your niece walked out in front of my truck," she added. "I almost hit her. Now my truck is in a ditch. Fortunately, your niece is fine."

"God," he muttered, smoothing his hand over his hair and eyeing Moisey. "Didn't we agree that you were going to take a nap?"

"I'm too old for a nap," Moisey responded.

"You're also too old to be punching and kicking when you don't get your way. Since you still do both, I figure you still need a nap."

"Sometimes children act out because they aren't sure how to cope with the emotions they're feeling,"

Rumer pointed out, ignoring the little voice in her head that was telling her to keep her mouth shut and walk away. This wasn't her mess. She sure as heck didn't need to stick around and clean it up.

He met her eyes again and frowned. "You're from the county?"

"The county?"

"Social services? CPS? Whatever the heck they call it now." The baby grabbed a handful of his hair, and he winced, gently pulling her dimpled hand away from his head.

"No. I'm—"

"You're from the state tax assessment board, then?"

"Of course not."

"Real estate agent? SPCA? County School board?"

"None of the above."

"Then you must be from the church. We have enough casseroles to last several lifetimes, and I promise I'll bring the kids back to Sunday school once we get a little more settled. Come on, girls. We need to get home before the boys tear the house down." He grabbed Moisey's hand and started walking away. He'd have kept going if Rumer hadn't opened her big mouth.

But, of course, she had.

"I don't suppose you know where Pleasant Valley Organic Farm is?" she called out as the motley little group departed. She hadn't come all this way so that she could go home before she found the guy who'd written the help-wanted ad.

"You're standing on it." He tossed the words over his shoulder but didn't slow his stride.

"I'm here to see Sullivan Bradshaw. Can you point me in the right direction?"

He stopped, turning so they were facing each other again. "I'm Sullivan."

Her heart thumped. One hard quick jerk of acknowledgment. *This* was Sullivan? The guy who needed a housekeeper/gardener/cook who had experience with kids?

"I came about the ad."

"What ad?" Sullivan asked.

"The one you ran in the *Benevolence Times*?" She pulled the newspaper from her oversize purse and tapped the ad. She'd circled it in blue marker. "Housekeeper/Gardener/Cook. Experience with kids a plus." She read it out loud, and he frowned.

"How about you girls go inside?" He handed the baby to Heavenly and released his hold on Moisey. The tween didn't waste time. She marched to the farmhouse like a martyr going to her doom. Moisey dawdled behind, the bouquet of nearly dead flowers losing most of its petals as she twirled and whirled away.

Rumer was so busy watching the girls, she didn't realize Sullivan was moving until he was standing so close she could see flecks of gold in his dark green eyes.

"Can I see that?" he asked, taking the paper before she could respond.

He scanned it quickly. "It's my number, my name, and my situation, but I didn't pay for the ad."

He handed her the paper, his fingertips grazing hers. Heat shot up her arm. She ignored it. Sure, he looked good. Great, even—all that thick black hair with those dark green eyes. Firm full lips, hands that were nicked and scarred and currently speckled with what looked like orange frosting. But he was a man. Men were trouble. At least they were trouble for the Truehart women.

"In that case, I'll get out of your hair," she mumbled, because working for someone like Sullivan was absolutely out of the question for someone like Rumer. That would be like a sugar junky working in a doughnut shop. She was addicted to men who were in the business of breaking hearts. If she found Sullivan attractive—and she did—he must be one of them.

"I didn't run the ad. One of my brothers must have. I've been a little . . . busy. That doesn't mean I'm not interested in hiring someone." His gaze dropped to the cuffs of her too long pants, and he smiled. "Do you normally arrive at job interviews without shoes?"

Damn. She'd forgotten about ditching her shoes. She'd have to hunt them down before she left. And, she *was* leaving, because that's what the new improved version of Rumer Truehart did. She didn't stick around waiting to fall for the next guy who was going to smooth talk her and then betray her. Nope. She walked away.

"Yes," she lied.

"Good. The kids would probably prefer someone who is a little . . . avant-garde."

"I'm sure you'll find plenty of candidates who fit that criteria."

"Currently, you're the one and only. If you're willing to stick around, I'll interview you and look at your résumé after I check on the kids." He glanced at the house and frowned. "They've been left to their own devices for too long."

"It hasn't even been ten minutes," she pointed out.

"With that crew, ten minutes is nine too many."

"Crew? How many children are you talking about?"

"Six."

"That's a lot."

"And, I sure as hell know it." He sighed. "If you're interested in the job, experience with kids is a necessity. Not a plus."

"Actually, Mr. Bradshaw—"

"Sullivan. You do have experience with children, right?"

"I have a bachelor's in special education, and a master's in early childhood development," she responded. "But, I think this job may be a little beyond the scope of what I'm capable of."

"Too bad. It pays well."

She'd already turned and was walking away, determined to listen to the voice in her head that was shouting that she needed to go while the going was good.

"What is your definition of 'well'?" she asked, still walking, because he was trouble, and she had the feeling that every one of his six nieces and nephews was, too.

He named a figure that was just about half her yearly teaching salary. More than enough to pay Lu's medical bills. With the extra, she could have Lu's barn painted, buy feed for the horses for a year and pay someone to plant alfalfa in Lu's sixty-acre field.

"How long are we talking? Six months? A year?"

"Two months. If things stretch out longer, we'll work up a new contract."

"Things?" She swung around to face him.

"My brother and sister-in-law were in an accident. He was killed. She's in a coma. We're not sure how long that will last."

"Moisey mentioned that her father had died and that her mother was in the hospital. I'm sorry for your loss."

"It's been tough. We're all grieving, but right now, making sure that Sunday and the kids are okay is our top priority." He glanced at the house and frowned. "Speaking of which, I really do need to check on them. Why don't you come and meet the rest of the crew? I'll interview you after that."

He headed for the house, and she found herself following, watching the subtle movement of muscle beneath his shirt and the oddly graceful way he carried himself. He was gorgeous, and she was no fool. If she walked in that house and met the rest of Sunday's sad and struggling kids, she wouldn't be able to walk away. That wouldn't be a problem except that there was no way she could work for Sullivan. He was too much of everything she'd told herself she would avoid.

"I think I'll—" *head home* was what she planned to say, but a curtain in one of the windows moved, and Moisey appeared. Face pressed against the glass, a smudge of orange on her cheek, she looked straight at Rumer and mouthed, "Help me."

Rumer smiled, because who wouldn't?

"You'll what?" Sullivan asked. They'd reached the porch, and he jogged up the four steps ahead of her.

"I'll—" She glanced at the window.

Moisey was still there, smiling impishly and licking what looked like a huge glob of orange frosting off her palm. Heavenly appeared behind her, scowled at Rumer and stalked away.

Trouble.

There was way too much of it inside the sweet-looking yellow house. Rumer might not want any more of it in her life, but she couldn't make herself walk away. Not while Moisey was watching.

"I'll enjoy meeting the rest of your nieces and nephews," she finally said. Then, she straightened her shoulders, lifted her chin and followed Sullivan to the front door.

He'd never wanted children.

He wasn't even sure he liked them.

He sure as hell didn't have a clue what to do with them.

How Sullivan had been nominated to be Mr. Mom to Matthias's crew of crazy kids, he didn't know.

Scratch that.

He knew.

He'd made the mistake of taking a sabbatical. He'd planned to spend the entire fall semester writing a research paper on the influence of eighteenth-century women artists. Instead of teaching art history classes at Portland State University, he'd been holed up in his apartment doing research. No obligations except to himself and his research deadlines.

Things had been going well.

Until the middle-of-the-night phone call from Matthias's pastor. Now everything was shot to hell, and—being the only one of the three remaining Bradshaw brothers who didn't have to report to work—Sullivan was in charge of putting out the fires.

There'd been a lot of those.

Both figurative and literal.

He held the door and waited for Rumer Truehart to step inside. Dressed in bright yellow bell-bottoms and a gauzy white shirt. No shoes. Five foot two inches and slender as the reeds that grew in the pond behind the house, she was nothing at all like what he and his brothers had been thinking the kids needed.

They'd been thinking the kids needed a prison warden, but since that wouldn't go over well with CPS, they'd decided a grandmotherly type would work. Not the soft Mrs. Claus kind of grandmother. A hard-nosed, sharp-tongued, gray-haired drill sergeant. Rumer looked more like a flower child—the type who'd pat little hellions on the head and tell them how special they were. She had a degree in special education, though. A master's in child development. Experience with children.

More importantly, she was there.

She might not be the kind of help he'd had in mind, but she was still the best thing to happen to him in weeks.

"Oh my," she said as soon as she'd crossed the threshold.

That was a nicer version of what he thought every time he walked inside. The once immaculate entryway was littered with Legos and Matchbox cars. To the left, a wide doorway opened into a living room that had been torn apart. There were couch cushions on the floor, books tossed on the coffee table, spilled milk on the area rug, a few soggy Cheerios marking the spot where a bowl of cereal had apparently been upended.

Not to mention the fact that Sullivan hadn't dusted or swept in . . .

Well . . .

He'd never done either. Not since he'd arrived. There'd been too many other things taking up his time.

"It's a bit of a mess," he said in what might have been the understatement of the century.

"Well," Rumer said "Okay."

"Okay what?"

"Okay, it's more than a bit, but I've seen worse."

"Really?" he questioned, and she smiled, a sweet little curve of her lips that made her look about the same age as Heavenly.

"No, but I thought you needed some encouragement."

"What I need," he responded, picking his way through the line of toy cars and trains that filled the hallway, "is exactly what the ad said: a housekeeper."

"I can see that." She stepped over Thomas the Tank Engine, her bare toes peeking out from under the too-long cuffs of her pants.

"And, a cook," he added as he walked into the kitchen. The burnt cake that he'd pulled from the oven sat on the counter, the weird pink strawberry color of it turning his stomach. The bright orange frosting was still in the mixing bowl, a spatula sunk to its hilt in the watery mess. This was attempt number three at making a birthday cake for Twila.

Attempt number one and two hadn't been fit to feed Bessie the hog. The kids had told him that. He'd have been more than happy to take it out to the scrap pile anyway, but Twila had been nearly hysterical, worrying that the hog might die from cake poisoning. He'd tossed both cakes in the trash, because he couldn't stand to see her cry. Twila was the easy one. Quiet. Bookwormish. Helpful.

Currently, she was sitting in a chair, a book in one hand, a stopwatch in the other.

"What are you doing?" he asked, grabbing a wad of paper towel and wiping pink cake batter from the counter.

As if that would help anything.

Every surface seemed coated with cake batter or

flecks of frosting. The floor was covered with a thin layer of dry cake mix. An egg had rolled off the counter, the yolk broken and seeping into the old cracked linoleum.

Even the kids were covered with stuff.

Moisey had gotten her hands in the frosting and had it smeared all over her face. Heavenly had orange streaks down the front of her too-short shirt. Little Oya had it in her hair and squeezed between her chubby fingers.

She needed a bath.

God help him!

He'd already been through *that* ordeal several times.

Soap and slippery skin and a chubby baby were not a good combination.

Yeah. Three of four girls were filthy, but Twila was clean as a whistle, glossy dark hair pulled into a neat braid, dark eyes flashing with worry and fear.

"I am watching the clock, Uncle," she said in that clipped precise tone of hers.

"Is there a reason you're doing that?"

"Do you know where the boys are?" she answered, her gaze darting to Rumer, her eyes widening in surprise.

"The boys?" Of course he knew where they were. They were playing forts in the living room.

He frowned.

Except they weren't. The room had been empty.

"Upstairs?" he answered, but he didn't hear them, and Maddox and Milo were never *ever* quiet.

"No. They have gone to get me a present, and I have told them to return in five minutes." She looked down at the watch. "They have two more."

"A present, huh?" Good for them. He'd sure as heck

dropped the ball on that one. He hadn't even known it was her birthday until Heavenly had dragged him away from his research at five o'clock in the morning and told him that they needed to make a cake. Stat.

Five hours later, and he was still trying to get that done.

"What kind of present are they getting you?" He grabbed another wad of paper towel and scooped up the egg. The scrap bucket was supposed to be in the mudroom, but it was sitting next to the door, the foul aroma of mixed-bag rot permeating the room.

He tossed the egg on top of the mess and lifted the bucket.

"A goldfish," she replied. "From the river."

He stopped. One foot in the mudroom. One foot in the kitchen. Entire body suddenly stiff with dread.

"Did you say the river?" he asked, meeting her eyes.

She nodded. Just a little tiny movement of her chin, but God!

The river!

And, two seven-year-old boys who either could or could not swim. He had no idea, because he didn't really know any of these kids. Sure, they were his nieces and nephews, but up until he'd become Mr. Mom, he'd spent a few hours a year with them. Tops!

"Are you sure?" he said, his body cold with fear.

Sunday had lost her husband. If she came out of her coma and found out she'd also lost two sons . . .

"Twila! *Are* you sure?!" he snapped when she didn't answer immediately, and then he felt like an ass, because her chin wobbled, and he knew she was fighting tears.

"Yes. I told them there were not goldfish there, but

they said they could probably find one," she finally said.

And then, of course, he was dropping the bucket, crap sloshing all over the floor and his feet as he took off out the back door, leaving the girls and Rumer Truehart, the burnt cakes, and the mess behind him.

Chapter Two

Rumer ran after Sullivan, because what else was she supposed to do? She certainly wasn't going to stand around hoping for the best. Lu had raised her to be proactive, to get her hands dirty, to act when others wouldn't. Truehart women weren't damsels in distress, sitting in their towers, praying someone would rescue them. They might be terrible at sewing hems and choosing men, but they were damn good at fighting battles for themselves and others.

She followed Sullivan past a new-looking SUV, a faded-red Chevy passenger van, a two-story garage. She chased him across the old dirt road and into a field of wild grass and brambles. In the distance, the Spokane River wound a lazy path across the horizon. Shallow and calm in some areas. Deep and dangerous in others.

People died there all the time. *Adult* people who should know better than to risk being swept away by the current. Little kids didn't usually think past the moment, and she could picture any one of the third-graders she'd taught going off on a goldfish-finding expedition, not giving a thought to rushing water, frigid temperatures, or slippery rocks. She didn't know how old the twins were, but if they were young enough to think there were goldfish in the Spokane, they weren't old enough to be near the river by themselves.

Thanks to Sullivan's quick pace, they crossed the field in record time, sprinted across a bed of wilted wildflowers and headed down the steep embankment that led to the river.

Sullivan seemed to have no difficulty navigating the nearly vertical slope.

Rumer, on the other hand, slipped and slid her way down, reaching for scrub-like bushes that jutted out from the rocky bank, doing everything in her power to not tumble headfirst into the water.

"Careful," Sullivan said, grabbing her hand and helping her the last few feet to the river's rocky shore.

"Thanks," she responded, her hand still in his.

She would have pulled away, but he was running again, tugging her toward a small shed-like structure a few hundred yards upriver. She couldn't see a dock. Just the blue-green river and the pine trees that jutted up from the opposite bank.

"Milo!" Sullivan shouted. "Maddox! You two had better not be playing in the river!"

No response.

"Boys!" he tried again.

Rumer could hear the desperation in his voice, feel the tension in the fingers that were still woven through hers.

He was terrified.

So was she.

The river was rushing past. Other than that, the

morning was silent and still. Eerily so. Nature had movement and sound. When it didn't, trouble was brewing.

"Milo?! Maddox?!" she shouted.

A towheaded boy ran around the side of the boathouse. Maybe seven. Scrawny. Feet kicking up pebbles and sand as he beelined it toward her.

Another boy ran after him, just as blond. Just as scrawny.

"Mom!" the second boy shouted, and Rumer's heart dropped.

He must have heard a female voice and thought his mother was home from the hospital. He was racing toward her, smiling as if every wish he'd ever made had come true.

She knew the moment he realized the truth.

He skidded to a stop a few feet in front of her, his smile disappearing.

"Who the hell are you?" he demanded as his brother stopped beside him.

"Maddox," Sullivan cautioned. "What did I tell you about language like that?"

"Not to use it at school," the boy replied, his eyes still fastened on Rumer. "And, I'm Milo."

"I told you not to use it at all," Sullivan corrected. "And, you're Maddox."

"Prove it." Maddox's hands were fisted, his jaw tight. He had a thick purple scar on the side of his neck that looked like it was from a burn. Another smaller scar peeked out from beneath his too-short jacket sleeves.

"Milo doesn't have a scar on his neck," Sullivan pointed out. "And you don't have one on your cheek."

Maddox's scowl deepened, his gaze cutting from Rumer to his uncle.

If looks could kill, Sullivan would be dead.

"I know things have been tough around here since your parents'—" Sullivan began, his voice gentler than Rumer would have imagined it could be.

"I'm going back to the house." Maddox cut him off, tossing the words over his shoulder as he raced to the embankment and began climbing.

His twin was right behind him, silently following in his footsteps. Aside from the location of their scars, they looked exactly alike: same height, same weight, same hair and eyes. Same lanky arms, long legs, and oversized feet. They'd be tall, one day.

If they survived childhood.

"Damn," Sullivan muttered.

"He seems a little angry."

"His dad is gone. His mother is in the hospital. He's got a clueless uncle living with him. He's a cauldron of boiling rage, and I don't blame him."

"What about Milo?" she asked, watching as the boys reached the top of the embankment and took off. Hopefully for the house.

"I couldn't tell you. He doesn't talk much, and I've been too busy trying to put out the fires his brother is setting to sit down and try to have a heart-to-heart." He started walking, and she followed, her feet digging into soft pebbly earth, the cuffs of Minnie's pants dragging. She would have hiked them up, but the damage had already been done. Both cuffs were stained. She wasn't sure, but she thought one might be ripped.

"A counselor might be able to help all the kids with

this transition," she suggested, picking her way across smooth river rocks and sharp twigs.

"They're seeing the school counselor."

"Is it helping?"

"Does it look like it is?" he asked wryly as he started up the steep slope.

"It's going to take time, Sullivan," she panted as she tried to get up the embankment. That seemed to be as treacherous as going down had been.

Maybe more so, because she wasn't panicking now. She was thinking things through, trying to find hand and toeholds, digging her feet into soft earth and wrapping her fingers around scraggly bushes. She slipped, rocks and dirt rolling out from under her and dropping straight into the river. She hadn't realized how easy it would be to tumble into the Spokane.

"You okay?" Sullivan called.

"Peachy, but falling into the river and drowning will make finding a job a lot more difficult," she murmured as she reached for the next bush.

"That's for damn sure," Sullivan responded, wrapping his hand around her wrist and pulling her up. One minute she was struggling. The next she was at the top, his warm hand still wrapped around her wrist.

And, God! It felt good.

"Thanks," she managed to say, tugging her wrist from his and rubbing at the spot where his fingers had been, trying to will away the warmth that seemed to linger there.

He noticed.

Of course.

His gaze dropped to her wrist, and then settled on

her face. "No problem. Now that you've met the boys, are you still game to be interviewed for the job?"

He was direct and to the point.

She liked that.

What she didn't like was the way she felt when she looked in his gorgeous eyes. The little shivery awakening in the pit of her stomach. The warmth in her cheeks. The way she had to fight to keep her hands at her sides rather than reaching to brush away the smudge of frosting on his neck.

"I might not be the right candidate for the job," she hedged. The pay was great. She could use the money. The kids obviously needed someone who could provide a little stability, a little maternal love, and a whole lot of structure. And, the house. God! The house! That was a mess she could have cleaned up in two shakes of a stick, if she wanted to.

But, Sullivan was trouble.

Lots of it.

And, she'd already decided she was going to avoid that.

"How about you let me decide that?" he asked.

"The thing is—"

"You came here, Rumer. You obviously need a job."

"Just until my grandmother's medical bills are paid off."

"Has she been ill?"

"She had a heart attack and triple bypass surgery. We're fortunate she survived. I took a leave of absence from my teaching job to help while she recovered."

"You're a teacher?"

"I did tell you I had a degree in special education," she pointed out.

"That doesn't mean you had a job in it," he replied.

"I did. I work at a Montessori school in Seattle. I've been there for six years. I'm contracted again for the fall of next year. This year, though, is a bust." They'd reached the road. If she turned east, she could find her way back to the truck, call someone to tow her out of the ditch and go back to the homestead.

But, of course, she kept walking with Sullivan, taking two steps for every one of his.

"And, that's why you're looking for work?"

"Like I said, Lu has medical bills that need to be paid."

"Lu?"

"My grandmother."

"You're on a first-name basis with her?"

"We didn't meet until I was fourteen. I called her Lu to annoy the hell out of her in the hope that she'd send me packing."

"I see," he responded, scanning her from head to toe again.

"I doubt it," she replied, and he shrugged.

"You didn't have an easy childhood. You probably spent time in quite a few different homes before Lu found you. You understand a lot more about being a tween girl like Heavenly than I ever could. As a matter of fact, I'm pretty damn sure you're a grown-up version of my oldest niece," he said matter-of-factly. "Am I wrong?"

No, damn it, he wasn't.

He'd hit every nail straight on the head.

"Look," she said, totally avoiding his question, because there was no way she'd ever admit how right he'd been. "It's obvious you need full-time help. I've got obligations to my grandmother. Until she's able to muck stalls, carry feed, and groom her horses, I need to be there on the weekends when her part-time help isn't. Obviously, that's not going to be a good fit for the job you're offering."

"Why not?" he asked.

"I've already explained," she said. "Lu owns Sunshine Acres. She trains horses for therapy work and has a few dozen clients with a variety of disabilities who come and ride. Most of them like to ride on the weekends. I can't just abandon her on her busiest days."

"I wouldn't ask you to."

"You wouldn't?"

"My brothers have been trying to fly in every weekend to help, so you can have Saturday and Sunday off. Probably Friday evening, too. Will that work?"

"Yes," she said without thinking.

"Great." Sullivan opened a dingy white gate that led into the overgrown backyard, smiling into her eyes as she walked past.

That's when she realized what she'd said.

What she'd agreed to.

"What I mean is, it could work. If you offered the job, and I accepted it. I'd really need to discuss things with Lu. She may need me more than I'm thinking. She's very particular about the way things are done at the homestead."

"Homestead?"

"The farm. That's what she's always called it. No television out there. No cable. No Wi-Fi. She didn't have running water in the house until the year I moved in. She needed it to get approved as my guardian. Otherwise, she probably still wouldn't have it."

"Your grandmother sounds like an interesting person," Sullivan commented, apparently determined to ignore the fact that Rumer had backtracked on her agreement regarding hours of employment.

"Lucille Ball Truehart is one of the most interesting people I've ever met." And, that was the God-honest truth.

"Lucille Ball?" He touched her back as she made her way up the back steps, and the little shiver in her stomach turned into a dozen butterflies taking flight.

"Her mother was big into television when Lu was born."

They'd reached the backdoor.

Finally.

Which was great, because she needed to say her good-byes and be on her way.

"You have an unusual name, too. What was *your* mother into?" he asked.

"Drugs." Once again, she opened her mouth without thinking. Once again, she spoke the God-honest truth.

"Like I said," he responded. "You're a grown-up version of my niece. Right now, she really needs someone like you in her life."

The sincerity in his voice was unmistakable.

It was in his eyes, too. In his face, and she couldn't resist it any more than she could resist loving six kids who were obviously hurting and troubled and in need of a person who understood that.

And, therein lay the crux of the problem.

Rumer never gave just a piece of herself. She was all in or she wasn't in at all, and the Bradshaw kids? They needed all-in. They needed someone who was willing to love them and then let them go. Rumer didn't think she could be that person any more than she thought she could spend five days a week working for Sullivan and not fall a little in love with him.

She knew her strengths and her weaknesses.

This man and those kids?

They were her Kryptonite, her Achilles' heel, the things most likely to shatter her heart.

"I need to go," she murmured, brushing past him and heading back down the stairs.

"Isn't your truck in a ditch?" Sullivan called as she reached the corner of the house.

Right. It was.

"I'll call a tow truck."

"Is it a pickup?"

"Yes."

"I can pull it out for you."

"There's no need—"

"Your truck wouldn't be in the ditch, if my niece hadn't walked out in front of you. The least I can do is pull it out so you can be on your way. Can I have your keys?"

He seemed to understand that she wasn't going to accept the cook / housekeeper / nanny job. That being the case, the sooner she got away from the house, the kids and him, the better.

"They're in the ignition," she said.

"My SUV is over near the barn. We can use that." He was already fishing in his pocket, dragging out car keys.

"You go ahead. I'll walk." Because, she wasn't getting in a vehicle with him. She wasn't going to sit in a warm cab, listening to whatever style of music he liked, making small talk.

That's how things had started with Jake—a broken-down car, a ride home. Three weeks later, their first date and then their second. She'd fallen for his charm and his smile, and she'd told herself that they had so much in common they were guaranteed a happily-ever-after. Both college students studying teaching. Both into jazz music and slow dancing. Neither drank to excess, smoked, or did drugs. Both wanted to settle down after college, get married, have a couple of kids.

Six years, two apartments, and a boatload of heart-ache later, she'd realized that only one of them wanted a monogamous relationship. It wasn't Jake.

"I don't bite, Rumer," Sullivan said with a smile that made her toes curl in the cool grass.

"I'm not afraid of you biting," she responded. *I'm afraid of you breaking my heart.* "I need to find my shoes before I go back to the homestead. They're my aunt's. Vintage. She'll be pissed if they're missing."

"All right," he agreed. "I'll pull your truck out and leave the keys under the mat."

He didn't mention the job again and she told herself she was glad. Walking away was the reasonable thing to do, the best thing.

But she couldn't stop thinking about Moisey dressed in a tutu and tiara wandering away from home. Or the twins, slipping and sliding down the slope that led to the Spokane River.

She reached the side of the house, turned toward the path that led across the field. She'd have followed through with her plan to leave if she hadn't smelled smoke. Not wood smoke, either. This was a burnt pop-corn kind of smoke.

Or burnt cake.

She frowned.

"Just keep going, Rumer," she said out loud, because she needed to hear the words, and she needed to listen to them. "It has nothing to do with you."

Except that it did. There were a bunch of kids in that house, and Sullivan was gone, pulling her truck out of a ditch. If someone died because she hadn't checked things out, she'd never forgive herself.

She hurried back the way she'd come, darting up the back stairs and reaching for the door.

It flew open, and she grabbed it, stepping to the side as smoke and kids poured out.

The twins. Twila. Moisey. Heavenly, the baby in her arms.

She counted heads, then walked inside, Heavenly standing on the threshold and watching as she made her way through black smoke and into the kitchen.

"Why aren't you gone?" Heavenly demanded.

"Take the baby into the yard until I get the smoke cleared," she responded.

Heavenly thrust the baby at Twila. "Hold her while I put out the fire."

"What fire?" Rumer asked, but she could see it now—a charred cake pan sitting in the sink, tiny flames shooting up from it.

She reached over the mess, turned on the faucet and coughed as smoke and steam filled her nose.

"Shit," Heavenly muttered.

"Language," Rumer replied.

"Sullivan is going to hit the ceiling when he sees this mess."

"Who says he's going to see it?"

"There's smoke everywhere." Heavenly dropped into a chair and made a production out of looking at her phone. Obviously, she wasn't keen on having Rumer around.

"The fire is out. Open the windows. Tell your siblings to come inside."

"I figured you were leaving, and you could tell them on your way out."

"You figured wrong." Rumer turned off the water and surveyed the wreck of a kitchen. No child deserved to have a birthday as bad as this one was shaping up to be. No cake. No presents that Rumer could see. Messes everywhere. The smell of slop and smoke filling the house.

"And?" Heavenly was still scrolling through her phone.

"This place is a disaster. So, how about you get your butt out of the chair and do what I asked? We have work to do."

That got Heavenly's attention.

She met Rumer's eyes, and there was no mistaking her surprise and irritation.

"Who died and . . ." Her voice trailed off, because someone *had* died, and she must have realized exactly how childish she sounded.

Smart kid with a big attitude.

The smarts could be cultivated and the attitude could be curbed, but that wasn't anything to do with Rumer. All she wanted was to make sure Twila didn't have the worst birthday of her life. At least, that's what she was telling herself.

She suspected it was a lie.

She really did.

Because, she knew herself, and she knew her weaknesses, and these kids and this house and their trouble? They were it.

"Go on," she prodded. "We don't have all day to make your sister's birthday nice."

Heavenly stared into Rumer's eyes for another couple of seconds, and then she slowly set the phone

down. Slowly got up. Sloooowly went to the back
door. Every bit of her scrawny body screaming her dis-
pleasure.

She probably wouldn't have done it at all if she
hadn't been so shocked by Rumer's insistence.

Rumer grabbed a bottle of dish soap and squirted it
into the blackened cake pan. She could hear Heavenly
yelling for the crew to come inside, and she grabbed a
few dishcloths from a pile near the sink, rinsed them
all with hot water, and was waiting when five kids
tromped through the mudroom and into the kitchen.

"It's time," she said before any of them could escape.
"To get to work."

"What work?" Maddox asked, his hands on his
skinny hips, his eyes flashing with ire. She figured he
was still angry that she wasn't his mother.

"Work that's going to make your mamma happy
when she finally gets home." She held out a rag and he
took it, frowning a little but not arguing.

"If she comes home," Heavenly said morosely. She
was holding the baby again, bouncing her gently to
keep her from fussing.

"I choose to believe that she will. When she does, do
you want her walking into a house caked with food,
mold, and soot?" She handed another rag to Milo and
one to Moisey.

"I do not," Twila said, opening a narrow closet and
pulling out a broom, a bucket, and a mop.

"That's what I thought," Rumer said cheerfully, because at least Twila seemed on board with the plan.
"You guys get to work. I'll start the cake."

"We used the last box of cake mix, so good luck with
that," Heavenly muttered, but she'd grabbed a clean
rag from a drawer and was wiping the baby's face.

"Boxed cake mix is a luxury for the uninspired. We can manage without," Rumer replied, opening the window above the sink and letting cold crisp air swirl in. The place still smelled like burnt food and pig slop. Three of the five old-enough-to-work kids were frozen in place, clutching damp rags and staring at her like she had two heads and a forked tongue.

Or, like she was nuts.

Which she obviously was.

She should be searching for her shoes, not pulling eggs out of the fridge and flour out of the pantry closet, but there she was . . . doing exactly what she shouldn't.

An hour.

That's how much time she'd give herself to make the cake and straighten the kitchen. Any longer than that and she might start feeling things she shouldn't. Like sympathy, obligation, concern.

Who was she kidding?

She already felt all those things, but she was still only giving an hour, because it was Saturday, and Minnie had probably gone off to do her weekly garage sale hunting. Lu's part-time employees only worked weekdays, and at noon, someone would have to check on the horses. Knowing Lu, she'd decide it needed to be done before Rumer or Minnie returned.

Yeah. An hour. That should be just enough time to finish and not enough for Lu to get into trouble.

She eyed the clock, grabbed a clean mixing bowl from a glass-faced cupboard, and began.

Pulling the truck out of the ditch took a little longer than Sullivan expected. First, it was an old truck—a

1970s Ford. Solidly built and heavy. Second, the back bumper was loose, and he'd had to jerry-rig it before he could attach the towline. He managed it with duct tape and rope he kept for emergencies. It felt good to let off a little steam doing something physical that wasn't related to housecleaning or kid herding.

Once he had the bumper secured and the towline attached, it took three tries to get enough momentum from his SUV to drag the beast out. He checked the truck, made sure there wasn't enough damage to keep it from running, placed the key under the driver's side floor mat, and climbed back into his vehicle. Rumer hadn't appeared, yet. She was probably still hunting for her shoes. Either that, or she'd decided to take her chances and hitchhike back to wherever she'd come from.

No way would anyone in her right mind take a job like the one he and his brothers were offering. Not after seeing the house, the kids, the chaos. No. A logical, smart and savvy person would take one look at the situation and run. If Matt hadn't been his brother, if Sunday weren't his sister-in-law, if the kids weren't his nieces and nephews, that's what Sullivan would have done.

As it was, he was stuck.

Matt had been his brother.

Sunday was his sister-in-law.

That made the kids his problem. His very big problem.

He sat in his SUV for a few seconds considering his options for escape. Which were just about none. He was there, thanks to his oldest brother Flynn's planning. "*You're on sabbatical. We both have things to tie up at*

*home. Give us some time to do that. We'll come back and
discuss long-term plans if they're needed."*

Sullivan couldn't deny that the plan was sound or
that it made sense. He'd helped create it, for God's
sake—he and Porter and Flynn sitting up into the early
hours of the morning hashing things out, deciding
what was best for a bunch of kids they barely knew.

God! What a mess!

Three bachelors. No experience. Six kids with backgrounds that would make the hardest heart melt with
sympathy. Sullivan didn't have to read the foster and
adoption files to know they'd all been through hell. He
could see the scars, the defensive postures, the anger.

He scowled, starting the engine and doing a U-turn,
heading back toward the house because it's what he'd
promised to do. He wasn't sure if Matthias had had a
premonition or if he'd just been worried about his
family, but three months ago, he'd called and asked
Sullivan if he'd be guardian to the kids if anything were
to happen to him and Sunday.

Hell no! had been Sullivan's response.

He regretted that now. Regretted that his brother
had gone to the grave with no certainty about the kids'
future. But, Sullivan *had* promised to keep an eye on
things, make certain that whoever was guardian would
do right by his nieces and nephews.

This was a lot closer of an eye than he'd planned,
but he couldn't walk away. Not with Sunday in the
hospital and everything up in the air. If she survived,
great. If she didn't . . .

He didn't want to go there.

Didn't want to contemplate what would happen to
the kids.

Matt hadn't named a guardian in his will.

Sunday hadn't either.

Which meant that the kids had no one unless one of their uncles anteed up and agreed to take them.

More than likely, they'd split the duties. Four-month stints at the farm, because they'd all agreed the kids shouldn't be shuttled from home to home.

They'd agreed, but none of them were happy about it.

Not one of them had planned to return to Benevolence for any length of time. Ever. They'd worked too hard, gone too far in their lives to be rerouted back to the place they'd all escaped. Porter had suggested buying a house in a central location and settling the kids there, but Pleasant Valley Farm was their heritage, and Flynn had every intention of seeing it succeed and watching his nieces and nephews take over running it one day.

The fact that he had a cattle ranch in Texas had probably influenced his perspective, but Sullivan had seen his point. Sunday's family had owned the acreage for five generations. It was the birthright of the next generation, and he wanted the kids to make their own decisions about whether to keep it or not.

Two votes for keeping the kids at the farm. One against.

Porter hadn't been happy, but he'd conceded defeat and agreed to the plan.

And now he and Flynn were back at their homes, tying up loose ends, putting things in place so they could return and be there when Sunday recovered.

Or didn't.

And, Sullivan was here. In the second level of hell, knee-deep in kid crap and attitudes.

He parked the truck and got out.

No noise from the house, so that—at least—was good.

One of the boys had left a scooter near the driveway, and he carried it into the two-car garage, setting it next to a row of bikes, trying not to notice the empty bay. His brother's car should be there. The fancy Corvette that a guy who had six kids didn't need and really couldn't use. Why he'd had it was a mystery, but Sullivan had seen the bent carcass, the crushed metal and shattered windows. The fact that Sunday had survived was a miracle. Matt and the drunk driver who'd hit them hadn't been as lucky.

The medical bills were being paid for. The insurance adjuster had already cut a check for the blue-book value of the Corvette. None of that could bring Matt back or cause Sunday to wake up completely healed. None of it could give the kids back what they'd lost.

He shoved the morose thoughts away.

He had a damn cake to make and a birthday to celebrate.

Twila deserved that. Even if her world was falling apart and all the pieces that had come together to bring her to the USA and to Sunday and Matt and the farm had separated again, she could have cake and a rousing off-tune rendition of "Happy Birthday to You."

He opened the mudroom door, expecting to hear the usual cacophony of noise—twins playing, Heavenly blasting music, Moisey singing something completely different, Oya crying.

He heard . . .

Silence.

And, that was terrifying.

"Kids!" he yelled, barreling into the kitchen, skidding across a wet floor.

"Careful," someone said. "The boys just mopped the floor."

Not someone.

Rumer.

Standing at the sink, scrubbing out a bowl, Moisey beside her with a rag, a pile of sparkling dishes in front of her.

The counter was sparkling, too.

The floor.

The cupboard faces and the pantry door.

All of it . . .

Clean.

"I've been gone twenty minutes," he said, his gaze on the rocking chair that someone had carried from the nursery and set right in the middle of the kitchen floor.

Twila was sitting in it, a plastic crown-like thing on her head, Oya in her arms. She was feeding the baby a bottle and humming quietly.

Tranquility. That's what he was seeing. Quiet. Order. Structure. All the things he'd dreamed about when he was a kid but had never had. All the things he wanted for Matt's kids but couldn't seem to achieve.

"Twenty-five minutes," Rumer responded, wiping her hands on a dishrag and tossing it into a laundry hamper that was sitting nearby. Empty. Not one towel, rag, or piece of clothing in it. "Not that we were counting."

"The truck's bumper was loose," he offered by way of explanation, and she nodded. No smile. Just that nod and steady gaze.

"It needs a little work. Kind of like this house." She said it deadpan, but there was a hint of amusement in her eyes. Blue eyes. Or violet. Or some odd shade in between. He wasn't sure, and found himself staring a little too deeply, searching for a little too long.

If that made her uncomfortable, she didn't show it. She sure as heck didn't look away. She just stared right back.

"By a little," he said. "I'm assuming you mean a lot."

"Something like that," she responded. "Fortunately, many hands make light work." She gestured around the sparkling kitchen. No ring on her left hand. Which he shouldn't have noticed but did.

"The kids did this?"

"Who else?" She walked to the stove, turned on the light, and peered inside. "This has another fifteen minutes. Don't open the door until the timer goes off. If you do it'll sink. Not cute and not yummy."

"It?"

"The cake? It's Lu's pound cake recipe. You'll want to poke it with a toothpick when the timer goes off. If the toothpick comes out clean, the cake is ready. Frosting is here." She opened the fridge and took out a bowl of what looked like whipped cream. "Twila said she wanted strawberry cake. I suggested strawberry-topped cake, and she thought that would be good. Right, hun?" She touched Twila's shoulder, and to Sullivan's surprise, to his absolute shock, Twila smiled.

A sweet, young, unguarded smile. The kind a kid offered when she trusted someone.

"Yes. I think that would be very nice."

"The strawberries are here." Rumer pulled a bowl from the fridge and held it up. "Just a little sugar to bring out the juices. Let the cake cool before you cut and top it. No need to frost the whole thing. Just slice it, plate it, and pile on the whipped cream and strawberries. Extra for our birthday girl."

She lifted the laundry basket and carried it into the mudroom, still talking about the cake and birthdays, candles and singing. He followed her, walking into the narrow room and watching as she tossed the dirty rag into the washing machine.

"I'm turning this on," she said, closing the door and pushing start. "If you forget to put the load in the dryer when it's finished, you're going to have a mess of stinky, moldy towels and dishrags."

"I may not know how to make a cake, but I sure as heck know how to do laundry," he said dryly, and she grinned.

"Great, because I had the kids gather all their dirty clothes and pile them on the couch in the living room. Milo is separating light and dark. He's been at it for a while. Must be quite a lot of clothes."

"There are seven people in the house," he pointed out.

Her grin widened. "Right. And, when was the last time any of you ran a load of laundry?"

"Probably . . ." Never. Not that he could recall. "Things have been a little crazy around here. Their mom is in a hospital in Spokane. That's a forty-minute drive each way."

"That's hard, Sullivan," she responded, all her amusement gone. "It's difficult on all of you, but kids need structure and order and routine. I don't want to stick my nose too far into your business, so I'll just say that a weekly chore chart would be a good idea. Incentives tend to work with kids. A little cash or a special treat. Some kind of carrot dangling in front of their noses."

She had a point.

A good one.

He wasn't all that keen on sitting down and putting the chart together, but Twila was the kind of kid who'd probably love it.

"And, don't ask Twila to make the chart just because she's the most organized," Rumer said as if she'd read his mind. "Heavenly is the oldest, and she's just as capable. Putting her in charge might win you a few points with her. Then again"—she straightened and moved toward the back door, grabbing her purse from a hook on the wall—"it might not. Good luck with everything! Thanks for towing the truck out. See you around!"

She was outside before he could respond, walking down the steps and into the yard. Bare feet and arms. Pretty little white shirt and butter yellow bell-bottoms. Wild curls and grass stains. And, his only chance of surviving the next few days or weeks or months. It wasn't like anyone else was knocking on the door begging for the job his brothers had advertised.

He frowned, walking back through the mudroom and into the kitchen. Someone had left the window cracked open, but the oven seemed to be keeping the room warm. He could smell the cake—sugar, butter, vanilla. Caught a hint of smoke and laundry detergent beneath it all. Somewhere outside, a kid was giggling, the sound carrying in on a cool fall breeze.

This was what home should be. He'd been working toward it since he'd arrived with no success. The kids fought him tooth and nail. They fought one another. They fought at school.

Every. Single. Damn. Day.

"I like her," Moisey said, breaking the tranquil silence. "You should bring her back."

"It might be hard to convince her to come after the mess she saw today," he said bluntly.

Too bluntly, because Moisey's face crumbled and a tear slipped down her cheek. She wiped it away with her sleeve.

No. Not *her* sleeve.

She was wearing a yellow jacket that hung off one shoulder and fell nearly to her ankles. Butter yellow. The same color as Rumer's bell-bottoms.

"Sorry, kiddo," he mumbled, crouching so they were face-to-face. He didn't touch her. He'd made that mistake the first time he'd seen her cry, trying to pull her in for a hug that she didn't want. She had a killer left hook. "Tell you what. Once the cake is done and we've had Twila's birthday, I'll call Rumer and talk to her."

"You will?" She eyed him with a mixture of suspicion and hope.

"Sure."

"You promise?"

He hesitated. Promises weren't his thing. He'd heard too many of them made, seen too many of them broken. But, this was a small thing. An easy thing. A phone call. He hadn't gotten Rumer's phone number, but there couldn't be many horse therapy programs in the area. He doubted there was more than one run by someone named Lu. It should be easy enough to track Rumer down. He'd make the call. He'd offer the job. She'd accept or decline and life would go on. "I promise."

"That you're going to talk to her, right?" Moisey said, still not quite believing him.

"I'll talk to her."

"Not just her voice mail?"

"Moisey Bethlehem, I said: I'll talk to her," he responded, exasperated.

Something flitted in her eyes and across her face. There. Gone.

"You sounded just like Daddy," she whispered, and then she ran off, the too-big jacket trailing on the floor behind her.

Chapter Three

Snow started falling right around sunset, giant flakes fluttering through fading light, coating the ground and trees with a glittery layer of white. Rumer watched the swirling flakes, listened to the soft whistle of wind beneath the eaves, and wished she were anywhere but in Lu's kitchen cleaning up after one of Minnie's infamous spaghetti pie dinners. She'd only eaten three or four bites, but she felt like she had a lead weight in her stomach. And, the mess.

God!

How could a woman as smart as Minnie manage to create this kind of kitchen chaos: sauce on the counters, the floors, the cupboards. Sticky bits of pasta everywhere. Cheese smashed into the grout in the tile floor.

Maybe cleaning it wouldn't have been so bad if she hadn't already spearheaded the cleaning effort at Pleasant Valley Organic Farm.

Two horrendous kitchen messes in one day was too much.

She dunked a bowl into steaming water, the scent of

garlic and parsley filling her nose. She wanted to gag, but she didn't think Minnie would appreciate it. She stood a few feet away, squirting cleaner on the oven and trying to scrub off caked-on goo. She'd been at it for ten minutes, and Rumer was beginning to think she was purposely being slow so she wouldn't have to deal with the rest of the mess she'd created.

"I'm thinking next time, we order in," Lu muttered, grabbing a plate from the drying rack, swiping a cloth over it, and placing it in the cupboard.

"That might be a good idea," Rumer agreed.

"Why?" Minnie was still scrubbing at whatever had been cooked onto the stovetop. "You didn't enjoy my cooking?"

"I enjoyed it about as much as I enjoyed my heart attack," Lu responded.

"That's real nice, Ma," Minnie mumbled, running the rag under the faucet and going back to the stove.

"I wasn't trying to be mean, Min," Lu responded. "I was just making a statement of fact. You're good at other things. No need to be upset if you don't have a talent for the culinary arts."

"What does talent have to do with it?" Minnie finished at the stove and went to work on the floor, swishing the mop around over bits of congealed sauce and noodles. "It's all about measuring," she continued. "If you measure the ingredients properly, the dish will always turn out."

"You must have been distracted and measured wrong," Lu insisted. Just like she did every time Minnie cooked. They'd been having this same tired argument for as long as Rumer had known them.

Thirteen years.

It seemed like forever and no time at all.

"Of course, I was distracted. Seeing my beautiful daffodil suit—"

"Daisy," Rumer corrected absently.

"What?" Minnie stopped mopping and speared her with a look that would have stopped the tongue of most people.

Not Rumer.

She knew her aunt well enough to know she was more bluster than bully. "There were daisy buttons on the jacket. Not daffodils."

"I was referring to the color," Minnie huffed. "The color it was before you dragged it through dirt and mud and stomped on it," she added.

"I explained what happened, Minnie, and I promised to replace the suit."

"Replace? Replace!? That is a genuine nineteen-seventies original. It can't be replaced."

"I'll get you something else, then. I'm sure I can find a vintage outfit at Goodwill or Andrea's Clothes Cupboard."

"Andrea's Clothes Cupboard is a disaster. Bugs and cigarette smoke. The stuff she's offering for sale reeks." Minnie smoothed her raven-black hair, the pixie cut she preferred only adding to her gamine appearance. Like Rumer, she had small bones and a delicate build. Rumer's mother had been tall and curvy and beautiful. At least, in all the photos Lu had, Victoria was those things. In Rumer's memory, she was sallow-skinned and blank-eyed, head thrown back and mouth gaping open. Scrawny. Anxious. Picking at her skin and refusing food.

"I'll drive out to Spokane. They'll have something there." Rumer wasn't in the mood for arguing with her aunt. She hadn't been in the mood for overcooked spaghetti pie. As a matter of fact, she hadn't been in the mood for much of anything since she'd left Pleasant Valley Farm.

The problem was, she kept picturing Heavenly—her scrawny body shoved into too-tight clothes, her eyes filled with more knowledge than a twelve-year-old should have. She kept wondering if she should have said something to Sullivan, told him to keep an eye on her, make sure she didn't get into the kind of trouble girls like her tended toward.

She could have named every single one of them.

She'd lived them all. Survived them. Overcome them. Thanks to Lu and Minnie.

Thinking about that made her soften, and she sighed, rinsing the last pot and draining the sink. "I really am sorry, Minnie. I should have been more careful."

Minnie raised a raven-black brow. "I accept your apology, and I'm sorry for being such a grinch about it. You know how I am about my stuff."

"Insane?" Lu cut in, and Minnie smiled.

"There's some truth in that. I'll admit it. But, I like what I like, and I'm not going to change that."

"As long as you have your own place to keep all that stuff you like, it's not my business. Speaking of which, Dana Wilson called me today. She said she was at your place for a consultation, and you had so many boxes piled up in the living room, she could barely make it through to your office."

"Dana needs to stop gossiping. That's why she's got so many problems with her stomach," Minnie said.

"Yeah. Well, she said the boxes are a hazard, and you know how she is. She'll probably mention it to Derrick, and then he'll put on his county inspector hat and pay you a visit. After all my medical stuff, that's the last kind of trouble either of us need."

"Derrick may be her husband, but he and I go way back. He's not going to come to my house without a warning. Not that it matters, I'm cleaning stuff out. Those boxes are filled with items I'm donating."

"Donating?" Lu sounded as surprised as Rumer felt.

"Don't act so surprised, Ma. Even old horses can be taught to carry a rider."

"You're not old," Rumer pointed out. "Or a horse."

"I turn forty in less than a month. It's time to make some changes. Besides, I'm a naturopath. How can I tell my clients to declutter, destress, and embrace peaceful living, if I'm not doing the same?"

"You've been a naturopath for fifteen years, hon. You've been heading toward forty since the day you were born." Lu swiped sauce off the counter, not meeting Minnie's eyes.

"And, I've suddenly realized it."

That was it.

Just that statement, and the kitchen went dead silent.

The old cuckoo clock on the wall ticked away the minutes while Rumer scrubbed the cupboard and tried to think of something to say.

Something besides *Are you thinking of moving away? Doing something different? Leaving Lu behind?*

"I'm thinking, that this means you're ready to do what your sister did," Lu finally said.

"If I'd been planning to do what Victoria did, I'd have run away at sixteen, gotten pregnant, raised the kid in a . . ." She met Rumer's eyes. "I'd have left a long time ago."

"But you are planning on leaving, right?" Lu demanded, tossing her cloth into the sink and putting her hands on her hips. She'd lost weight since the bypass surgery, her well-padded hips now narrow, her bones jutting out from beneath a fitted T-shirt.

"I never said that."

"That's no answer."

"Lu," Rumer interrupted. "You're getting upset. The doctor told you that you have to take it easy."

"I've done nothing but take it easy for weeks, and of course I'm upset. Minnie is planning to leave."

"Ma, really . . ." Minnie sighed. "Look, you've been bugging me for years, telling me to get rid of some of my stuff. I'm finally doing it. You should be thrilled."

"I'd be thrilled if I weren't suspicious."

"Of what?"

"We'll see," Lu said cryptically, dropping into a chair, her face pale. She'd be sixty-five in the spring, but she looked older, years of sun exposure and decades of smoking creasing her face and aging her skin. She'd given up smoking in exchange for Rumer's promise to attend college. That had been eleven or twelve years ago. Even after all this time, she still tapped her fingers on the table when she sat for too long or patted her pockets as if searching for a cigarette.

"How about some tea?" Rumer offered, wanting to move the conversation away from Minnie's plans. She'd walk over to the trailer later, sit down with her aunt, and have a cup of coffee or a glass of wine. Maybe Minnie would tell her what she didn't seem to want to share with Lu.

If Minnie left the homestead . . .

Rumer didn't want to think about that.

Lu was great at training horses, working with clients, and helping families. She did okay with the books and with payroll, but Minnie had set up the nonprofit. She filed the taxes, kept the accounting logs, calculated how much feed and hay needed to be ordered each month. Along with being licensed as a naturopathic doctor, she had a master's in business administration. Without her, the business might fail, and if it failed, Lu might not have a reason to get out of bed in the morning, do her therapy. Heal.

"No coffee for me," Lu said, rubbing the back of her neck and eyeing the clock. "I've got to go feed Hamilton. Otherwise, he'll be standing outside my window tonight, yowling for dinner."

"I'll take care of him." Rumer grabbed her coat from a hook by the back door and shoved her arms into it. She'd rather feed the barn cat than stand in the kitchen worrying about a future she couldn't control.

"Thanks, hun. I'm tired. I think I'll go tuck myself in."

"It's not even eight yet," Minnie protested.

"My body doesn't care what time it is. Neither does my brain. It sucks to get old, girls. Take my advice. Don't do it." Lu shuffled across the room and probably would have gone to her room and locked the door if the doorbell hadn't rung.

"Who's that?" Minnie whispered as if some demon were standing outside the door.

"Good question. Nobody I know would come for a visit at this time of night." Lu grabbed a frying pan from the dish rack. "Which means it's a stranger. And, what kind of stranger would show up here?"

"Just about any kind," Rumer responded.

"We live in the middle of nowhere. Strangers don't just show up. They come for a reason or they don't come at all. I'll go get the shotgun." Minnie sprinted down the narrow hallway that led to the bedrooms before Rumer could tell her not to bother with the gun.

The doorbell rang again, and Rumer reached for the doorknob.

"Don't," Lu commanded. "It could be a serial killer, a thief, a druggie hopped up on PCP thinking he's hunting zombies."

"Have you been watching horror movies on your computer?"

"This is the reality of the world we're living in," Lu huffed, lifting the frying pan above her head as Rumer opened the door.

She wasn't expecting a killer, a thief, or a druggie. She sure as heck wasn't expecting Sullivan, either. But there he was, standing on Lu's front porch, his dark hair gleaming in the dim light, Minnie's daffodil jacket in his hand. No apron this evening. No kids that Rumer could see. She glanced past him, eyeing the shiny SUV that sat in the driveway.

"I didn't bring them. If that's what you're wondering," Sullivan said before she could ask. "I asked someone from their church to sit with them for a few hours."

"Who are you? What do you want?" Lu asked, her knuckles white from clutching the heavy pan, her dark eyes drilling into Sullivan.

"Sullivan Bradshaw. I came to return Rumer's jacket." He held it up, and Lu scowled.

"That's what most killers say."

Sullivan's lips quirked but he had the decency not to smile. "That they're returning a jacket?"

"That they have a good excuse for being where they shouldn't." She lowered the pan, gave him a good once-over, and called, "Forget the shotgun, Minnesota. He looks shifty, but I think we can take him down if we need to."

"Minnesota?" Sullivan mouthed as he met Rumer's eyes.

"My aunt. Minnie."

"The one who let you borrow the suit?"

"That's right."

"She might be happy to know her jacket has been returned." No judgment. No condescending smirk or angry diatribe about his ability to fend off a couple of women. He seemed more intrigued than scared. More interested than annoyed.

Which was a whole heck of a lot better than Jake had done the first time he'd been to the homestead.

But, then, Jake didn't like animals. He hated dirt, fresh air, sunshine, heat. All the things that Sunshine Acres had in abundance during the summer. He'd spent his first night there mourning the fact that there was no television, no air conditioner, no comfortable king-size bed.

And yet, for some reason, Rumer had still thought they were the perfect match.

She shoved the thought away. She'd promised herself she wasn't going to waste time thinking about all the time she'd wasted on him and on their joke of a relationship.

The fact was, she hadn't been heartbroken when she'd discovered his infidelity. She hadn't even been all that angry. She'd been . . .

Relieved?

That wasn't quite the right word, but it was close enough.

"I'm sure she'll be thrilled to have this back." Rumer took the jacket Sullivan was offering. "Thanks for bringing it by."

"It's the least I could do. The cake was delicious. Twila enjoyed it."

"What cake?" Minnie emerged from the hallway, the shotgun in hand. Of course. Because not only could the Truehart women not find a good man or sew a straight hem, they also tended to attract men who couldn't be trusted. Minnie had the worst record of all of them—married twice to men who'd used her as a punching bag and a doormat. She'd divorced the second bastard on her twenty-third birthday. As far as Rumer knew, she hadn't been in a relationship since.

"I made Lu's pound cake recipe," Rumer explained, taking the shotgun and checking to make certain it wasn't loaded. As far as she knew, there wasn't ammunition in the house. That was kept in a locked box in the attic. Still, it didn't hurt to be cautious.

"For my niece. Today is her tenth birthday," Sullivan added. He didn't seem intimidated by the shotgun or Minnie. As a matter of fact, he'd stepped across the threshold and was standing in the tiny foyer that separated the entry from the living room. Melting snow dripped from his hair onto the old linoleum, and he swiped moisture from his face. "I'm sorry I startled all of you. I tried to call but your voice mail is full, Rumer."

"Is it?" She knew it was. Jake kept calling about stupid things. Like whether she wanted the photos she'd hung on the wall in their living room.

His living room now.

She had her own place—a cute little apartment within walking distance of the school. She'd moved in three months before Lu's heart attack, and she had no intention of filling it with reminders of the past.

"It is," he replied, his attention on Minnie, who'd put on the jacket and was buttoning it over her stained white apron.

"I'm sorry about that." Rumer grabbed his arm and tugged him back outside. "Thanks for bringing the jacket. Drive safely."

"Actually," he responded before she could retreat, "I was hoping to discuss the position with you."

"Position?" she repeated as if she didn't know darn well what he was talking about.

The job she'd gone out of her way to apply for.

The one she'd been thinking about most of the afternoon.

The one she'd sworn to herself she wouldn't take if it was offered, because she didn't need that kind of trouble.

"The one you interviewed for this morning," he responded, flashing his dimple.

"I'd love to discuss that with you, Sullivan," she lied, "but, I have a cat to feed."

She walked back inside, and would have closed the door, but Lu was standing in the entry with a bag of cat food in one hand, Rumer's coat in the other.

"Hamilton hates to wait," she announced, shoving both into Rumer's arms.

"I'll go out the back door," Rumer replied, but Lu refused to move.

"It's quicker out through the front. I'll keep the porch light on, so you can find your way back. Go on now," she insisted.

So, of course, Rumer did.

That was the way Lu had raised her. From age fourteen on, she'd been taught to respect authority, to follow the rules, to be responsible for her actions.

So, yeah, she stepped back outside.

Lu closed the door with a quiet thud, and Rumer was standing out in the cold with cat food in one hand and her coat in the other. She hadn't even put on her snow boots.

She set the bag of food on the old rocker that had been there longer than Rumer had been alive. She wasn't surprised when Sullivan took the coat and helped her into it.

"Thanks," she muttered, sounding about as irritated as she felt.

She knew what Lu was doing, because she knew Lu. Good-looking guy? Shove her granddaughter at him, because all the decades and generations of romantic failures by Truehart women couldn't stop her from wanting at least one of them to have a happily-ever-after.

"You're annoyed," he responded, pulling the collar of the coat up, his knuckles brushing the side of her neck and then her jaw. She refused to acknowledge the way her heart jumped at the contact, the way her entire body seemed to want to lean toward him.

God!

She was an idiot.

"Not with you," she replied, grabbing the cat food and heading down the slippery porch stairs.

"With your grandmother?" he guessed, following her across the yard and around the side of the house.

"You didn't drive all this way to discuss my family problems," she replied as they reached the wooden fence that separated the yard from the fallow field beyond it.

The barn was just across it, a pale shadow in the swirling snow.

"That doesn't mean it has to be off the table," he replied, following her as she opened a gate and headed across the field.

"You came to offer me the job, right?" She didn't want a personal discussion, and she didn't want to drag out the inevitable.

"Right."

"I can't accept it."

"Okay."

Just that.

No argument.

No fishing for an explanation. Just okay, and she wasn't sure what to think about that. She sure didn't want him to beg or plead. She didn't want him to give a dozen reasons why she should take the job, and she didn't want to have to explain the reasons why she couldn't.

He opened the barn door, holding it as she walked inside.

She caught a whiff of strawberries and cream as she walked past, found herself wondering how the celebration had gone. Wondering if they'd sung happy birthday to Twila, if she'd smiled, if the twins had managed to stay out of trouble for long enough to enjoy a slice of cake.

"Not my circus. Not my monkeys," she mumbled.

"What's that?" Sullivan asked.

"Nothing." She flipped on a light, illuminating the cavernous space. Horse tackle hung from one wall, saddles from another. Plastic bins of chicken and goat feed sat in the center of the space, discarded farm equipment piled near the back.

A few mice scurried away from the pellets of food that had fallen near the bins. She could hear them scrabbling into their nests behind the walls.

She walked to the back, knowing without looking that Sullivan was following.

"You don't have to hang around until I finish," she said, opening a door that led into Lu's office. The cat bowl was there. Right next to the spindle-back chair. Rumer had bought a comfortable office chair for Lu a few Christmases ago. It was in the stable, sitting near the entrance to the indoor riding arena. As far as she knew, Lu had never once sat in it.

"I don't mind."

"It's snowing hard out there." She poured food into the bowl, shaking it around to try to draw Hamilton out of his hiding place.

"My SUV does well on snowy roads," he replied, walking into the small room and looking around. She could almost see it through his eyes—the unpainted walls and card-table desk. The metal file cabinet shoved against a wall, one drawer opened a crack. No computer. No modern conveniences. Not even a space heater to keep it warm.

"Even with a vehicle that handles them well, the roads will be difficult. It's going to take time to get home, and the kids might get worried." She shook the bowl again, eyeing the corners of the room and then the exposed rafters. Still no sign of Hamilton.

"My guess is that they're having a lot more fun with Renee Wheeler than they would be with me."

"She's the church lady?"

"The twins' Sunday school teacher. She helped with

the funeral and has made a bunch of meals for us. I think one of the boys let her know that I'm not much of a cook."

"So, it's not just baking you struggle with?" she asked, and he grinned.

"I can open a can and heat soup. I also make a mean grilled cheese. Other than that it's precooked meals or takeout."

"Most kids love takeout."

"Sunday was all about wholesome, healthy eating. Every time I feed the kids McDonald's, I feel like I'm betraying her." He was still smiling, but some of the amusement was gone from his eyes.

"I'm sure she'd understand."

"You're right. And, that's the problem. Sunday would understand. She'd tell me it was okay, that the kids would survive a month or two or three of less-than-nutritious meals. And, that makes me want to honor her wishes, make sure the kids have as many healthy meals as I can provide. Which, if it were totally up to me, would be none."

"It's not that difficult to learn to cook." She set the bowl down, determined to turn off the light and head back home. She didn't want to stand in the tiny office listening to Sullivan talk about his sister-in-law, the kids, and his own desire to do right by all of them. It made it all too real—the little family going through a horrible time, the uncle who'd stepped in to try to help, the tragedy of it all.

"That's what I've been told a dozen or more times."

"By Heavenly?"

"She's too busy giving me attitude to give me advice."

"Twila, then?"

"Right. I keep telling her that I'd be happy to do a

little culinary studying if I weren't busy trying to keep up with six kids, housework, and my research paper."

"You're in school?"

"On sabbatical. I teach art history at the Portland State University."

That surprised her.

She wasn't sure why. It wasn't like she'd spent any time thinking about what he might do for a living. It was more that if she'd had to guess, she'd have guessed military or law enforcement. He had that look: tough, rugged, unflappable.

"You're surprised." He spoke into the silence, and she shrugged.

"I guess I've just never seen an art history professor outside his natural habitat."

He laughed, the sound ringing through the barn and chasing a few starlings from their nests in the eaves. "We do tend to keep close to our ivory towers. Only my tower is more like a broom closet on the third floor of the fine arts building."

"A broom closet, huh?" She was amused and shouldn't be. He was just a guy who she happened to have crossed paths with. For an hour, their lives had converged. In a week, they'd both have forgotten the meeting.

"It's a little bigger than that but not much bigger than this. I do have a real desk, though. And, a nice chair."

"Lu had both. She gave the desk to Minnie and the chair is in the stables."

"She probably spends most of her time there."

"She did. Before her heart attack." She reached for the light switch, ready to be done with the conversation because it felt too friendly, too nice. Too much like they could have continued talking forever and not gotten tired of it.

"Hold on." He grabbed her hand, and she was so surprised, she didn't pull away.

"What?"

"I thought I saw something moving in the rafters." He pulled her back, his attention on the ceiling.

"There are dozens of mice in here. Birds. Sometimes raccoons. That's why we have . . ."

Her voice trailed off as Hamilton appeared, his oversize body perched on tiny paws. Even with his extra weight, he was graceful, leaping from one ceiling joist to another.

"That," Sullivan said, "is the fattest cat I've ever seen."

"Shhhh," she responded, watching as Hamilton disappeared behind the drywall, "you'll hurt his feelings."

"You sound like Twila. She's always worried about the hog, scared it's going to be too cold or too hot or eat something that'll kill it."

"With what I saw coming out of your kitchen, that last worry isn't too much of a stretch."

He laughed again, the sound fading away as Hamilton's furry face appeared in a hole that was about as big as the palm of Rumer's hand.

"He's not going to try to get out through that," Sullivan said.

"Watch him," she responded.

Sure enough, the cat stuck his head through the hole, his golden eyes and black-and-gray face framed by drywall. He meowed softly and somehow managed to shimmy his plump body through the small opening. Seconds later, he had his head in the bowl and was purring loudly.

"I've seen a lot of things these past few weeks, but

that was, by far, the most entertaining." Sullivan squeezed her hand and then released it.

Funny, she hadn't realized he was still holding it until that moment.

Or, maybe, it wasn't funny.

She'd never been a touchy-feely person. As a matter of fact, she'd been the kind of kid who'd refused hugs and barely accepted handshakes. She liked to keep distance between herself and others. Maybe because she'd spent so much of her childhood in tiny apartments or single-wide trailers or packed into an old car with all her mother's crap.

"Hamilton has eaten. I can tell Lu that I saw him consume half his weight in food. My job here is done," she said lightly, flicking off the light and stepping out of the office.

He followed, grabbing the bag of cat food on his way out and holding it as they walked back through the barn.

His cell phone rang as they reached the door, and he pulled it out.

"Damn," he said so softly she almost didn't hear.

"Home?" she asked.

"The hospital," he responded as he answered.

He didn't say much. A question or two about treatment options. An assurance that he'd be there soon. Then he tucked the phone back in his pocket.

"Bad news?"

"Yeah. Sunday's brain is swelling again. She's going into surgery. I need to get to the hospital. Thanks again for everything you did today." He was jogging, moving back across the field, snow still swirling in the darkening twilight.

She could have let him go.

That would have been the easy thing to do.

It probably would have been the best thing, too, but she kept picturing little Moisey standing in the middle of the road in her oversize tank top and shimmering tutu. She kept remembering Heavenly's scrawny frame shoved into too-tight clothes. She kept thinking about six kids whose lives had been upended, and no matter how much she told herself to, she couldn't go inside and pretend she didn't know that something horrible might be happening.

She followed Sullivan to his SUV, the voice of caution and reason screaming in the back of her mind, telling her she was making a mistake. Warning her to retreat.

Sullivan handed her the cat food and hopped in the driver's seat. That was her cue to back away, to offer some easy platitude that would sound nice and mean nothing.

"Are you bringing the kids to the hospital?" she asked instead, and he stilled, the key halfway to the ignition.

"I wasn't planning to."

"It might be good for the older ones to see her before surgery." She didn't say *just in case,* but she was pretty certain he heard the unspoken words.

He raked a hand through his snow-damp hair and grimaced. "You're right, but I can't bring the older ones and leave the younger ones at home. I'll take all of them. Except Oya. She's not allowed in the ICU."

"Will the boys' Sunday school teacher be willing to stay with her?"

"Probably. Maybe. I don't know. I'll figure it out when I get to the house." He smiled but it was more of a grimace than anything else.

"If you think you might need help," she began.

Don't! her brain screamed. *Do. Not. Say. It.*

"I could follow you over," she finished, the words tumbling out.

For a split second, she thought he was too busy starting the SUV to hear her.

Then, he met her eyes, and she could see his fatigue, his worry, the weight of the responsibility he was carrying.

"I can't ask you to do that," he said.

"You didn't. I offered."

"How about you ride with me, then? This thing can handle seven passengers, and it's probably better on the road than your truck."

No! Just no! A thousand times no! her brain shrieked.

"Give me a minute to grab my purse and put on some boots," her mouth said, and then she was sprinting across the yard and up the porch steps, the cat food bouncing out of the still-opened bag as she barreled into the house and ran for her shoes.

Sullivan had always appreciated irony.

He loved it in art, in books, in musical scores.

He didn't like it much right now, though, because Sunday looked better than she had since the accident. The bruises on her face were healing, fading from dark purple to green and yellow. The swelling was down, too, the broken bones slowly healing. The gash on her temple was a jagged purple line, dotted on either side from the staples the doctors had used to close it. They'd been removed a few days ago, and now she had no staples, no stitches in her cheek or the side of her neck.

She looked better, but she was dying.

The irony of that nearly stole his breath.

She'd been three years behind him in school, but they'd been in the same classes. She'd been smart, driven, and passionate about learning. She'd also been kind, generous, warmhearted. It hadn't surprised him when Matt had fallen for her, but it had surprised everyone that she'd fallen, too.

She wasn't the kind of girl that anyone thought would go for one of the Bradshaw boys. They were trouble. She wasn't.

Somehow, it had happened.

Somehow, she and Matt had made it work.

Now, he was gone, and she was hooked up to machines that measured her pulse, her oxygen, that breathed for her because her lungs had been punctured by jagged pieces of her broken ribs.

She was fighting for her life, the head injury she'd suffered causing her brain to swell. Again. This would be the second surgery to relieve pressure. If it failed . . .

He didn't want to think about that.

He sure as hell didn't want to have to make decisions about it. Especially not with Moisey sitting beside him, but the surgeon was asking about living wills, trying to be subtle because there was a child in the room. Sullivan and his brothers hadn't been named guardians in the will, but they'd been named co-executors of the estate. They'd also been given medical power of attorney for all six kids and for Sunday and Matt.

That had surprised all of them.

None of them wanted the responsibility. None of them were willing to turn away from it. When his brothers had been around, they'd made decisions together, hashing things out, deciding what was best for all the kids and for Sunday.

But, Sullivan was there now. Alone. He was the one who would have to sign on the dotted line, agree that if Sunday's heart stopped, they would revive her.

Or not.

He'd already called Porter and Flynn. Neither had picked up. He'd sent texts. No response to those either. Not surprising. Flynn worked long hours in areas where there was very little cell phone reception. Porter worked private security for a company in Los Angeles. When he was on a job, he didn't take calls or answer texts. Sometimes for days.

That left Sullivan to make the choice, because Sunday didn't have a living will.

He squeezed the bridge of his nose, trying to concentrate on what the surgeon was telling him. Mostly he heard disparate words. Skull. Section. Replaced. Expand.

He might have heard more if he hadn't been watching Moisey watch Sunday. She was leaning toward the bed, her hair a mass of wild curls, her hands resting on the rail. She'd painted her nails. Or someone else had. They were bright green and red. Christmas colors, maybe.

"Do you have any questions, Mr. Bradshaw?" the surgeon asked.

He did, but he doubted a doctor could answer them.

He wanted to know why a kid like Moisey, one who'd been born into abject poverty, who'd lost both birth parents to famine, was having to face the possibility of losing another set of parents. He wanted to know what he could say to make things better, what he could do to keep Sunday around for her kids.

"No," he responded.

The doctor nodded as if she understood.

"I'll have you sign the forms electronically." She moved to the computer that sat on a rolling table. "We're readying the OR. The sooner we get started"— she glanced at Moisey—"the better the chance of a good outcome."

Moisey turned to look at them. There were circles beneath her eyes, dark smudges against her coffee-colored skin.

Had they been there that morning?

Had he looked?

"Is she going to die?" she asked bluntly, her voice falling into the silence and filling it.

"We're going to do everything we can to make her better," the surgeon responded, all business as she typed something into the computer.

"Everything you can do might not be enough," Moisey said.

That got the doctor's attention. She stopped typing, her gaze going from Moisey to Sullivan. It settled there. As if she expected him to say something, maybe expected that he'd have a better response than anything she could come up with.

He should have.

He was an adult, for God's sake.

He'd lived through a lot of tough times, faced a lot of tragedy. He worked with angsty teens and young adults, kids who were worried about grades, about the future, about relationships. It wasn't his favorite part of the job, but there hadn't been a time yet when he hadn't known what to say.

Now he was struggling.

Afraid to overstate things or understate them. Afraid whatever he managed to come up with would only fan the flames of Moisey's fear.

"I think your time is up. Your siblings are going to put up a fuss if they think you've gotten an extra minute when they didn't," he said. It was a total cop-out. Absolute evasion at its finest.

He wasn't proud of it, but it worked.

She leaned forward and kissed Sunday's cheek, avoiding the fading bruises and finding one tiny spot of unblemished flesh.

"I love you, Mommy," she whispered.

The door opened before she moved away, and Rumer peeked in.

"Moisey?" she said quietly. "It's someone else's turn."

"Who's someone? I'm the youngest kid here, and I was last to see Mom, so no one should be waiting," Moisey responded.

"Your pastor. He wants to pray with your mom before her surgery."

"She can't pray with that tube down her throat." Moisey sniffed, and Sullivan had the horrible feeling she was about to cry. He could handle her spunk and her backtalk a lot more easily than tears.

"We don't have to speak out loud for God to hear," Rumer said, holding out her hand.

To Sullivan's surprise, Moisey crossed the room and took it. She looked tiny, her legs sticking out from beneath a bright orange skirt, thick purple tights pulled up over shins that he knew were covered with scrapes and bruises. She'd dressed for the weather because Renee had insisted, but she'd chosen her own color scheme—fuchsia snow boots with faux fur trim that had once been white but was now dotted with colored marker, grape-colored gloves, spruce-blue coat. He couldn't see her shirt, but he'd lay odds it was as bright as the rest of her outfit.

She looked back at Sunday, a single tear sliding down her cheek.

And, God! His heart hurt for her, for her siblings, for Sunday, who'd have given anything to keep them from ever being hurt again.

"It'll be okay," he said.

She met his eyes, and he saw a world of maturity in her gaze, a lifetime of knowledge she shouldn't have. She knew it might not be okay. She knew Sunday might die. She knew how fragile life could be.

"I think I'll have a cookie and hot chocolate," she said, her voice wooden and raspy, the tear still damp on her cheek.

Then, she bounced out of the room as if none of it had happened, and there was nothing left for Sullivan to do but sign the online forms and pray things really would be okay.

Chapter Four

The cafeteria smelled like overcooked broccoli and fried eggs.

Not something Rumer would have noticed if Heavenly hadn't been mentioning it incessantly for the past twenty minutes.

"It really does," she said, her nose wrinkling, her attention darting from Rumer to the table next to them to the doorway and then, to the line. Restless. Unhappy. Sure as heck not afraid to show it. "It's the most disgusting smell in the world. Like dog sh—"

"Don't," Rumer warned, and she scowled.

"Dog *poop* on hot cement."

"I wonder if they're cutting her skull open right now," Maddox said, stabbing his grilled cheese sandwich with a fork. "Or maybe they've just started shaving off her hair. I asked the doctor, and she said they were going to do that. All of it. Off." He touched his head, his eyes wide.

"Poor Mommy," Twila said with a sigh. "She's going to be sad when she wakes up and her hair is gone."

"Dweeb," Heavenly growled, "that is the last thing Sunday is going to be worried about."

"If she were conscious enough to worry about anything," Milo agreed, "it would probably be about the fact that Dad is dead and we're all acting like hooligans."

It was the first time Rumer had heard him speak.

Surprised, she turned her attention away from Heavenly and her cornrow hair and skin-tight shirt and eyed the little boy. His brother wore a look of perpetual anger: furrowed brow and flashing eyes. Milo's expression was softer, his eyes wide as if he were in a constant state of curiosity or fear.

He met her eyes and just . . .

Watched. As if he were waiting for a reaction.

"You're not acting like a hooligan," she finally said.

"One of us has to behave."

"And, Mr. Perfect has to be the one. Just like always," Heavenly snapped, her cornrows nearly shaking with frustration.

"I'm not perfect. I just know how to follow the rules."

"Because you're a kiss-up who wants to be the favorite. You're not going to be. Ever. None of us are. Our own damn mothers didn't want us. Do you really think someone else actually does?" Heavenly nearly spat.

"Our parents do too want us!" Maddox bellowed, lunging across the table, obviously not quite getting the gist of what Heavenly was saying. Not that Sunday and her husband hadn't wanted them. That their biological parents hadn't.

Rumer grabbed him by the back of the shirt and hauled him away before he could do any damage.

"You two obviously have too much time on your hands," she said, her focus on Heavenly. She'd known the girl was trouble. She'd obviously been right. But, she couldn't help feeling sorry for the tween. This was a tough situation, and she seemed new to the family. Not quite in sync with the rest of the crew, not quite jibing with the way the others interacted.

"And?" Heavenly stared her down, muscles tense, posture combative. She was itching for a fight, but Rumer had given up on those a few years after she'd moved in with Lu.

"I have some jobs you can do at the homestead. That should keep you occupied on the weekends and after school. I'll talk to your uncle about it and see what he thinks."

"He's not my uncle," Heavenly said, some of her defiance slipping away. "And, this"—she waved her hand in a wide arc that encompassed everyone at the table—"is not my family. So, I really don't care if you send me to some kids' ranch."

"Kids' ranch? The homestead is where I live," Rumer said gently, because she suddenly realized her mistake. She'd forgotten Heavenly's past, her worldview, the secrets she hid from everyone.

And, she did have secrets.

Rumer understood that the same way she understood the defiance, the cavalier attitude toward her siblings, her mother, her family.

"You live on a homestead?" Twila asked. "That's what they did during westward expansion. Do you have an outhouse? Do you have to pump your water and cart it inside in a big tin pail? Is it like in *Little House on the Prairie?*"

"No. Nothing like that," Rumer said. "It's a small farm with a few barns and a big stable. We train horses so that they're gentle enough for kids with disabilities to ride."

"You have horses?" Moisey jumped out of her seat, her upper lip smeared with hot chocolate. "Can we see them?"

"I'd be happy to have you visit, but we have to check with your uncle first."

"Check with me about what?" Sullivan asked, and Rumer swung around, the chair scraping the floor as she stood.

God, he was handsome!

Even tired. Even with a stubble on his chin and shadows under his eyes, he looked good enough to kiss.

Whoa!

No!

He did *not* look good enough to kiss.

And, if he did, she was definitely not going to notice.

"We don't have to check with you about anything," Heavenly muttered. "And, if we did, it wouldn't matter. I'm too young to work."

"What work?" he asked, meeting Rumer's eyes.

"Lu could use some extra help in the stables. We have several volunteers who come a couple of times a week, but we don't have anyone on the weekends."

"Volunteer? I only work for money," Heavenly muttered, but she looked intrigued.

"That's pretty mercenary of you," Sullivan said. "Volunteer work is about others. Not ourselves. And, you'd be doing it for a good cause."

"What? You getting rid of me for a while on the weekends?" Heavenly snorted. "Because, I know that's what you're hoping for."

"That has nothing to do with it."

"I'd like you better if you weren't such a liar," she spat.

"What's that supposed to mean?"

"It means that you're sure as hell not the kind-hearted uncle who is happy to take on childcare duty. And, before you try to say anything different, I've heard you talking to your brothers about us."

His jaw tightened, and Rumer was certain she was about to witness a shouting match of epic proportions. Sullivan denying. Heavenly insisting. All of it playing out in the middle of the hospital cafeteria.

"You know," she began, hoping to distract them, "this is a really stressful time, and—"

"I'm sorry. I shouldn't have said anything about any of you," Sullivan interrupted, surprising the rest of what Rumer planned to say right out of her head. "This is a big job for one person. Especially a person who has no experience with kids. It's not easy on you guys, either. I understand that. We're all just going to have to make the best of it for however long your mother is in the hospital."

"What if she . . . ?" Heavenly's gaze cut to her siblings, and she pressed her lips together. "Fine. I'll take the stupid volunteer job, but nobody better expect me to like it. Now, if you don't mind, I need a smoke. See you around."

She turned on her heels and sauntered away like she was a twenty-year-old with every right in the world to take a cigarette break.

Sullivan just stood there and watched her go.

"Aren't you going after her?" Rumer prodded. "Because, if you don't, I will. She can't smoke. Even if she could, she shouldn't. Not to mention the fact that she's got no business wandering around on her own at twelve years old."

"She's not smoking. She's crying," Twila piped up, her hair still in perfect plaits, her face clean of crumbs or cocoa. No stains on her shirt, coat, or knee-length skirt. No rips in her tights.

"Why do you say that?" Rumer asked, tracking Heavenly as she continued across the cafeteria.

"That's what she always does. She says she's smoking, but Mom says she's never smelled one bit of cigarette smoke on her, and she's never found cigarettes, either. Heavenly just says that so she can be alone and cry."

"She can be alone at home. Here, she's sticking with us." Sullivan finally moved, following Heavenly across the room. He caught up with her before she reached the door.

He touched her arm, and even from a distance, Rumer could see her flinch, the reaction saying a lot about the tween's background.

Whatever Sullivan said, it seemed to do the trick. She went from angry, to frustrated, to resigned, the emotions flashing across her face one after another until she finally nodded.

They walked back together. Not touching. Not speaking. Both tense.

"Come on, dweebs," Heavenly said as she reached the table. "Pastor Mark is waiting in the lobby. We're going home with him." She grabbed Milo's hand, and he stood, sidling up close, his shoulder bumping her side. Maddox scowled but followed suit, standing with his arms crossed over his chest, his eyes flashing with irritation.

"What about Mom?" Moisey asked, swiping the back of her hand across her mouth. All she managed to do was smear the chocolate more.

"She's in surgery," Sullivan said, grabbing a napkin from the chrome dispenser and wiping her mouth. He did it gently. As if she were a porcelain doll and he was afraid of breaking her.

She was probably more of a rugby player—tough and invincible—but the gesture was still sweet to watch.

"Here," Twila said, dipping a napkin in her cup of water and dabbing at Moisey's face, probably mimicking what she'd seen her mother do.

Rumer looked away.

She didn't want her heart softening toward this family.

Didn't want it softening?

Who did she think she was kidding?

It *had* softened.

But, that didn't mean she should get more involved.

Sure, the money was good.

Sure, she needed it.

Taking the job would mean paying off Lu's medical bills well before it was time to return to Seattle in the summer.

The thing was, she didn't want to witness the downward spiral of this patchwork family. She didn't want to watch as the stitches that held it together came apart. She sure as heck didn't want to be the one trying to stitch it back together.

She'd seen Sunday, though.

Lying in that hospital bed. Breathing tube down her

throat, ventilator forcing air into her lungs. IVs and tubes and beeping machines, her kids all waiting and hoping and praying that she'd wake up.

And, maybe she would.

Maybe what they were believing in would happen, and Sunday would recover and return to them.

In the meantime, they needed someone.

That was as obvious as sunrise on a cloudless morning.

What wasn't obvious was who that someone would be.

She followed the group as they walked to the exit. Pastor Mark was waiting near the door. Very tall and a little stooped as if he'd spent most of his life ducking to avoid low-hanging light fixtures and short entryways.

He met Rumer's eyes and smiled. "I only have enough room in my Chevy for the crew. I'll bring them to the house and then come back and bring you home," he offered.

"There's no need. I can get a ride," she lied. No way was she calling Aunt Minnie. The woman might be an ace at naturopathic medicine and bookkeeping, but she couldn't drive to save her life or anyone else's. She was fine close to home. On clear days. With full sunlight. Having her make the forty-five-minute drive to Spokane during a snowstorm was like asking her to jump out of an airplane without a parachute. It would end badly. No doubt about that.

But, she didn't want the pastor making the drive again, either. From what she'd gathered, he was married and had a couple of kids. They needed their dad around more than she needed a ride.

"Are you sure?" he asked, his dark eyes looking straight into hers.

"Positive," she lied again, and immediately felt guilty about it.

She'd spent the last half of her teenage years attending church. Lu might be a hermit, but she didn't believe in hiding from God. Sunday morning meant dress clothes, makeup-free faces, and a half-hour drive to the little chapel on the hill. It meant hard pews and old organ music and a pastor who preached fire and brimstone and eternal damnation. It also meant women's auxiliary on Tuesday night, stew and home-baked bread brought to shut-ins. It meant a tiny community of people who'd cared about one another.

She'd loved that part of it.

Even if she hadn't quite appreciated the pastor's sermons.

"All right. If you can't find someone to come out here, give me a call." He handed her a business card and turned his attention to Sullivan. "Keep me posted on things, okay? I may be able to come back once we figure out who's going to stay with the kids tonight."

"Don't risk the roads," Sullivan responded. "I'll call you once she's out of surgery. I'm thinking I'll be home in the early morning. It could be sooner or later depending on how things go."

"Sunday is strong, and the Lord is stronger. She'll get through this. Ready, guys?" He opened the door, and all five kids filed out without a word of protest or a wave good-bye.

"That's sad," Rumer said, watching as they disappeared into the swirling snow.

"Yeah. It is. Their dad is dead, and they need their mom, but she's probably . . ." Sullivan didn't continue.

Maybe he was afraid to speak it aloud, afraid that giving voice to the fear would make it a reality.

"What are the doctors saying?" she asked, falling into step beside him as he walked back to the cafeteria.

"That if she survives, she probably won't be the same. There's some damage to the frontal lobe of the brain. The surgeon mentioned a dozen things that could impact. I got the impression that she wasn't very hopeful for any kind of recovery."

"The surgeon is one person with one opinion," she reminded him.

"It's not just the surgeon. It's the attending physician, the neurologists, the nurses. Sunday has been in a coma since the accident. The longer it goes on, the less hope for a full recovery. That's a fact. Not an opinion."

"Here are a few other facts. The human body has an incredible capacity to heal. Doctors don't know everything. Nurses don't, either."

"Yeah. I know."

"But?"

"Someone has to decide how far treatment should go, how much disability Sunday would want to live with. My brothers and I have medical power of attorney. If it comes down to it, we decide whether to keep Sunday on life support or take her off it."

"That's tough," she said, feeling herself being pulled into his story, into his life and drama. She didn't want to be. She wanted to say good-bye and walk away, maybe hitchhike through the storm until she found her way back to the homestead. Anything but stand there listening to the depth and width and volume of the tragedy he was going through.

"I think she'd want to be here for the kids. No matter

what." He grabbed an insulated cup from a cafeteria counter and poured coffee into it. "Want a cup?"

"No. Thanks. I need to get going." There. She'd said what she should, given herself the out she needed.

"Your ride is on the way?"

"No," she admitted before she realized the mistake.

He poured a second cup of coffee, dumped in two packets of sugar and three creamers, and handed it to her. "Might as well drink the coffee, then. If your ride is coming from anywhere outside of Spokane, it's going to take a long time to get here."

She peered into the cup, eyeing the light-brown brew. Somehow, he'd made it exactly the way she would have. Two sugars. Three creams.

"I'll probably wait in the lobby," she murmured.

"Too much drama?" he asked, taking a sip of coffee and watching her over the brim of his cup.

"It's not drama. It's real-life tragedy, and you've got way more on your plate than anyone should. It will be easier for you to deal with everything if you don't have an extra person underfoot." That sounded reasonable. It sounded professional.

It sounded exactly like the excuse it was.

"We met because you were responding to a help-wanted ad. The help-wanted ad was in the paper because I needed help. Help is not another person underfoot." He took another sip of coffee, grabbed two prepackaged pastries from a basket, and walked to the long line that stretched out from the only open cash register. "But, I'm sure you know that, so I'll take this conversation to mean you're no longer interested in the job."

He sounded so weary, so defeated, she didn't have

the heart to say that it did. "I'm sure you'd rather find someone who doesn't have other obligations."

"Rumer, I'm desperate enough to take Bozo the Clown if he shows up on my doorstep. You've seen what those kids are like. They're—"

"Wonderful?"

He smiled, a slow, easy smile that softened all his sharp angles and hard edges. He looked sweet. The kind of guy Rumer would be happy to do a favor for.

Which, of course, meant nothing.

She was a Truehart.

Truehart women had notoriously bad luck when it came to knowing the good guys from the bad ones.

"See? That is exactly why I want to offer you the job."

"Sullivan—"

"I'll pay you what I quoted earlier. Plus, an extra thousand dollars a week if you accept my offer now."

That would pay off Lu's bills and cushion her account. She'd be able to feed the horses, pay to have the alfalfa planted, hire some weekend help. Get things back on track with the nonprofit. No stress. No fuss. Just Rumer taking care of six kids and a house for the next couple of months.

It was an offer almost too good to refuse.

And, he knew it.

Darn it all!

She could see the calculation in his eyes. He might be grief-stricken and struggling, but he sure as heck knew how to get what he wanted. "That's an awful lot of money, Sullivan."

"To take care of an awful lot of problems. Six to be exact. Plus cooking. Housework." He shrugged. "It seems fair."

"I'd really need to take some time to think about it."

"The thousand dollars extra is a bonus for not thinking about it. Or, at least, not thinking about it any more than you did this morning when you donned that yellow suit and drove to Pleasant Valley Farm. I could have been anyone on the other side of that ad. You took a chance then. The only thing different now is that you've met me and the kids."

He was right.

She'd driven to his place with absolutely no idea of what she'd find. For all she'd known, she was going to knock on the door of a serial killer. "I—"

His cell phone rang, and he frowned, trying to balance the coffee and pastries in one hand while he dragged it from his pocket.

She took the coffee and waited while he answered the phone.

It would have been easy enough to leave if he hadn't offered so much money and if he didn't look frazzled and concerned, the phone pressed to his ear, the pastries being crushed in his hand.

He didn't say much. Just listened. Then nodded, cleared his throat, grunted out, "Yes."

"I need to go up to surgery. Can you pay for this?" He dug a twenty out of his wallet, shoved it and the pastries toward her, his knuckles brushing her abdomen as he rushed to get everything out of his hands.

Coffee sloshed on the floor and on the sleeve of her coat. They were making a royal mess of the cafeteria, but he didn't seem to notice or to care. He was already running toward the door, sprinting into the hall and disappearing from view.

Which left her in the line with too many things in her hands.

Coffee dripping from her arm.

Twenty dollars crushed in her fist.

Not sure what was happening, but certain it wasn't good.

She felt sick with worry over a woman she didn't know, over a family she'd just met, and she couldn't stop picturing little Moisey, marching down the middle of the road in her boots and tutu.

What would happen to her if her mother didn't return?

What would happen to Heavenly, Twila, the twins, and Oya?

Would their uncles step up or step away?

And, why was she wondering when it really wasn't any of her business?

"It *isn't*," she told herself just to emphasize the point.

"Isn't what?" a man responded.

She glanced back, realized an older gentleman was in line behind her. Medium height, gray hair, eyes filled with amusement, he was holding a cup of coffee and a giant pink bear.

"My business," she answered mostly because she liked the twinkle in his eyes.

"Ah. So, you're thinking about making it your business."

"Absolutely not."

He snorted.

"I'm not."

"And, I'm not here to visit my granddaughter and her new baby."

"Are you?"

"Of course." He held the bear up so she could get a good look. "Another little girl. This is my second great-granddaughter."

"Congratulations." She smiled, and he seemed to take that as an invitation to continue.

"Thank you. I'm hoping for a few more."

"Great-granddaughters?"

"Great-grandchildren. Girls or boys. I've got no preference. I figure nine would be a good number. Three from each of my granddaughters."

"Are they aware of this?"

"You're damn right they are! I've made it very clear that one of them has to produce the heir to my chocolate empire."

"You have a chocolate empire?"

"Some people would call it a chocolate shop. Me? I say it's an empire. Chocolate Haven has been around for more years than the two of us combined."

"Is it here in Spokane? My grandmother loves good chocolate," she said, happy to continue the conversation. Lu did love chocolate. *Rumer* loved people who had twinkles in their eyes, smiles on their faces, and stories to tell.

"Nah. Chocolate Haven is in Benevolence. Ever heard of it?"

"I have. It's just to the east of where I grew up."

"And, you've never tried my chocolate? Now, you listen." He reached into his pocket and pulled out a wallet. "I'm giving you my business card. You go to Chocolate Haven next time you're near Benevolence. Someone there will hook you up with a pound of the best fudge you've ever eaten. On the house. Just tell whoever is there that Byron sent you."

He dropped the card into her purse and grinned.

"It's nice to meet you, Byron," she said, setting the pastries down near the cash register and paying the cashier. "I'm Rumer. Maybe we'll see each other at your chocolate shop one day."

She was already moving away, the two cups of coffee

in her hands, the pastries in her purse, Sullivan's change in her pocket.

"That's an unusual name, kid. You wouldn't happen to be Rumer Truehart, would you?" Byron called as she headed toward the exit.

Surprised, she stopped and turned to face him again. "That's right. Have we met?"

"I know your grandmother. Lu. She's come into Chocolate Haven every few months since she was a kid. Gets herself a pound of s'more fudge and leaves. Not much for talking, that one."

"No. She's not," she said, surprised to meet someone who'd known Lu when she was young. There were no photos of Lu as a child, no class pictures or yearbooks. Nothing that anchored her in time. It had always seemed to Rumer that Lu had been born a crotchety old woman with a big heart, that she'd never been a child or a young woman with dreams.

Of course, she obviously *had* been all those things, but the past had been off-limits in their conversations. Lu liked to deal in the here and now. She hated waltzing down memory lane. Her words. Not Rumer's.

"She does talk about you, though. Says you're the best of the Truehart bunch."

"That doesn't sound like Lu." She wasn't one for effusive praise. She said it like it was and didn't bother stroking egos. Ever. Bragging? That was about as likely as Lu going to the casino to gamble away her hard-earned cash.

"God as my witness. She says it every time I ask about her family. How is she? It's been a while since I've seen her."

"She had some heart problems. She's recovering. We're hoping she'll be one-hundred percent soon."

"I'm sorry to hear that. What room? Maybe I'll pop in for a visit after I deliver the bear and chocolate."

"Lu's already home. I'm here with someone else." They were moving down the hall, talking like old friends. He was obviously going up to the maternity ward. Rumer had no idea where she was heading.

Not to the surgical unit, because that would be a mistake. She didn't think she could spend much more time with Sullivan and still manage to walk away. She didn't think she could look into his tired face, listen to him talk about his sister-in-law, watch as he grieved, and still refuse the job.

Plus . . .

The money.

Yeah.

That was a big deal.

One that she could only discount if she could convince herself that the offer wasn't valid, that maybe he was reeling her in and then planned to renege on the agreement. She did, after all, have a terrible record when it came to putting her trust in the wrong people.

Look at Jake.

She'd believed every lie he'd told her until the evidence of his infidelity was right in front of her face. Even then—even looking at the silky thong tangled in the sheets of their bed—she'd tried to believe something other than what she was seeing. She was a Truehart woman, after all.

"Well tell her I said hi. I've missed seeing her. How's Minnie?" Byron said, pulling her from memories she shouldn't be dwelling on.

"Same as ever."

"I heard she's got some kind of doctoring business. One of the ladies from church goes to see her."

"She's a naturopath."

"That's a fancy word for a doctor who doesn't like to give traditional medicine, right?"

"Something like that." They'd reached the bank of elevators and he jabbed one of the buttons. "What floor?" he asked as they stepped inside.

"Four," she responded, because the truth was, she had Sullivan's coffee, his pastries, and his change. She also had a need to know what was going on and a deep desire to make all that extra money.

"Surgical unit is up there. You got a loved one going under the knife?"

"A . . . friend of mine does." That was the easiest explanation. "He asked me to take care of his kids while she's in surgery and recovering."

"I hate to tell you this, but you're doing a piss-poor job of it. Near as I can tell, you don't have a kid anywhere near you." He smiled, and she grinned.

She might be allowing herself to be pulled into more trouble than any one person needed, but at least she was meeting interesting people along the way!

"They went home with their pastor. They live just outside of Benevolence, and with the roads getting bad, it seemed best for them to head home."

"My daughter-in-law would tell me not to point this out, but I can't help myself—if you're watching the kids, wouldn't it make sense for you to go home with them?"

"It's complicated."

"Life is complicated. That's what makes it interesting." He winked, and she couldn't help herself. She laughed.

"You're right about that. The fact of the matter is, I don't know the person having surgery. I don't know the family. I don't know the kids. This morning, I was looking for a job, hoping to make money to help Lu with her medical bills. I drove out to an organic farm and planned to interview with a guy who advertised for a housekeeper and cook. Somehow, I ended up here."

His eyes narrowed, and he cocked his head to the side, studying her like she was a bug under a microscope. "Organic farm? Are you talking about Sunday Bradshaw's place?"

"That's right."

"The ad ran in the *Benevolence Times* this morning. Saw it myself and wondered who would be foolish enough to take on the task." He must have realized what he said, because his cheeks flushed and he shook his head. "What I mean is—"

"You don't have to explain. I've been asking myself the same question since I walked into the farmhouse and saw the . . . need for help."

"The mess, you mean? The way I hear things, Sullivan is struggling trying to get it all done." The elevator doors slid open, and he should have stepped out. Instead, he stood on the threshold. "I didn't realize Sunday needed another surgery."

"I got the impression it was unexpected."

"Well, it's not unexpected now. Now, it's known. Obviously, the need for help is even greater during a time like this."

It wasn't a question, but she found herself nodding in agreement.

"Here's what we're going to do. You go on up and tell Sullivan that help is on the way."

"I don't think—"

"I'll make a few phone calls, and we'll have an entire contingent of people up here waiting with him."

"I don't think he needs anyone to wait with him."

Too late.

He'd already stepped off the elevator.

The door closed, and she was by herself, staring at the silvery walls and wondering what in the heck had just happened.

Byron Lamont made fudge, chocolates, and candies that Sullivan had dreamed about and drooled over when he was a kid. He also owned the longest-lived shop in Benevolence, Washington. Fifty or so years after taking over from his father, he was still running the shop and making a profit. By all accounts, he was a great chocolatier, a savvy businessman, and a good friend.

And, he was currently sitting beside Sullivan in the waiting room, asking Rumer dozens of questions she seemed more than willing to answer.

How old was she?

Where had she attended college?

What degree did she have? What kind of job? Was she married? Dating? Engaged? Did she have any kids?

If Sullivan had been the subject of the interrogation, he'd have put a stop to it twenty minutes ago, but Rumer was going with the flow, allowing Byron to ask as many questions as he wanted.

He seemed to want to ask a lot.

Sullivan gave Rumer points for patience. It was a good quality to have. One that he was running very low on. He wasn't meant to be a parent. He'd known that before he'd been old enough to have kids. He'd listened to his father rant and rave, and he'd realized how easy it might be for anyone to become that person. The one who'd brought kids into the world, but didn't want anything to do with them. The one who was more judgmental than understanding, more harsh than gentle, more hate-filled than loving.

Of course, his father hadn't just been harsh, judgmental, or hateful. He'd been purposely cruel to his kids and to his wife. He'd taken everything that was given to him and demanded more. The way he'd viewed things, it had been his right as the head of the home to have what he wanted when he wanted it. When he didn't get that, he flew off the handle, breaking whatever he could get his hands on. Including his wife's wrist, her nose, and her heart.

She'd been in a terrible marriage, but she'd managed to be a loving and compassionate mother. Sullivan remembered that. Just like he remembered that she'd been their protector until she died of cancer, putting herself in the crosshairs of her husband's anger to keep her children from being harmed. It wasn't long after she died that his father had turned his rage on the four kids she'd left behind. Sullivan had been punched, kicked, and pushed down a flight of stairs. His brothers had been treated similarly. None of them had asked for help from the community. None of them had believed they'd get it. Their mother's silence had become theirs.

They'd talked about that over the years, about the way silence and secrets had bound them together.

Eventually, they'd learned to avoid being home. They'd spent hours wandering around town, finding more than their fair share of trouble to get into. And, while they were finding trouble, they were planning their escape. They might have been troublemakers, but they'd done well in school. They'd gotten jobs as soon as they were able, and they'd helped one another put aside enough money to leave town for good.

The only one who'd stayed was Matthias.

Stayed and married and had kids whom he'd loved and protected the way a good father should.

Sullivan wanted to do the same for his nieces and nephews. He'd woken up every morning for the past week reminding himself that kids were kids and they sure as hell couldn't help it if they were up half the night crying for their mom.

The problem was, it hurt to hear them. It hurt to know that Heavenly was in her room, pretending she didn't care, that Moisey was in bed plotting an escape to some far-off country where magical flowers could create healing potions. It hurt to see the boys struggle and Oya cry and Twila try to be perfect day after day. He felt helpless in the face of their sorrow, and he wasn't sure what to do with that. Sure as hell not scream and rant and punch like his father had.

"All right, son. That's it." Byron nudged his arm, pulling him back from the memories and from his worries.

"That's what?" Sullivan asked, glancing at Rumer. She looked about as bemused as he felt.

"The end of the interview," Byron responded. "She's a perfect candidate for the job you posted in the *Benevolence Times*."

"My brothers posted it," he explained, and Byron scowled.

"Does it matter? She's still perfect. A teacher." He held up one finger. "Years of experience." He held up another. "Hardworking, smart, knowledgeable, single."

"What's single have to do with it?"

"Nothing. Just wanted to make sure you were paying attention. I guess you were. So, how about we discuss terms?"

"Byron," Rumer cut in. "Sullivan and I already discussed terms."

"You did?"

"Yes," she said, standing and stretching to her full height. She wasn't much taller than Heavenly, and she didn't look all that much older.

Although, if he could get Heavenly to scrub all the makeup off her face and wear clothes that didn't cling to her skin, she might look like the twelve-year-old she was. If Sunday knew how her daughter was dressing . . .

But, she didn't.

Which was the entire problem. She didn't know about Heavenly. She didn't know that Maddox had nearly been suspended three times since Matthias's funeral. She didn't know her husband was dead or that her family was falling apart.

"And?" Byron demanded, getting to his feet and taking a cigar from his pocket.

"The terms are good." Rumer tucked a stray curl behind her ear and met Sullivan's eyes. The salary he'd quoted *was* more than fair for the job, but he'd pay her more if it meant he didn't have to deal with the kids on his own.

"That's what you think." Byron clamped the cigar between his teeth and spoke out of the corner of his mouth. "Let me talk to him for a few minutes alone. I can probably get you more money. I've been in the business world for a long time. I know how to negotiate."

"More isn't necessary. Sullivan's offer was generous."

"Then, you plan to take the job?"

"Well, I . . ."

"You said the terms were good," Byron reminded her.

"I know but . . ."

"And, with your grandmother being poorly, I'm sure you could use a little extra cash around the homestead. Plus, you said there were medical bills to pay."

"That was the reason I applied for the job," she admitted.

"Then, it's settled. She'll take the position you're offering." He grinned.

"I think I'd better hear that from her," Sullivan said, meeting Rumer's eyes. They reminded him of summer skies and spring flowers, of cool rain on hot days.

She reminded him of those things.

Comfort. Warmth. Home.

If he'd had a sketch pad, he'd have drawn her—the sharp angle of her cheekbones, the softer curve of her chin, the slight upward tilt at the corners of her eyes, her expression—the one that said she wasn't sure if she should say yes, but she couldn't quite make herself say no.

"What do you think, Rumer? Do you want the job?" He pressed his advantage, and he didn't feel a twinge of guilt about it. She'd walked into a chaos, and she'd created order. The kids needed that.

He needed that.

"You can have Saturday and Sunday off," he continued. "If you can stay a few nights a week, that would be a big help. Especially if things don't improve, and I have to spend more time here. If you can't, that's okay, too. We'll work around it."

"Lu is fine at night," she said, smoothing her hair and sighing. "And, I can't pass up the money, so I'll say yes to the job."

"Your enthusiasm is overwhelming," he responded, and Byron laughed.

"She'll warm up to the idea. No one can resist those kids. They're a handful, but there's only ever been one sweeter bunch."

"Your granddaughters?" Sullivan guessed. He'd gone to school with the Lamont sisters. Every one of them had had red hair and bright eyes, freshly washed and pressed clothes, and an air of confidence that came from being loved and valued at home.

"Who else?"

"Not me and my brothers. That's for damn sure."

Byron's bark of laughter mixed with the sound of voices drifting in from the hallway.

"Looks like my backup is here. Better hide this." Byron shoved the cigar back in his coat pocket. "There's always a snitch in every crowd."

"Afraid one of your granddaughters will find out?"

"You're damn right. Those girls won't leave me alone about the cigars. They think I should quit for health purposes." He snorted. "As if a man my age could be any heathier. I fish. I boat. I hike. I even went horse riding a couple of weeks ago."

"If you want to go again, you should come out to the homestead. I'm sure Lu would love to show you around," Rumer offered, her gaze jumping to the doorway.

The people they'd heard in the hall were there, filling the doorway, bustling into the room.

"I may take you up on that, kid, and for the record, I haven't actually smoked a cigar in over a year. I carry them around. Just in case I decide I need one," Byron said, waving at one of the women who'd walked in. Maybe in her fifties, with short dark hair and hazel eyes, she tapped her watch and smiled.

"That's Laurie Beth. She drove all the way out here to see my granddaughter. I can't keep her waiting. See you two around." He hurried away, taking the woman's arm and escorting her from the room.

"An old-fashioned gentleman," Rumer murmured. "Or someone who pretends to be."

"What you see is what you get with Byron," Sullivan responded. In all the years he'd lived in Benevolence, he'd never heard anything different. Byron played by the rules. He conducted his business in a way that benefited his family and the community. If he had a problem with someone, he said so. No gossip. No whispering behind people's backs. No undermining new business or bad-mouthing old ones. Over the years, he'd earned a solid reputation and made a lot of good friends and staunch allies.

Sullivan's father hadn't been one of them.

Then again, Robert Bradshaw hadn't been friends or allies with anyone. He'd grown up in town, left to get a degree, returned with a wife and four young kids after he'd earned a fortune in software development. He'd bought a huge old house right off Main Street and fixed it up to be the most impressive property in town—the best materials, the best fixtures, the most expensive appliances and furniture. Lawn-care crews to keep the yard beautiful. Flashy cars to park in the driveway.

He wasn't the kind of guy who explained anything to his kids or his wife, but Sullivan figured Robert had had something to prove. Maybe that he hadn't turned out to be a drunken bastard like his father.

Yeah. He hadn't been a drunk.

The bastard part? Sullivan was pretty damn sure he'd qualified.

"That's good to know," Rumer responded. "I'm tired of being surprised by the men in my life."

"I'll keep that in mind," he said, and she offered a quick, hard smile that didn't reach her eyes.

Obviously, she had some baggage.

Who didn't?

He might have asked her about it, but Kane Rainier had crossed the room. The sheriff of Benevolence, he'd been the first responder to the accident and had pulled Sunday from the burning wreck of the car. He hadn't given Sullivan many details. Based on the conditions of the two vehicles involved, there was probably a reason for that.

Not much had been left.

Just burnt-out metal carcasses sitting in a state police impound lot.

"How's she doing?" Kane asked, his gaze shifting to Rumer and then back to Sullivan.

"They stabilized her. I haven't heard anything since then."

"I was hoping the last surgery would be it." He swiped moisture from his hair. "She seemed to be improving when I was here yesterday."

"She looks better, that's for sure."

"But?"

"Her brain was swelling again. The neurosurgeon wasn't sure why. Hopefully, they can relieve the pressure and get her back on track. I'm sorry Byron had all of you come out here. There's really nothing anyone can do but wait."

"Byron didn't ask anyone to come. He called the church and got the prayer chain started. I got a call from someone who wanted a ride out here. Next thing I knew, I had four people in my SUV." He nodded toward four women who were sitting a few feet away. Hand in hand, heads bowed, tight-curled white hair tinged with blue, they were obviously praying.

He was struck by the beauty of that, by the sharp contrast of arthritic hands and smooth polyester fabric, powdered cheeks and red-rouged lips.

Another thing he would have sketched if he'd had his sketch pad: those gnarled hands linked together. Those heads bent so close bluish curl touched bluish curl. Those four sets of legs, ankles crossed just so, boots pulled on to cover nylon-clad legs.

Friendship.

That's what he'd have called the sketch.

Or, devotion.

"It would have been safer for them to stay home," he commented, oddly touched by their presence and by the fact that they'd braved the storm to come and pray.

"Sunday never stayed home," Kane responded. "Every Monday, Wednesday, and Friday, she brought a meal to each one of those ladies. Always hot. Always home-cooked. It didn't matter what the weather was. Snowstorms. Rain. Wind. She never made a big deal about it, but she enlisted my help a couple of times when one of the kids was sick and Matthias was out of town. I'm sure there were other people who helped. People don't forget those kinds of things. Deeds done without any expectation of repayment."

"Obviously, she was well liked by the community," Sullivan responded, watching as a few more people joined the prayer. He counted fifteen men and women praying or talking quietly with one another. He recognized most of them either from his childhood or from the funeral.

He could have done the rounds, said hello, thanked each and every one of them for coming. It probably would have been the right thing to do, but he didn't want to look in their eyes and see their sorrow. He already knew how deeply Sunday was loved and how desperately she'd be missed.

What he didn't know was why he'd insisted on staying away for so long. Why he'd refused so many of Sunday's invitations to birthdays, Christmases, adoption finalizations.

How many times had she called and asked him to come?

How many times had he said no because he hadn't wanted to return to Benevolence?

It was the place he'd escaped, and he'd never planned on coming back. Once a year, though, he'd trekked up the Oregon coast and across Washington State. A two-day drive and a three-day visit. He'd always arrived the day after Christmas, handed out a couple of gift cards to the kids, and stayed up late chatting with Matthias and Sunday, filling them in on his life and letting them fill him in on theirs.

He should have listened more closely. Maybe he'd have learned a little about the kids before he'd become their guardian.

He grimaced, rubbing the tense muscles in his neck.

"Sunday sounds like a wonderful person," Rumer said, cutting into the conversation and pulling his attention away from the regret that had been eating at him since he'd learned of the accident. "I'm looking forward to meeting her once she recovers." There was a hint of censure in her words and in her tone, and he realized they'd been discussing Sunday like she was already gone.

"She'll be happy to meet you, too. She'll probably want every detail of everything the kids have done while she's been in the hospital." He tried to lighten his tone. He thought he was mostly successful.

She smiled. "I'll keep a notebook. She can read it when she's ready. Photos would be nice, too. Did you take pictures of Twila's cake?"

"I probably should have."

"Of course you should have. Things have been crazy, though. You've had a lot on your mind. Now you've got help. I'll make sure we document the kids' important events."

"Like the choir competition?" Kane asked, his gaze on Rumer. He seemed curious. Sullivan could understand why. Rumer was a stranger who'd suddenly appeared in the middle of a tragedy.

"Is there one?" she asked.

"Benevolence is hosting the regional choral festival at the high school two weekends from now. A thousand or so competitors from fifth grade up to twelfth. Heavenly is performing with the middle school choir. She's also singing a solo."

"She is?" Sullivan had heard nothing about that.

"I take it she didn't mention it to you?"

"She doesn't mention anything." Except her desire to go back to wherever she'd been before she'd joined the Bradshaw clan.

"Things have been a little difficult for the family," Kane reminded him. "She probably forgot."

"I'd think something like that would be difficult to just forget. Assuming she has a choir director or music teacher who's prepping her, she has to have been reminded of it every day at school."

"*Supposed* to be prepping her. Heavenly hasn't shown up for the last four rehearsals. I only know because I got lassoed into providing traffic control during the event. April Myers is the middle school choir director and music teacher. She's also on the board of directors for the festival. She's obviously concerned about Heavenly and doesn't want to put pressure on her or your family, but she's mentioned it to me and probably just about anyone else who has anything to do with the competition. I thought I'd mention it to you. From what I hear, Heavenly has some real talent. Maybe that's her key to staying focused on where she is rather than where she's been." He smiled to take any sting out of the words.

"I'll talk to her," Sullivan said. As if that would really happen. As if the taciturn, irritable kid would suddenly want to have a nice, friendly conversation about anything.

"No pressure," Kane responded, his gaze shifting to Rumer again. "I just wanted to mention it since you were discussing documenting things. I'm Kane Rainier, by the way." He offered a hand, and she took it.

"Rumer Truehart. I'm the Bradshaws' new house-keeper, nanny, cook, and—"

"Jack of all trades," Sullivan offered, and she laughed, the sound reminding him of the summer brook that used to run through the backyard when he was a kid.

"That's as good a title as any."

"You live in Benevolence?" Kane asked.

"I'm in River Way. Or, right outside of it."

"One of my deputies grew up there," he said. "Susan Brenner? She was probably a few years ahead of you in school."

"Then, I probably didn't know her. I didn't move there until I was a teenager." She smiled, but Sullivan thought she was finished answering questions.

She glanced around the room, gestured to a coffeepot that sat empty near a coffee maker.

"How about some coffee?" she asked, completely ignoring the fact that there were two cups of it sitting on an end table nearby.

She'd set them there when she'd arrived, fished money from her purse and thrust it into his hands along with the two pastries he'd abandoned her with.

He wasn't sure what he'd done with those or the money.

"I'm good," Kane responded.

"Sullivan?"

"Actually, I think I'll see if there's any news." He was walking before either of them responded, weaving through the small group and making his way into the hall.

He didn't realize Rumer was behind him until he reached the nurses' station and she nearly barreled into his back.

"Sorry," she mumbled, moving up beside him, head down as she typed a message into her phone. "I wanted to let Minnie and Lu know I wouldn't be home tonight."

"Kane can probably give you a ride back," he responded, his attention on the nurse. She was typing something into a computer, studiously avoiding him. Probably because she knew he wanted an update that she couldn't give.

"If I go anywhere, it will be back to your place," Rumer responded, and the nurse looked up, her gaze shifting from Sullivan to Rumer.

"Lucky you," she said.

"Not so lucky. There are six kids at my place and about twenty loads of unwashed laundry."

"Six kids? Girlfriend, he must be really good to you!" She grinned.

"Oh. He is, but they're not his kids. They're his nieces and nephews. Their mother is in surgery. Sunday Bradshaw? We're obviously really anxious to get updates on her condition."

"Sunday Bradshaw." She typed something into the computer and frowned. "I remember hearing about the car accident on the news. Her husband was killed, right? On their anniversary. Poor thing. She's been through a lot. Hopefully, she'll recover and go back home to her kids. Looks like she's out of surgery as of a minute ago. Someone should be out momentarily to update you."

Thank God!

That's all Sullivan could think.

She'd survived. There'd been no further need for resuscitation. Which meant no more tough decisions.

Not tonight anyway.

"Are they bringing her to recovery?" Rumer asked as if she were family and had every right to the information.

"Soon, I'm sure. Surgery is just around the corner. You'll see the sign on the door. You can't go in, but you can wait there if you want to see her. I doubt she'll know you're around, but sometimes the family finds it comforting."

"Great! Thanks." She grabbed Sullivan's hand and started dragging him in the direction the nurse had indicated.

He went because it beat the hell out of pacing the waiting room.

They rounded the corner, and her hand was still in

his, the warmth of it suddenly registering. The smooth silky skin and long narrow fingers. The fine bones and dry palm. He wanted to slide his hand along hers, feel the thrumming pulse in her wrist, the velvety flesh there.

She dropped his hand, nearly jumping away.

As if she'd known his thoughts or felt the same heat zipping through her veins that he did.

She was gorgeous. There was no doubt about it. Smart. Savvy. If he'd been in the market for a relationship, she was exactly the kind of woman he'd have been looking for.

He wasn't.

He'd dated Sabrina for six months and broken things off two weeks before the accident. Even if Matthias hadn't been killed and Sullivan hadn't been thrust into this mess of a situation, he'd have waited a while to find someone new.

The truth was, he'd gotten tired of the game. Tired of the flirtation. The façade. The women who pretended to want one thing while they tried to get another. He was tired of keeping things shallow and light and easy because sharing more than a few pieces of himself made him seem more available than he was.

No leading women on. No hurting them.

That had been his motto for as long as he could remember.

Because, he didn't want to be his bastard father. A wife at home. A mistress or two on the side. All of them trying to be everything to him while he strung them along.

No kids plus no long-term relationships equaled an easy stress-free life. The equation was simple, and he'd solved it effectively. Until now.

Now, all hell had broken loose, his life had gone up in flames, and the only person standing between him and total destruction was a child-whisperer with silky skin, silvery-blue eyes, and the most tempting lips he'd ever seen.

Chapter Five

She'd been holding his hand, for God's sake!
Holding his hand!
Like he was a child.
Or worse, her boyfriend, significant other, lover!
"Idiot," she muttered.

"Who?" he asked, so, of course, she looked at him, stared right into his beautiful green eyes. He had long thick lashes. The kind good-looking guys always seemed to have. The kind every woman in North America seemed to drool over.

Not Rumer.

She didn't drool over anything but chocolate cake and iced sugar cookies.

"Me."

"For accepting the job? You can still back out. It was a verbal agreement, and I can't legally hold you to it. Even if I could, I wouldn't. The kids need someone who wants to be there. Not someone who's obligated."

Like you? she almost asked, and then thought better of it.

He was there because it was his family, and that was a lot better than some people would have done.

"I'm not going to back out." And, she wasn't going to explain why she'd called herself an idiot.

"Thank God for that," he responded, stepping back as the double doors that led into the surgical wing swung open.

A nurse pushed a hospital bed out, the shrouded figure lying on it so small, Rumer thought it was a child.

"Sunday?" Sullivan said, and she realized her mistake, saw that the ghostlike creature was the woman she'd caught a glimpse of in the ICU. Eyes closed, face gaunt, she had the kind of wholesome good looks Rumer had always wanted but had never been able to achieve.

"She's still sedated," the nurse said, checking one of the lines that snaked out from under a sheet.

"Things went well?" Sullivan asked, moving aside and letting a crew of medical personnel file out through the doorway. An orderly rolled the IV pole and portable oxygen machine. Right behind her, the surgeon was reading Sunday's chart.

"After the initial rough start? Yes. We're hopeful this procedure has curtailed any further injury to the brain."

"Has she shown any sign of regaining consciousness?" Sullivan asked, walking beside the doctor as they entered an elevator.

No one told Rumer she couldn't go along, so she followed, stepping in as the doors were sliding closed, listening as the doctor explained the procedure, the possible complications, the prognosis.

It all sounded more than grim.

It sounded dire, and she couldn't help studying Sunday's face, wondering if she could hear and understand what was being said.

Probably not.

Hopefully not.

But, if she could, she'd be terrified, listening to all the ways that things could go wrong, hearing the surgeon say over and over again that chances of a full recovery were zero. There would be disabilities. There would be long-term issues. There would be a dozen things that would keep her from living her life the way she had.

They arrived at recovery, and Rumer thought they'd stop her there. She knew how these things worked. She'd gone through it with Lu. Only one person in recovery at a time, but instead of telling her she'd have to wait, they ignored the fact that she was following.

Maybe they were too caught up in the details of the surgery and recovery to notice.

She kept out of the way, half listening and half wondering, her mind drifting along, trying to connect the unconscious woman with the six children she'd met. They obviously weren't all biologically hers. As a matter of fact, Rumer wouldn't be surprised if all the kids had been adopted.

Not that that changed anything.

The magnitude of the tragedy couldn't get any bigger. Six kids had lost their father. From the way the surgeon was talking, they were going to lose their mother, too.

Sullivan was obviously hearing the same pessimism she was. His jaw was tight, his expression grim. He had a day's worth of stubble on his chin and looked like he was ready for a fight, fists clenched, eyes flashing.

"So, what you're saying," he said, "is that you're giving up on her recovering."

"Mr. Bradshaw, if we'd given up, we'd have never done the surgery. We're simply being realistic. She's been in a coma for weeks. That could stretch into months, or even years."

"Or, it could end today," Rumer cut in, showing her hand and letting everyone know that she'd walked in uninvited.

No one told her to leave, but the doctor sighed. "It could. We don't know, and that's the limits of medicine. With all the high-tech images, all the peer-reviewed studies and documented successes and failures, we still can't predict a person's outcome."

"Exactly." Rumer stepped up to the bed, looked down at the woman who had six children depending on her, believing in her, hoping and praying she'd come home to them.

She didn't know Sunday Bradshaw from Adam, but after seeing the Bradshaw kids, she was pretty darn sure she knew her heart. She lifted her hand and held it gently. It felt warm, blood pulsing just beneath nearly transparent skin.

The surgeon was talking again, outlining the next step. Stabilize her. Get her breathing on her own. See if her vitals stayed good. Make sure her bones had knit together well, that her lungs had healed, that her body was in working order, and then, send her to a rehab facility.

Or a long-term care facility.

Depending on how things progressed.

"You're going to progress just fine," Rumer said, leaning down to whisper it in her ear. "Your kids need you to come home. You should see them—Heavenly wearing the teeniest shirt she can squeeze into. Moisey kicking every person she disagrees with. And, the twins . . . well, they're cute little buggers, but they sure do need a firm hand. Twila is trying to keep everything under control, but I've got a feeling that little one has some deep water running beneath her stillness. I haven't spent much time with the baby, but I'm sure she's missing you as much as the rest of them."

Sunday's fingers twitched, and Rumer was so surprised, she nearly released her hand.

"Are you trying to squeeze my hand?" she asked, and felt another twitch.

"Is something wrong?" Sullivan asked, cutting off whatever else the surgeon had to say.

"I swear she's trying to squeeze my hand."

"Hun," the nurse said, "that's just a muscle spasm. Sometimes it happens after surgery."

"Does it happen at exactly the time the patient is asked to respond?" Rumer asked, because she didn't think Sunday's muscles were twitching unintentionally. She thought the young mother was trying to communicate.

"Sometimes." The surgeon stepped to the other side of the bed, frowning slightly as she lifted Sunday's other hand. "Sunday? Can you hear me?"

Another little twitch, and Rumer's heart started racing faster than Ezekiel the pony when he heard the food buckets being rolled out.

"She did it again," she said, and the surgeon's frown deepened.

"I didn't feel anything."

"Maybe because my hand is the one she's trying to squeeze."

"We all want to believe that she's making conscious movements. Trust me, I'd be as thrilled as anyone if she did, but sometimes love is blind. Sometimes we see what we want to see rather than what's there."

"What does love have to do with anything?" She was getting annoyed now, frustrated by the surgeon's un-willingness to believe the clear-cut evidence.

Or, at least, what *she* thought of as clear-cut evidence.

The medical community obviously didn't agree.

Even Sullivan looked doubtful, his brow furrowed, his focus on Sunday.

"You're her sister-in-law. You want her to improve. It's natural and it's right. She needs you rooting for her, but I don't want to give you false hope. We see these kinds of unconscious movements all the time."

"I'm not—" she began, planning to correct the as-sumption, but Sullivan put a hand on her nape, his palm calloused and warm.

"It *is* hard to see *family* suffering," he said, emphasiz-ing *family*.

She might be distracted by his warm, rough skin against hers, but she sure as heck could still take a hint.

"Right. It is," she agreed as his hand slid from her nape to her shoulder and settled there. "But, I know what I felt, and I know she was trying to communicate. Weren't you, Sunday?"

Nothing for a heartbeat, and then the twitch again.

"She did it again."

"Ms. Bradshaw," the surgeon began.

"Call me Rumer." *Otherwise, I might not realize you're speaking to me, seeing as how Bradshaw isn't my name.*

She kept the last part to herself.

"Rumer, I know you want to believe that she's improving, but, as I've said—"

Sunday's free hand shifted, moving across the blanket the doctor had set it on. Just a little slide. Maybe an inch, but it was enough to stop the surgeon's words, to make the nurse freeze, her hand on a probe she was trying to attach to Sunday's heart monitor.

"Did you see that?" the nurse asked, and the surgeon nodded, pulling out a penlight and checking Sunday's pupils.

"Sunday?" she said.

Another small movement.

Rumer's heart was galloping now, pounding so hard, she thought it might burst right out of her chest.

"You are in there, aren't you?" she asked, and Sunday's hand tightened on hers. No mistake this time. It wasn't just a twitch. She was holding on, clinging as if she were trying to keep from floating away, and then her hand relaxed and it was over, whatever had drawn her close to consciousness gone.

"That didn't look like unconscious movement," Sullivan said, his hand still on Rumer's shoulder.

She could have stepped away.

She should have, but she was a Truehart and prone to making lousy decisions when it came to men.

So, of course, she stayed right where she was.

"I'll admit, that surprised me." The surgeon smiled, and since it was the first smile Rumer had seen from her, she was counting it as a good sign.

"Do you think she might be coming out of the coma?" Sullivan asked.

"It's hard to say. Once we get her back to her room, I'll run a few tests and see how the results compare to our baseline. I don't want to give you undue hope, but it did seem like she was responding. We'll be moving her back to her room in ICU soon, if you two want to meet us there."

What Rumer wanted to do was keep standing right where she was, holding Sunday's hand and waiting for another sign that she was in there.

Sullivan leaned past her, his hand falling away as he touched Sunday's cheek. "The kids are fine, Sunday. They're doing great, but they'd really love for you to come home. I'd really love it, too, because as much as I appreciate all the little rug rats, I'm just not parental material and the only one of your kids who doesn't know it is Oya. If you stay here too long, she might just figure it out."

Not even a hint of movement from Sunday, and he sighed, stepping away. "I guess I'd better go fill people in on what's going on."

He sounded so tired, so overwhelmed, Rumer did exactly what she shouldn't. She opened her mouth. Again. "Why don't you let me take care of that?"

"I don't think running interference between me and Sunday's friends is part of your job description," he said as they walked into the hall.

"I thought my job description was jack-of-all-trades?"

"Around the farm, maybe. Everywhere else, I think I can handle things." He smiled, touching her back as the elevator door opened. Sure as God made sunrise and dandelions, that was all she could think about. His hand. Right there at the base of her spine.

She engaged her brain for a change and moved

away, because she had already decided she didn't need Sullivan's brand of trouble.

She'd take the job.

She'd do her best for the kids and for Sunday, but she was going to give Sullivan a wide berth while she did it.

No way was she getting pulled in by his gorgeous eyes and dimple-flashing smile.

"I really don't mind passing the surgeon's information along. Maybe I can ask the sheriff to give me a ride back to your place while I'm at it. The kids need some consistency. It will be good for me to be there when they wake up."

And, better for her to be far away from him.

"So, you haven't changed your mind?" They stepped off the elevator again. The waiting room was just ahead, and she could hear voices drifting out from it.

"About the job? No."

"I'm relieved. I don't have the time or the patience to interview more people."

"You didn't interview me," she reminded him.

"True. I'll have to thank Byron for convincing you."

"The kids convinced me, and the pay."

"I was trying to make you an offer you couldn't refuse. I'm glad it worked out. The kids need someone like you around."

"They need their mother, but I'll do what I can to make things easier while they wait for her."

"You'll do a hell of a lot better than I've been doing."

"From what I saw—"

"I hope you're not going to say that I was doing fine, because we both know that I wasn't."

"I was going to say that from what I saw you were in over your head but managing to tread water."

"Barely. But, thanks for not adding that." He smiled, flashing his dimple again.

God!

Did he have to have a dimple?

They walked into the waiting room, and he fielded dozens of questions from a bunch of well-meaning people who seemed to really care about Sunday and her family. They wanted to know what the doctor had said, how Sunday looked, if it seemed like she was recovering. The four blue-haired ladies who'd been sitting side by side stood in a semicircle at the head of the group, lobbing questions as quickly as he could answer, talking about meal trains and after-school activities, pulling binders out of their oversize purses and taking notes.

Rumer glanced at *her* oversize bag. Besides the fact that it was bright blue, it was a close match. She had the sturdy boots, too. Thick-soled no-frill ones that she'd borrowed from Lu. And, the curly hair.

She smoothed her hair, trying to get a feel for just how curly it had become, and realized the hair she'd straightened for her interview had become tight ringlets. If she cut off a few inches, bleached it white, and tinged it purple, she could probably join whatever group these women belonged to.

A church prayer group maybe, but they weren't there because of some vague religious obligation. They were asking questions about the kids as if they knew them and Sunday well, as if they'd been a part of their lives for years and considered them family.

That wasn't something Rumer had much experience with. Lu might be a great businesswoman with a heart for special needs kids, but she wasn't social. Aside from church every Sunday morning, she didn't spend much time making connections. Not that there were many people to connect with in River Way. The town was tiny by anyone's standards. Just a dot on the map, a pit stop on the way to somewhere else—rural properties owned by people who wanted to be left alone, one small grocery store, a couple of ramshackle businesses that sold mostly junk, a gas station with one pump, a seedy bar, and the little white church on the hill that attracted people from River Way and from the unincorporated land that surrounded it.

Benevolence was a different cup of tea—vibrant and thriving, a mecca for people who wanted small-town life and a slower pace. She'd been there a few times when she was a kid—buying feed and tackle from the saddlery with Lu. She'd been with Jake, but they hadn't done the normal Main Street thing—walking through shops and buying local goods. No. He'd wanted to attend wine-tasting festivals and try out the local bars. One year, they'd spent hours at a brewery twenty miles outside of town. Another year, they'd spent most of the night at a wine shop learning how to pair the right cheese with the right wine.

The cheese had been good.

The wine had been fine.

The beer had been okay.

But, she'd have rather gone berry picking in the orchards near town, or rented a kayak and taken it out on the river. Not to fish. Just to enjoy the hot sun, the brown-blue water, the golden landscape. She'd have rather had chocolate or ice cream or cake, but she'd gone along with Jake's plans because she'd thought a good relationship was based on compromise and mutual respect.

Not that she'd ever actually been witness to one. She'd read books and watched movies and listened to the couples at church who'd been married forever. Based on those things, she'd figured compromise and respect were key, so she'd given a lot of both.

And ended up finding a thong in her bed, an e-mail trail of infidelity, and a secret bank account Jake had been using to buy gifts for his lover.

Lovers?

Probably.

He hadn't admitted it, but that was Jake—die-hard denial until she'd walked out. Now he was living in the apartment they'd shared with the woman he'd insisted he hadn't cheated with.

Yeah. She should have bypassed compromise and gone straight for chocolate shops and berry picking.

Lesson learned.

"Are you okay, dear?" a well-dressed woman asked. Maybe in her early fifties. Thin. Perfectly pressed and coiffed. Not a hair out of place or a piece of lint on her wool coat.

"I'm fine. Thanks." She patted her hair, realized there was absolutely nothing she could do to tame it, and let her hand drop away.

"My father-in-law tells me that you're the Bradshaws' new nanny."

It wasn't a question, but she nodded. "That's right."

"I'm glad to hear that someone is willing to take on the task."

"It *is* a paid position."

"That's what Byron said, but my friends and I didn't think there'd been anyone in town who'd be . . ."

"Stupid enough to take it?"

"Brave enough," she replied. "I'm Janelle Lamont, by the way."

"Nice to meet you, and congratulations on your new granddaughter."

"Thank you. She's precious. Absolutely precious. I'd show you a photo, but then I'd end up showing every photo I took of her and my other granddaughters. The other two are just as gorgeous, of course."

"I thought Byron said this was number two?"

"Technically, she is, but we've got a third. She's not quite official yet. My oldest daughter and her husband will finalize the adoption in a couple of months."

"That's wonderful!"

"Isn't it? Byron doesn't usually talk about it. He's afraid it'll jinx things. Me? I know little Merry was meant for our family, and I don't have a doubt that the adoption will be finalized." Her cheeks were pink with pleasure, her eyes shining. "We've been very fortunate. I wish I could say the same for the Bradshaws. It just seemed like one tragedy after another with that family."

"What do you mean?"

Her smile fell away, and she shook her head. "Nothing. I shouldn't have said anything. Gossip travels through Benevolence at the speed of light, and I've vowed to never be part of it."

"We're not in Benevolence," Rumer pointed out, and Janelle smiled again.

"You're quick. That's good. Those twins are going to keep you on your toes, and don't believe Milo's sweet-as-pie perfect-gentleman act. He's as much trouble as his brother. He's just quieter about it. I had them in Sunday school last summer. And, the stories I could tell . . ." She sighed. "But, I wouldn't want to scare you away."

"If the kids haven't managed to do that already, I don't think a story or two will." As a matter of fact, she wanted to hear them. Forewarned was forearmed, and based on what she'd seen so far, she thought that getting Sunday's kids to toe the line could be an epic battle of wits and fortitude.

"You'll be fine, and if you run into any trouble, call Chocolate Haven or Benevolence Baptist Church. They're the disseminators of all local information. One call, and you can have an army of help lined up at the door. I'd better head out. I'm giving a couple of the ladies a ride home."

She walked away, and Rumer realized that most of the rest of the group was leaving too. Apparently, Sullivan had answered enough questions, and they were ready to head home. They moved toward the door, quietly talking to one another, discussing the details they'd been given, making plans for meal trains and homework help, for fund-raisers to help pay medical bills and keep the farm going.

She liked what that said about Sunday and what it said about the town. Benevolence had to be a decent place to live if it had so many decent people in it.

And chocolate.

It had chocolate.

Which she was absolutely going to try. If for no other reason than to prove that she could do whatever the heck she wanted.

Enough of the compromises.

Enough of the caving to someone else's whims.

She dug through her purse, trying to find the business

card Byron had given her. She pulled out a scarf, mittens, a notepad, and a pair of scissors. Three pencils. A pen. The nub of a crayon and her wallet.

"Need some help?" Sullivan said, and she nearly jumped out of her skin.

"Good golly! You nearly scared the life out of me!"

"Sorry about that." He didn't look sorry. He looked amused. "I didn't realize you were so engrossed in your hunt."

"It's not exactly a hunt. I was looking for the business card Byron gave me."

"Feeling the need for chocolate?"

"Just thinking that I'd like to visit his shop one day. It sounds quaint."

"It is. Penny-candy jars on shelves. Old-fashioned cash register. A glass display case that's been there since the doors opened. And chocolate so good people come from all over the country to try it."

"Really?"

"That's what they tell me. I haven't lived around there since I was a teen."

"You're living there now."

"Hopefully not long-term," he responded.

"You don't like Benevolence?"

"I don't *not* like it."

"That's not an answer, Sullivan."

"No. I guess it isn't." He took the purse from her hand and pulled the business card out. No fuss. No muss. No digging through whatever else Rumer had tucked away. "Here you go."

"Thanks," she muttered, taking the card and the purse, one of the mittens falling from her hand, the scarf trailing the floor as she bent to pick it up.

"Here." He took everything except the card, somehow managing to grab it all before she could stop him.

"What are you doing?"

"Helping." He put everything back in the purse and handed it to her.

"You do know women don't like their purses messed with?"

"What women?"

"Me."

He smiled. "I'll keep that in mind."

"It's a little too late for that. You already messed in it." And found the card that she would have sworn wasn't there.

"Then, I'll have to make it up to you. I'll bring you to Chocolate Haven one day."

"That would be . . ."

Fun was the word she almost used.

Because going to a quaint chocolate shop in a quaint town with a guy like Sullivan sounded interesting and exotic and nice.

For once, her brain was working faster than her mouth could speak, and she didn't say what she was thinking.

". . . hard to do while I'm taking care of the kids," she finished.

"Like I said, the kids love Chocolate Haven."

Oh.

Okay.

Not the two of them.

The eight of them going for chocolate.

That she could handle. "Is the shop big enough to fit all of them?"

"Probably. If we order quick and get out fast."

"We could go after Heavenly's choir competition."

"If she participates, and I doubt she will."

"Why wouldn't she? You don't get volunteered to be in things like that. You have to sign up."

"Can you actually see Heavenly signing up for anything?" he asked.

"No, but, then, I've never seen her when her mother wasn't in a coma and her father wasn't . . ."

"Dead? It's okay to say it. The words don't make things any worse or any better. And, you're right about Heavenly. It's hard to say what she was like before this happened."

"Has she been in the family long?"

"They fostered her for a year or two, I think. I'm a little hazy on the timeline. The adoption was finalized a couple of months ago. I do know that."

"Poor Heavenly," she murmured, remembering her own journey through foster care—the constant revolving doors, the neat little ranchers, the tiny apartments, the smiling foster parents and the grouchy ones. The unknowns had been the hardest part, getting into the caseworker's car and being driven off to the next place and the next.

None of them had ever been home.

Even Lu's place had never really felt like that.

"I feel sorry for her, but there's not a hell of a lot I can do to make things better. I've tried to be patient. I've tried to explain things." He raked a hand through his hair. No ring on his left hand.

Not that she'd been looking. She'd just happened to notice. In passing. "I can tell you from my experience in the foster care system that all the patience in the world isn't going to help. All the love and support you offer won't be enough to change things if she doesn't want them to."

"Teacher and foster parent, huh? You're way overqual-ified for the job."

"Foster child," she responded.

"Lu adopted you?"

"No. I was in foster care because my mother was a hardcore drug addict and lost custody of me when I was a kid. Since my mom was a runaway and not using her real name, it took a couple of years for CPS to re-alize I had relatives. Once they did, they contacted Lu, and she agreed to take me in." She knew she sounded cold and unaffected. She knew she was wearing the look that she'd perfected years ago. The one that said she didn't care and it didn't matter.

But, of course, she did and it did, and she was too old to pretend things that weren't true.

"I'm sorry, Rumer."

"Why? Lu is great. So is Minnie. They may be a little odd, but they're good people, and I'm fortunate they agreed to finish raising me. If they hadn't, I'd probably be living the same kind of life my mother did."

"Did?"

"A figure of speech, Sullivan. She's still alive. As far as I know." She turned away, done with the discussion. Her past wasn't something she shared. Not with anyone.

She wasn't sure why she'd shared it with him.

He was nearly a stranger, for God's sake! A man she'd met a few hours ago. She'd spent four years living with Jake, and she'd never mentioned a word about her early childhood.

Then again, he'd never asked.

She frowned. "I guess we should go to Sunday's room."

"Why? So, we can stop talking about your past?" he asked, and she turned to face him again.

"Because, I'm worried about her. The surgeon doesn't seem to believe that she's improving. I do."

"She's been unresponsive since the accident, Rumer."

"She wasn't tonight."

"Maybe not, but I'm not telling the kids that. They don't need to get their hopes up and then have them dashed."

"We all need hope sometimes," she argued.

"But most of us would prefer not to have it crushed because we were given wrong information and had wrong expectations."

"I didn't take you for a pessimist, Sullivan."

"I'm a realist. There's a difference."

"Not from where I'm standing."

"Then, maybe you're standing in the wrong place," he offered with a quick smile that made her heart jump and her pulse race.

Not good.

Not good at all!

"We're both standing in the wrong place. We were heading to Sunday's room. That seems like a better plan than hanging out here," she responded, and then she walked into the hall and away from Sullivan as fast as her clompy oversize boots would allow.

They spent an hour in Sunday's room.

She didn't move a hand or twitch a finger.

To Sullivan's surprise, Rumer was almost as still.

She packed a lot of energy into her small frame, and he'd seen her put it to good use with the kids, but she'd turned that part of herself off. Instead of bustling around and organizing, she'd spent the entire time sitting beside Sunday's bed, holding her hand and talking quietly about the farm and the children.

He wasn't sure if she expected a response, but she seemed determined to fill the quiet with soft, easy words and sweet descriptions of Twila's birthday party.

She made it sound like a princess party—the kind where little girls danced, rode ponies, and jumped in bouncy castles.

She didn't mention the burnt cakes, the boys' jaunt down to the river, or Moisey's wandering. She didn't say that the house was a mess or the kids were running wild, or that she'd been hired because Sullivan didn't know what the hell he was doing. She said the things he'd have wanted to hear if he were the parent lying in the hospital bed. And, he appreciated that, because he'd run out of words days ago. He'd used them up talking to teachers, casserole deliverers, kids, random people from random government entities who were all there to get a piece of whatever pie Matt had left.

He hadn't left much—minimal life insurance, a few thousand dollars in the business bank account. Matt hadn't paid property taxes the previous year. He owed money on farm equipment that had been purchased a couple of years back. There'd be an insurance settlement eventually. The truck driver who'd killed him had been on company time, driving a company rig. No amount of money could bring Matt back, but at least Sunday wouldn't lose the farm. Sullivan and his brothers had already sent a check to the county for past taxes. They planned to pay off the equipment, too. Porter and Flynn would be back in a week to sit down and go over the finances.

They'd been in crisis mode before and during the funeral.

Now, they were planning things out, trying to prepare a future for six kids who might or might not get their mother back.

His phone rang, and he pulled it out, glancing at the number. Porter. *Finally.*

"It's about time," he said by way of greeting.

"Sorry, bro. I just finished with a client." A former marine, he'd spent ten years serving the country. Now he served overpaid celebrities, high-level government officials, and just about anyone else who was willing to pay the price for personal security. "How's she doing?"

"She's stable. They had to resuscitate her twice."

"Were you able to get in touch with Flynn before the surgery?"

"No. He's probably out in the middle of nowhere without cell reception. God alone knows when I'm going to hear from him."

"Sorry you had to make the decision on your own. We agreed to do this as a team. Flynn and I are falling short on that."

"So am I," he muttered, and Porter chuckled.

"Don't sell yourself short. I'm sure you're great at playing Mr. Mom. And, for the record, I would have made the decision to resuscitate, too, and I'm pretty damn sure Flynn would have. Those kids need their mother."

"Not if she's got no quality of life and they have to spend the rest of theirs watching her suffer," he muttered, and regretted it immediately.

"Shhhhh," Rumer hissed. "She might be able to hear you."

"Who's that?" Porter asked. "A nurse? If so, see if

she'll talk to me. I have a couple of medical questions I want to ask."

"She's the new housekeeper you and Flynn advertised for."

"Really? I just wrote up the ad and sent it in a couple of days ago."

"And forgot to tell me."

"That was Flynn's job. I did my part."

"I guess my desperation was obvious."

"Nah. We just figured you needed some time to work. None of us are going to be able to do the full-time parent thing. Not for long stretches of time. Not with that many kids. Eventually, we may have to split the kids up and each of us take a couple—"

"How about we discuss that when you're here next weekend?" Much as he wasn't enjoying the responsibility of taking care of six kids, he wasn't ready to contemplate splitting them up.

"That's fine. Tell me about the hired help. Is she as old as Methuselah?"

"Not even close."

"A former marine?"

"No."

"A glutton for punishment, then? You know the kind: dour. Mean-looking. Has a dozen cats and a couple of those yappy little dogs."

"Not even close. She's a teacher."

"Of what? Primates? Does she work at a zoo?"

"No, but in a couple of days, she'll be able to add that to her résumé."

Porter laughed. Full-out. Bold. Just like he'd always been. Out of the four Bradshaw brothers, he'd been the most daring. Not the oldest, but usually the leader. At least when it had come to getting into trouble.

"Good point. You hired her quickly. Afraid she'd figure out how bad things were and run?"

"Desperate," he admitted, meeting Rumer's eyes.

She smiled. Just a quick curve of her lips, but it caught his attention. Held it. Because, the angle of her jaw was perfect, the curve of her cheek, the misty blue-gray of her eyes—they were a Renaissance painting, alive with detail and texture and color.

And, suddenly, he wanted to cross the room, run his palm up her nape, let his fingers tangle in her hair. He wanted to drink in every detail of her, explore every angle and curve and plane.

"You still there, Sullivan?" Porter asked, breaking the spell, chasing away the quick heat that had been flooding through him.

"Yeah."

"Did you hear the question?"

"I missed it." He turned away, irritated with himself. Frustrated that he was in the middle of a mess of problems, and had been thinking about creating another one.

"Did you check her credentials?"

"Whose?"

"The new hire?" he asked.

"I haven't had time. Things have been crazy here."

"They're probably not going to be any less crazy anytime soon. Send me her résumé. I'll run a background check through the system at work. Actually, I'm at the office. Give me her name. I'll get things started. I don't like the idea of her spending nights in the house with the kids, if we're not sure of who she is or where she came from."

"She doesn't look like a knife-wielding lunatic to me, so I think we're good."

Rumer laughed.

Porter did not.

"I'm not worried about knives or lunatics. After growing up the way we did, I've got no doubt you can handle yourself. I'm worried about pedophiles, child traffickers. Basic scum-of-the-earth evil that should never get within two hundred miles of a kid."

"I don't think she's any of those things, either," he said. "She was a teacher until a couple of months ago. She had to have a background check for that."

"Why'd she leave teaching?"

"Her grandmother had a heart attack. Look, Porter, I know how you are. Every rock turned, a light shined in every corner and closet and hole, but we don't have time for that. The kids need someone. She's here, and—"

"How about I explain things to him?" Rumer asked, suddenly beside him, her curls brushing his shoulder as she grabbed the phone, held it to her ear. "This is Rumer Truehart. The Bradshaws' new housekeeper and nanny. Can I help you?"

She listened for a moment. Nodded. Listened some more.

Finally, she shrugged. "That's fine by me. Run whatever kind of background check you want. My juvenile record is sealed, so I doubt you'll turn up much dirt." She paused. "No. I'm not kidding. I was a wild child with an attitude. Just like one of your nieces. Maybe I can teach her to have some sense, so she doesn't make the same mistakes I did."

She paused again. Smiled. "Yeah. I make a mean apple pie, a to-die-for pound cake, and fried chicken even the pickiest eater will love. Mashed potatoes. Fresh green beans. Grilled corn with lots of melted butter. Unfortunately, the terms of my contract stipulate that I have the weekends off. You and your brothers will have to cook for yourselves while you're here. Now, if you'll excuse me, I need to go polish my knives and check in with my parole officer."

She handed the phone back to Sullivan, winked, and sashayed out of the room.

And, God help him, he was smiling as he watched.

Because, it took a ballsy person to go up against any of the Bradshaw men. They'd been raised hard, and they'd become hard. Only Matthias had been gentle. He'd been like their mother—kind to a fault, easy to talk to, a rule follower who toed the line.

They'd all expected him to do what their father wanted—go into software development and make a fortune before he turned thirty. Instead, he'd married his high school sweetheart and helped run her family farm. As far as Sullivan knew, the day Matthias married, Robert had cut all ties with him. Just like he'd cut ties with his other three sons. Utter disappointments. Every last one of them. Or, so he'd said dozens of time while they were growing up.

Fun memories, and he wasn't smiling anymore.

Robert Bradshaw had been a bastard. Maybe, he'd been raised by one himself. Sullivan didn't know. His father had never talked about his past or the family he came from. He'd been too busy using his fists and his tongue to control his sons.

That had only worked for as long as they'd allowed it.

Eventually, they'd become too big, too strong, and too hard to be beaten down by an aging man with an anger problem. Robert must have known that. By the time they'd reached high school, the physical abuse had mostly stopped. All that remained were the verbal slings and arrows. Those had been easy enough to ignore. It wasn't like he and his brothers spent much time at home. By that point, they'd created their own closed group. The four Bradshaw brothers against the world.

He supposed they were still like that.

No matter the trouble, they were there for one another.

Even now. Even in this. Even with Matthias dead, they had his back. They'd do what they had to for his family. For as long as it took.

He walked to the bed, lifting Sunday's hand and giving it a gentle squeeze. "Don't worry. We'll do right by your kids. I may not be able to promise much, but I can promise you that."

She didn't give even a hint of a response.

He set her hand back on the mattress, eyed the machines that blipped along with her heart rate. God willing, she'd recover. In a week or two or twenty, she'd be back at home with her children, gluing the pieces of their shattered lives back together.

If she wasn't . . .

They'd cross that bridge when they came to it.

For now, he'd be thankful for the small things—the tiny movement of her hand after surgery, the cake that hadn't burnt to a crisp, and the help-wanted ad in the *Benevolence Times* that had somehow made its way to the exact place it needed to be at just exactly the right time.

Sullivan had never been much for believing in miracles. He'd spent too much of his early years hoping for and never getting one. He'd listened to his mother pray to a God who didn't seem to hear, and he'd wonder why she kept believing and hoping. Miracles, it had always seemed, were for other people and other families. Not for his broken one.

This though? It seemed like the real deal, the answer to unspoken prayers, the life preserver thrown to the drowning man. The thing he hadn't even known he needed until it walked right out in front of him wearing bright yellow bell-bottoms and a gauzy white shirt.

Chapter Six

So . . .

Caring for six kids and a huge house was a lot harder than teaching third grade. It was also harder than mucking stalls, cleaning pigsties, and herding sea monkeys. Rumer was only guessing about the latter since she'd never actually attempted to herd brine shrimp.

She might be tempted, though.

After this gig, just about anything seemed possible.

She finished scrubbing the last of the dinner dishes, the glass casserole finally free of the weird mixture of noodles, mystery meat, and red sauce it had contained. It hadn't been quite as bad as Minnie's spaghetti pie, but it had come darn close. The meal train conductor had dropped it off after school, offering a quick explanation before thrusting it into Rumer's hands. She'd left a cloth grocery bag, too, filled with wilted salad in ziplock baggies, tomatoes with bits of molded flesh, and a store-bought cake that had been about as hard as the rock Milo had begun carrying around.

Yeah.

A rock.

That he'd named Henry.

Apparently, Milo had been wanting a dog for a couple of years. His parents had promised that he could have one on his birthday if he proved that he was responsible enough. A pet rock, according to Milo, was the first step in proving that he was.

Not that his parents were around to see it.

And, maybe that was the point.

Maybe he just needed to feel like he was still connected to them, that somehow, despite the fact that they weren't there, they would follow through on the promise they'd made to him.

Just thinking about it made Rumer's throat tight and her eyes sting. She'd only been working for the Bradshaws for three days, and she was already getting a little too attached.

But, that was the point, right? To love them exactly the way their mother did until she returned to them.

She dried the dish and slid it into a cupboard, wiped down the counter, and grabbed the bucket of slop from the mudroom. Carrying it out to the hog was supposed to be Heavenly's job, but she was in her room with the door closed and locked, fuming because Milo had cut up one of her teeny-tiny shirts to make clothes for Henry.

She'd been mad as a hatter, her eyes flashing, her cornrows vibrating with fury. She'd wanted him punished, and she'd wanted it to happen STAT. Rumer would have been happy to give some consequences if Milo hadn't found the shirt lying on the floor in the mudroom. He'd assumed it was an old rag. He'd explained the entire thing in excruciating detail as he'd clutched the cloth-covered rock like it was his best friend.

In Rumer's estimation, a teeny-tiny shirt left on the mudroom floor could easily be mistaken for trash or rags. She couldn't punish him for making a mistake. She'd told Heavenly that and suggested that the tween's attitude was a great way to get out of eating the mystery meat casserole they'd been gifted, because if she didn't cool it with the death glare, she'd be dismissed to her room.

Heavenly hadn't waited to be dismissed. She'd pushed away from the table and stomped to her room, slamming the door for good measure.

Not a bad show, but Rumer would have done a lot better at that age.

She unlocked the back door and stepped out into the cold night air. It was quiet here. Peaceful in a way she'd never found the homestead. Maybe because they were farther from the highway. There were no visible house or streetlights. No noisy traffic passing by. Nothing but the velvety darkness and the quiet.

She made her way across the yard, opening the gate that led into the pasture. Bessie's pen was a quarter mile away, its dirt floor layered daily with fresh hay. She'd helped the twins do that, the same way she'd helped Twila fix fence posts near the west edge of the pasture, helped Moisey make lunches for all her school-age siblings, and helped Heavenly with her math homework.

Keeping the kids busy was part of the plan.

So far it was going as well as could be expected.

She made it across the field without sloshing too much of the mystery casserole goop. Too bad for the hog, because Rumer had tasted a piece of mystery

meat, and she'd nearly gagged. Hopefully, Bessie
wouldn't get sick and die from it.

She approached the pen as quietly as she could.
Bessie seemed sweet enough, but she was a hog, and
she might squeal and bellow if she was woken from a
sound sleep. Rumer had managed to get all the kids in
bed on time, and she didn't want to give any of them
an excuse to get up again. After three long days of kid
and housekeeping duty, she needed a little peace.

She also didn't want Sullivan to emerge from his
room.

He'd been there most of the day, working on his research paper. He'd come out once or twice to check on
Oya and to ask if the school had called yet.

They'd both known that a phone call was inevitable.
Rumer had been up to the school three times in three
days. Currently, Moisey was back at school and Maddox
was out—suspended for tackling another little boy
who'd told him his mother was going to die.

The elementary school teachers and principal were
being as patient as anyone could be expected to be, but
Benevolence Elementary wasn't a haven for troubled
kids. It was filled with middle-class students from
middle-class backgrounds. Most of them went home to
people who cared about them. Those who didn't hid
their troubles with façades of polite civility. No fights in
the halls. No shoves off swings. No throwing a handful
of crumbled cookie into a rival's hair. The Bradshaw
bunch had done all those things and more. Rumer had
seen the files. The trouble the kids were having hadn't
begun with the accident, and it wasn't going to end
when Sunday came home.

Obviously, the problems—whatever they were—
needed to be dealt with, but Rumer had no background

on the kids, no idea where they'd come from or what they'd experienced before joining their family. She'd asked Sullivan, and he'd seemed just as clueless. He wasn't even sure which child had joined the family first.

She'd figured that out by asking Twila. The boys had been first, adopted through foster care. Then, Moisey, who was from Ethiopia. Twila had joined the family three years ago, and a year after that the Bradshaws had taken in Heavenly as a foster. Oya was Heavenly's half sister, and she'd joined the family three days after she was born. That adoption had been finalized before Oya was a month old. Right after that, adoption paperwork was filed for Heavenly. She'd become an official member of the family a few months before the accident.

Rumer might not have case files and backgrounds, but she could imagine what their lives were like before they'd become Bradshaws. Their heartbreaking beginnings should have had a great ending. Everyone she spoke to mentioned how loving Sunday and Matt were, how determined they'd been to provide a loving home for their children.

That was great. It was even noble. Sometimes, though, love wasn't enough. Sometimes kids needed firm rules and set boundaries. She wasn't sure if that's what Sunday and Matt had done, but it was what she was attempting.

Excusing behavior because of background and circumstances would only set the kids up for failure. That was Rumer's opinion, and the school shared it. You punch, kick, or tackle another student and you're suspended. Three suspensions, and expulsion was possible. It didn't matter what your reasons were, it didn't matter how justified you felt. Do the crime, do the time. Period. No exceptions.

Moisey was on suspension number one.

Maddox was on his second.

At the rate they were going, they'd be expelled before Christmas break.

She shuddered, opening the gate that led into the pigpen.

"Hey, Bessie," she called. "It's just me, bringing you some dinner. Hopefully, it won't kill you off."

"Is there a reason why you think it would?" Sullivan asked, his voice so unexpected, she jumped. The slop splashed her shoes and jeans.

"Dang, you scared the stuffing out of me. Again," she muttered, trudging over to Bessie's trough. She'd have dumped the slop in, but Sullivan had followed her through the pen.

He took the bucket, poured the slop into the trough, and stepped away as Bessie nosed her way toward the food.

"Is something in here I should be worried about feeding her?" he asked. "Because, if she dies, Twila will never get over it."

"Nothing but the casserole someone from the meal train brought."

"Is that what I smelled cooking?"

"I'm afraid so."

"Did the kids eat it?"

"A few bites each, then I relented and let them have sandwiches."

"And, they're still alive?" he asked.

It took a moment for the question to register. When it did, she laughed. "God! I hope so. I didn't think to check their pulses before they left the table."

"Assuming they are—and since I heard the twins

whispering in their rooms before I came out here, I think that's a safe bet—Bessie should be fine."

"The twins are awake? Last time I checked on them, they looked sound asleep."

"They're good actors." He rubbed the back of his neck, watching as Bessie chowed down on the slop. "Then again, based on how badly that stuff stunk when it was cooking, it's possible they passed out for a few minutes."

"You could smell it?"

"Couldn't you?"

"Yes, but it's a big house. I was hoping it hadn't permeated the walls."

"It had, and it was bad enough to turn my stomach."

"Is that why you didn't come down for dinner?" She'd sent Moisey up to tell him it was ready. Moisey returned saying that he'd eat later.

"No. I'd finally made progress on my research, and I didn't want to stop. Of course, if the food had smelled as good as last night's dinner, I probably would have stopped anyway." He smiled, and her heart skipped a beat.

Literally. It beat and then nothing. Just an empty feeling in her chest and the odd thought that in all her years of dating, she'd never had a guy's smile stop her heart.

"Maybe I should ask for the recipe. I could make it every time you're feeling unproductive. The smell might motivate you to stay in your room and keep working."

He chuckled. "That won't be necessary. With you at the house, I'm getting a lot more done."

"You never told me what you were writing about."

"I didn't want to bore you."

"Who says I'd be bored?"

"My experience tells me that most people aren't nearly as interested in art as I am."

"I'm not most people."

"I've noticed," he said so quietly she almost didn't hear.

Almost, but she did, and she wasn't sure if she should feel complimented or criticized.

"So, tell me," she prodded, anxious to move past his words, to put them out of her head and forget them, "what are you working on?"

"A research paper about eighteenth-century women painters and their influence on romanticism." He walked out of the pigpen, waited for her to follow, and closed the gate.

"Were there eighteenth-century women painters? Good ones, I mean. Ones who influenced art movements," she asked, curious and a little surprised. He'd said he taught art history, but she'd imagined him to be the kind of guy who preferred modern to antique and masculine to feminine.

"Women are in every aspect of art history. Just like they are in the history of everything else: medicine, architecture, science, literature, music, design. We just don't hear much about them, because their work was often overlooked or hidden away."

"Or appropriated by a man who claimed it as his own."

"Sometimes, but I'm not doing cultural or gender studies. I'm looking at the past and trying to see how esthetic movements changed and morphed into other things. Women haven't been given enough credit for their part in that. I want to make sure they do."

She ran that around in her head for a moment. The

words. The purpose. The passion she heard behind them.

"See?" he said. "Boring."

"If you're taking my silence for boredom, don't. I'm quiet when I'm interested in something."

He smiled. "Nice save, Rumer Truehart."

She'd heard her name a million times, but the way he said it—with warmth and humor and understanding—made every extra word and thought fly away. She was left with nothing but the truth. Plain and simple and straightforward. The way Lu had always encouraged her to be.

"I've never been much of a liar, Sullivan. Not even for good causes. My childhood was chaos. Loud and dirty and mean. I learned to talk fast and think faster, and my first nine years happened at warp speed. I still tend to talk fast, move fast, and act fast, but when something interests me, I slow down enough to take it in. Otherwise, I might miss the beauty of it."

"You have an interesting perspective. One that a lot of people could benefit from."

"Do any of them happen to be Bradshaw children?"

"Probably. As far as I can tell, the only one of them who ever stops is Twila," he said.

"Heavenly is pretty quiet, too."

"But, she doesn't stop moving and doing. Haven't you noticed? If she's not picking at one of her siblings, she's wiping a counter or taking out garbage or up-stairs dancing or singing or writing."

"I've noticed, and I've been trying to put that energy to good use. I'll be taking the kids to Lu's Saturday morning—"

"You have the weekends off," he reminded her.

"And?"

"You might want some time away from the kids."

"I told Heavenly and Maddox they could help at the stables. I never go back on my word. Not when it's given to children. They're going to help. The rest of the kids might as well do the same. Except for Oya, of course. You and your brothers will have bottle- and diaper-changing duty."

"Three to one are good odds. I'm sure we can handle it." He stopped at the old-fashioned water pump, moonlight glinting off his dark hair and a pair of glasses he only wore when he was working.

Reading glasses?

Maybe, but she hadn't wanted to ask, because she had no business being curious about him.

"And, maybe you can get more research done. Are you close to finishing?"

"Not as close as I'd like to be. It's not easy to find influential female painters from the time period, and what we know about them is limited. I'd planned on visiting a few libraries in DC and New York, maybe taking a trip up to Boston to speak with some colleagues, but this happened."

"And suddenly you were parenting six kids instead of going on research trips?"

"Right. If I'd known I was going to be playing Dad to this bunch, I'd have chosen an easier research project."

"I doubt it," she said, and he set the bucket under the spout and met her eyes.

"Why do you say that?"

"You don't seem like the kind of person who backs down from a challenge. I mean, look at all this." She waved toward the dark fields that stretched out as far as she could see, then the farmhouse. "There are a lot of people who wouldn't do what you and your brothers have. Some of them would have parceled the kids out to other people. Some would have let the state take the kids and place them in foster homes."

"Truth?" He grabbed the pump handle, his biceps well defined beneath a flannel shirt that he'd layered over a black tee. "I'm one of those people. I wouldn't do this. I don't want to do it. I never planned on doing it but Matthias was my brother. These are his kids. I'm not going to turn my back on family."

"Like I said, there are a lot of people who wouldn't do what you're doing. A research paper on women painters in the eighteenth century is tame in comparison."

"Yeah. We'll see how things look in a couple of weeks."

"What do you mean?"

"The hospital called a few minutes ago. Sunday still hasn't improved. They want to move her to a rehab facility."

"That doesn't sound like a bad thing."

"It's for long-term palliative care. The kind you give to people who aren't going to get better."

"Oh." That was it. All she managed to say, and it wasn't nearly enough.

The kids were counting on their mother getting better.

Right now, their entire lives were wrapped up in that hope.

Every night at dinner, one of them prayed for their mother's return. Every night when Rumer tucked them into bed, she listened to each one ask for the same thing.

Except for Heavenly.

She didn't pray. She didn't ask to be tucked in. She didn't talk about Sunday's return or plan what they'd do to celebrate once she came home. Heavenly's heart had been broken before. She wasn't willing to let it be broken again.

Rumer could see that as clearly as she could see the moon rising over distant mountains.

"Poor kid," she murmured, and she thought Sullivan must have known who she was talking about. He nodded, leaning over to pump water into the bucket and rinse it out.

She watched, because . . .

What else was she supposed to do?

Walk back into the house and leave him outside alone?

Stare out toward the river or toward the house?

When he finished, he straightened, turning to face her again. "I'm not sure what to tell them, Rumer. That's the problem."

"You don't have to say anything, yet."

"If nothing changes, the hospital plans to move her Monday. People in town are going to know at least some of the details. They're going to come to conclusions and discuss them in front of children. Those children—"

"Are going to get tackled by Maddox when they say Sunday is going to die?"

"Something like that." He ran a hand down his jaw and shook his head. "He only has one more shot after this last one."

"The school made me very aware of that."

"They're great that way," he said dryly. "Not so great at stopping the kid before he does something stupid."

"Twenty-six kids. One teacher. The odds are always against her."

He smiled. "You have a point. And, my point is that

I'm going to have to tell the kids something. There's no way to avoid it. I'm just not sure how much to say."

"Have you called your brothers yet?" she asked.

"I planned to do it out here. Where Heavenly couldn't hear. I don't want her telling the younger kids that their mother will never get better." He handed her the bucket, and took out his phone.

"You know," she said, before he made the call, "the kids haven't been to the hospital since her surgery."

"Life has been hectic. You see how it is—school, homework, after-school activities. There aren't enough hours in the day to pack it all into, so I've only been bringing them on the weekends."

"Maybe she'd like to see more of them."

"Rumer, she doesn't see or hear anything."

"You don't know that."

"No, I guess I don't, but the kids are always worse after they visit her. They cry more, they fight more, they hide in their rooms more. I want the best for Sunday, but I have to protect the kids, too." He sounded . . . heartbroken.

"Damn," he continued. "I wish my brothers were here making these choices with me."

"They're coming this weekend, right?"

"Friday night."

"When does the hospital plan to move Sunday?"

"If she doesn't respond to stimuli before then, Monday."

"And, if she does?"

"They'll send her to a different facility. One that specializes in brain injuries. Either way, the doctors have done all they can. The ball is in her court, and she's either going to come out of this or she's not." He turned away. "I need to call Porter and Flynn and let them know. The drunk driver's insurance is covering the hospital bill, and the trucking company he was working for has set up a trust fund for future expenses, but long-term palliative care might be outside the scope of that."

"There are a lot of logistics involved in all of this, and I don't want to downplay that, but I really think we should bring the kids to see her tomorrow and the next day and the next."

"Rumer," he sighed, but he hadn't walked away.

"I know it sounds crazy, and I know it's a long shot, but she responded to me when I was talking about the kids. I know she did." She touched his arm. Just fingers on warm, soft flannel, but he met her eyes, and her palm settled right where it was. Against fabric and muscle and warmth. Whatever she meant to say was lost in that moment, in the weight of that touch and the quick heat of their connection.

"It doesn't sound crazy," he said, shifting his arm so that her hand slid away. But, they were still so close, she could feel the warmth of his body, the tension in his muscles.

"Then, let's do it. We've got nothing to lose, and everything to gain."

"Your mother should have named you Pollyanna," he muttered, tucking a curl behind her ear, his finger lingering against her skin. There for a moment longer than they needed to be, and then gone.

"My mother didn't name me. She was too stoned."

"Someone named you," he responded, and she could see the questions in his eyes.

She could have told him everything—the story she'd been told on her birthday every year for as long as she'd lived with her mother.

She didn't, because she didn't want to explore whatever was building between them. She wanted to walk away from it and from him, pretend he was just part of the bargain she'd made, a job requirement she had to meet to get the money she needed. "One of my mother's suppliers."

That was it.

All she would say.

"And?"

"And, some things are better left in the past. Should I tell the kids we're going to the hospital after school tomorrow? They have a few activities scheduled, but we can cancel."

She changed the subject, and he let her.

Why wouldn't he?

They were employer and employee and there didn't need to be anything personal between them.

"I'm willing to give it a shot. Anything is better than waiting around, hoping for the best." He took a step away, and she could breathe again.

Which was funny, because she hadn't realized how tight her chest had become, how little oxygen she was inhaling.

She waited as he walked away, watching as the moonlight cast his shadow across the wheatgrass. She thought he'd keep going. That's what every other man in her life would have done. Walk away and move on to the next activity, the next conversation, the next more interesting thing on the horizon.

Instead, he glanced back. "Aren't you coming?"

"I thought I'd take a walk and get some fresh air." She hadn't really been thinking that, but she was now, because going back into the house and up to her room suddenly seemed like the loneliest thing in the world.

"I'll come with you," he said, walking back and taking her arm, his fingers curved around the crease of her elbow.

"That's not necessary, Sullivan."

"I'm not going to leave you out here by yourself."

"I don't see why you shouldn't," she responded, telling herself to step away. But, of course, she didn't.

There was something about him. . . .

Something that reminded her of childish dreams and girlhood crushes, of days when she'd thought that maybe she really could be the first Truehart woman to find true love.

"It's dark," he responded. "You're a beautiful woman—"

She snorted.

"What?"

"I've been called a lot of things in my life, Sullivan. Beautiful isn't one of them."

"Then, you've been hanging around the wrong people." He said it as if it were fact. As if there was no way on God's green earth she could have been hanging around the right ones.

"Or, the honest ones," she replied, and felt his fingers tighten on her arm. Just a quick twitch of tension where there'd been none, there and gone so quickly she thought she might have imagined it.

"You're not the only one who strives for honesty," he said as they reached the gate and stepped out of the field. "I don't make it a habit of buttering people up to get what I want."

"I didn't realize you wanted anything."

"Of course I do," he replied, stopping near an old elm that stood in the middle of the yard. "I want you to stay."

"And, I already said I would."

"Exactly. So, how about we start the conversation again. Or, finish?"

"What conversation?" she said, backing up because they were so close she could see her reflection in the lenses of his glasses, so close she could have levered up on her toes and brushed her lips against his.

"The one where I say it's dark and you're a beautiful woman?" he reminded her, and she was certain his gaze had dropped to her lips and rested there for a moment before returning to her eyes.

"Right," she muttered, taking another step back and bumping into a wooden swing that hung from a thick branch. "Go ahead. Continue."

"You are a beautiful woman, and it's dark. We're out in the middle of nowhere with nothing but hay and cows for miles around."

"Bessie's around."

"Bessie is too full of casserole to be of any help if some transient decides to see what's going on here at the farm and finds you walking around alone and un-armed."

"This is small-town America, Sullivan. The likelihood of that happening is slim to none."

"The likelihood of a well-qualified job candidate showing up out of the blue to interview for a position I didn't know I was offering is slim to none, too, but it happened."

He had a point.

He also had firm lips and gorgeous eyes and the kind of rugged good looks that made her think of fire-fighters and military men, heroes and heartbreakers and knights in shining armor.

She took another step back and bumped into a swing that hung from a thick branch.

Not a tire swing.

No. That would have made things too easy.

This was a long plank of wood that hit at thigh level. She stumbled, fell backward, and probably would have done the least graceful flip in the history of mankind if Sullivan hadn't grabbed her by the waist.

He pulled her upright, his hands resting just above her hip bones, his fingers splayed along her lower spine. Her heart did that thing again. The one where it just kind of stopped and then started beating so fast she thought it might jump right out of her chest.

"Thanks," she murmured, and he nodded, but he didn't release her.

She didn't want him to.

Which was stupid and dangerous and asking for trouble.

But, she couldn't make herself move away, and she couldn't make herself tell him to let her go.

"I think," he said, looking into her eyes and her face, studying her like a painting that he wanted to memorize and re-create, "you should probably go inside."

"I think you're probably right," she responded, but her hands had found their way to his arms, her fingers curling into the sleeves of his coat. She wanted to slide them along his biceps and shoulders, run her fingers through his thick hair.

For a moment, neither of them moved. She wasn't even sure they breathed. Then his hands dropped away, and he stepped back, cold air rushing in where nothing but warmth had been.

"I'm going to call my brothers," he said, his tone gruff, his voice gritty. Apparently, he wasn't any more excited about this *thing* that was between them than she was. "I'll be in after that. Unless you still want to get some air. If you do, I'll walk with you and call my brothers afterward."

She thought about that for all of two seconds. Thought about walking through fields of wheatgrass with Sullivan beside her, about moonlight in his hair and on his face, about the way it would feel and what it might be—the beginning of something they'd both regret.

"No. I've had enough air for one night," she managed to say, and then she did what any turkey with a good sense of self-preservation would do on Thanksgiving Day: She ran.

Sullivan watched as she reached the house and ran into the mudroom. He continued watching as the kitchen light went off, imagining that he could hear her footsteps on the wooden stairs the same way he had for the past three nights. Moments later, the light in the attic bedroom went on, and she was a shadow at the window, pulling down the shades.

And Sullivan?

He was still standing there like some love-besotted fool, staring up at the window.

"Damn," he muttered, dropping onto the swing that she'd almost fallen over. What the hell was wrong with him?

He had a million problems, and Rumer wasn't going to be one of them. She was beautiful and tempting, and he'd come *this* close to kissing her under the elm tree.

He hadn't.

He wouldn't.

Because, that wouldn't be fair to either of them.

Life was currently at an all-time high level of crazy. He had big decisions to make, limited time to make them, and a lot of pressure to make them right.

He didn't have time to lose himself in the arms of a gorgeous woman. Even if he did, he didn't think Rumer was the kind of woman who'd want to get lost. Not unless it was forever.

And for Sullivan, forever was about as likely as a beam of moonlight landing on Sunday's face and waking her.

Another one of Moisey's fantasies, and he let himself concentrate on that, on wondering what kind of trouble she might get into in her bid to make that happen.

A moonbeam on her mother's face. Magic flowers to make a potion. Moisey had dozens of ideas for bringing her mother back from the brink of whatever chasm she was standing on.

He could imagine her climbing out the window of her second-story bedroom and using the downspout to scramble to the ground.

He could also imagine her falling and breaking her neck.

He frowned, walking to the front of the house and eyeing the window in question. Moisey shared a room with Twila—white twin beds with soft gray sheets and comforters, small desks shoved up against a neutral blue wall. The light was off. Of course. Twila was great at following the rules to a T. She liked order and predictability. She loved organization and neatness. Her side of the room was a clutter-free zone. Moisey's was filled with origami creations and dried flowers, yarn dolls and bits of bright fabric.

Twila never complained, but then, she seemed to enjoy Moisey's free-spirited approach to life. Maybe she lived vicariously through her sister. Whatever the case, the two seemed to get along well, their room one of the few argument-free zones in the house.

He eyed the window and the downspout that was a few feet away from it. Too far for Moisey to reach, and hopefully, too far for her to think much about. He knew his niece well enough to know that once a seed was planted in her, it grew quickly.

He wasn't sure who had told her that moonbeams could wake people who were in a coma, but someone had, and she'd told him all about it when he'd said good night. She'd also told him it was going to be a full moon—the perfect time for magic to happen.

And, probably, for little girls to get lost or hurt or worse.

He made a mental note to check the window and the integrity of the screen. He could imagine Moisey opening the window and pressing her nose to the mesh, trying to figure out a way to get down without falling. He could also imagine the screen coming loose and Moisey tumbling twenty feet to the ground.

Not a good image, and not a good thought.

He shoved it away. Tomorrow, he'd talk to Moisey and make certain she understood that magic wasn't real. He'd also talk to Rumer and let her know that Moisey might be hatching another plan to escape. He should have mentioned it tonight, but he'd been sidetracked by other things—the hospital's call, Sunday's lack of improvement, Rumer's full lips and sweet smile.

"Damn," he said again, because there were no kids around to hear it. He'd cleaned up his language for them, and been doing a pretty good job of keeping it clean.

Sometimes, though, he wanted to go back to the time when he didn't have to worry about what little ears were hearing and little mouths were repeating. He wanted to go back to a time when the kids he dealt with were college age and no responsibility of his.

Sometimes?

Every minute of every day, because this life wasn't something he'd ever have signed up for.

His cell phone rang, and he answered, stepping away from the house, because he could picture Heavenly in her room, ear pressed to the floor or the vent or the window, trying to get as much information as she could.

"Hello?" he barked, all his frustration seeming to spill out in that one word.

"You sound cheerful," Flynn said.

"I'm about as cheerful as a mouse trapped in a cat carrier."

"Have things gotten worse?"

"With Sunday or with the kids?"

"I just got your message about the surgery."

"I left it four days ago," he said dryly.

"I know, and I'm sorry. I was out in the middle of nowhere finding and branding calves. That's a week-long process that I squeezed into four days because I didn't want to be off the grid for too long."

"I figured it was something like that."

"You know if there's an emergency, you can call the house, right? My housekeeper will send someone out for me."

"It wasn't an emergency. Or, at least, not one that you could have done anything about."

"How'd the surgery go?"

"Okay." He paused, because this was going to be hard to say. Admitting that they might have reached the end of the road, that there might not be any more improvement, didn't feel right. It felt like a betrayal of the deepest kind of trust. As if he'd given up on Sunday much too soon.

"I hear the word *but* in your voice," Flynn said quietly. That was Flynn. Of the four Bradshaw men, he was the calm one, the quiet one. The one who thought a lot of things he'd never say.

"The doctors are talking about palliative care."

A heartbeat of silence, and then, "They don't think she's going to wake up?"

"That's the impression I get."

"What do you think?"

"I wish I knew. I'd like to have some hard facts to share with the kids. Right now, we're all just in limbo. Thank God for Rumer. If she weren't around—"

"Rumer?"

"The housekeeper."

"You found one already?"

"That was the purpose of the ad, right? For me to find someone to help around here."

"It was the purpose, but Porter and I weren't sure if you'd get a response. We were thinking we'd have to run the ad in Spokane, Oregon, and Seattle. Just to get a bigger pool of potential candidates. Is Rumer local?"

"To Benevolence? No. She's from River Way."

"That tiny town to the southeast?"

"If you can call it a town, yes."

"And, she just happened to be in Benevolence and picked up a copy of the local paper?"

"I have no idea how she got a copy of the paper, but she had it, she saw the ad, she applied. I hired her."

"How long has she been working there?"

"This was day three. Night four."

"She's a live-in?"

"On the weekdays. On the weekends, she goes home."

"Her credentials?"

"A special education teacher with a master's degree."

"And, she was living in River Way and just happened to see our ad?"

"As implausible as it seems, yes."

"You know what I think about things that are too good to be true? They usually are."

"Agreed, but Porter ran a background check. It was clear. He spoke to her employer in Seattle, and she's in good standing with the school. They're looking forward to her returning in the fall."

"So, why isn't she there now?"

He explained as quickly and succinctly as possible. Flynn might be the quiet brother, but he was also the most opinionated and the most stubborn.

"I guess that sounds reasonable," Flynn said when he finished.

"I'm a lot of things, Flynn. Stupid isn't one of them. I wouldn't let someone with an unknown background care for Matt's kids."

"I know." Flynn sighed, the sound carrying a world of worry, concern, and frustration. "I hate being out of the loop, and I hate not being there. If I didn't have this ranch, I'd quit my job and move back to that area, but this is a thriving business with a dozen people counting on it for income."

"You don't have to explain."

"I feel like I do. I'm the oldest. I should be making the sacrifice."

"What sacrifice? I'm still working. I'm just doing it in a different location." The last thing he wanted was for either of his brothers to feel guilty. Sure, he'd had the bad fortune to be the only one who could relocate immediately, but they were a family, and they were working together to solve the problem.

"You're downplaying things, Sullivan. None of us want to parent that crew. You're the one who's doing it."

"With some help."

"The housekeeper. Right. I guess I'll meet her this weekend."

"What time are you flying in?"

"Early. I'm leaving here Thursday night, and I'll land around five a.m."

"I'll be there."

"No need. I'm renting a car. I've got a meeting in Seattle Monday morning, so I'm flying out from there."

"Are you coming here first, or heading to the hospital?"

"There. We need to sit down and come up with a plan of action. I'm not in love with the palliative care idea. Unless they can prove to me that she's not going to get better, I want her in a rehab facility."

"I agree."

"Good. Sounds like you have things under control there. If you have issues between now and Thursday evening, give me a call. I may be able to change my flight arrangements and get there earlier. You shouldn't have to deal with all this on your own." From anyone else that might have sounded condescending, but Flynn didn't have an arrogant bone in his body. He was tough as nails, hard as rock, and intimidating as hell. When he had to fight, he won. As far as Sullivan knew, he'd almost never had to.

"I'm about as close to having this under control as I am to solving the mysteries of the universe," he admitted.

"You're doing a better job than I would be. I can manage ten thousand acres and five thousand head of cattle, face down rattlesnakes and rustlers and not even blink an eye, but kids? They scare the hell out of me. I'll see you Friday, okay?"

"See you then," he responded, disconnecting the call and looking up at Moisey's window again. Still dark. Still closed. Not even a hint that she was plotting something.

She was. He knew that.

Just like he knew that Heavenly was in her room with earbuds in and her music turned up, and that the twins had pushed their beds together so that they could whisper to each other when they were supposed to be asleep. He knew Twila had a book under her pillow and a little flashlight under her mattress and that Oya would wake up in the morning smiling. He hadn't figured things out, but he at least knew that.

It wasn't much.

It wasn't everything.

But, it was a start. And that, he guessed as he walked back inside, would have to be enough.

Chapter Seven

Getting six kids ready for a hospital visit had taken its toll. Rumer had rushed them home from school, signed their daily planners, looked through their assignment books, and gotten them snacks. As soon as that was done, she'd sent them to comb their hair, brush their teeth, and get ready to go.

That, of course, had meant helping kids find shoes and combs and—God help her—toothpaste lids that had fallen into sink drains. It had meant separating the twins when they got into a fight over whose toothbrush was whose, untying the knots in Moisey's favorite laced boots, helping Twila choose just the right lip gloss and hair accessories, and ignoring Heavenly's irritable glares and muttered curses every time she was reminded that she needed to get ready.

At some point, Rumer had convinced the tween to get moving. Heavenly had one-upped the request and taken Oya with her, claiming that if she was going to be forced to go, she might as well get the baby ready, too.

Now, nearly an hour after Operation Getting Ready to Go had commenced, Rumer was shoving herself into the only clean clothes she could find—a poodle skirt and sweater set. They'd been packed in the suitcase Minnie had dropped by on Rumer's first day of work. There'd also been makeup, hair products, a few herbal headache cures, three romance novels, and a box of emergency chocolate.

The emergency chocolate was gone.

The rest of the stuff was sitting in the bottom of the suitcase. Aside from the 1950s getup Rumer had donned, all the clothes Minnie had brought were dumped in the hamper, most of them splattered with pig slop, baby spit-up, or good old-fashioned dirt from working on the farm.

She zipped the poodle skirt, running her hand down the front to smooth out a few wrinkles. The sweater was a little short, the bottom edge of it hitting right above the waistband of the skirt. She tugged it down as far as it would go, ran fingers through crazy-wild hair, and hoped to Heaven she didn't look as frazzled as she felt.

She glanced in the mirror and winced. Yep. Frazzled in the extreme: hair poking out in a million different directions, light pink poodle skirt falling nearly to her ankles, one earring in and one missing.

She thought she might have lost it in the middle of the night and been walking around all day without it. Moisey had woken screaming around midnight, and she'd run downstairs to see what was wrong. The screaming had woken Oya, whose crying had woken Heavenly. Eventually, every one of the six kids was down in the kitchen having warm milk and toast.

Sullivan had been there, too, wearing dark blue pajama bottoms that clung to his lean hips. That was it.

No shirt. No robe. She'd been fiddling with the darn earring, trying not to notice his lean, hard muscles, the smooth expanse of his skin, the contraction of biceps and triceps as he helped kids get toast and clean up messes.

Yeah.

She'd probably lost the earring then.

She scowled, grabbing her purse, her cell phone, and the journal she'd purchased that morning. The handmade leather-bound book contained hand-pressed paper. No lines. No margins. Just beautiful raw edges and the thick, uneven feel of pulped wood.

She'd already written in it, outlining a conversation she'd had with Moisey. The girl thought moonbeams could cure her mother's coma, and Rumer had jotted down all the details of her theory. When Sunday woke, she'd be amused by it.

If she woke.

Sullivan had been quiet since his conversation with the hospital. She'd noticed that. Just like she'd noticed the fact that he still hadn't shaved. Soon, he'd have a full-out beard and mustache.

He already looked sexy as heck.

That was going to be the frosting on the cake, the ice cream on the pie, the—

"Rumer!" Twila called, her voice faint but audible.

Rumer could picture her standing near the front door, holding a stopwatch and a checklist.

The kid had more organizational skills in her left pinkie than most people had in their entire bodies.

Knowing her, she'd already herded her siblings to the foyer and had them lined up by age or height or troublemaking ability. That was good, because they were leaving in T minus—Rumer glanced at her watch . . .

Now!

They were leaving now.

"Darn it," she muttered, tossing the notebook into her bag and grabbing the baggies of snacks, the packages of crayons, and the coloring books that she'd purchased for the visit. She tossed them in with the journal, flicked off her light, and ran down the stairs.

She hit the lower landing and skidded across the wood floor, nearly slamming into the wall.

"Smooth," Heavenly said. She was a foot away, Oya in a baby carrier strapped to her chest. Both were wearing dresses. Oya's was a frilly teal concoction that had been paired with thick white tights and black patent-leather shoes. Heavenly's dress skimmed her narrow frame and fell to an inch above her knees. She'd taken her hair out of cornrows and it hung around her face in glossy dark blond strands. No combat boots or holey tights. She was wearing cute ankle boots with purple laces and patterned tights that matched the dress.

"You look lovely, Heavenly," Rumer said, both pleased and discomfited by the tween's choice. She'd never seen her in anything other than skin-tight holey rags.

"Whatever," she muttered, stomping to the door. "Are we going? I have stuff to do tonight."

"Like what?" Sullivan asked, walking out of the kitchen, a sketch pad in his hand, a pencil behind his ear. He'd dressed in denim and flannel again, the T-shirt he wore beneath the flannel shirt the same bold green as his eyes.

"Homework," Heavenly snapped, opening the door and walking outside, her siblings filing out behind her.

Twila in a knee-length skirt and navy peacoat, Moisey in a wool blazer and a bright pink dress, the twins dressed in slacks and ties and suit coats.

She did a double-take at that, skimming them from the top of their combed hair to the toes of their polished shoes. Not a smudge. Not a speck of dirt. Their clothes looked freshly washed and pressed. Even Henry was wearing a suit, the gray-black rock shrouded in what looked like a Ken-doll suit coat.

"What the heck?" she muttered.

"I was wondering the same," Sullivan responded, touching her lower spine and urging her outside.

"Did you tell them to dress up?"

"I figured you had," he responded, his gaze on the kids. They were marching single file toward the old red van.

"I told them to brush their teeth and comb their hair. I didn't mention clothes. I didn't think—" She glanced at the kids. They stood next to the locked van staring somberly in her direction, listening to every word she said. "I didn't think of how wonderful it would be if everyone dressed up for the occasion. If I had time, I'd go change into something a little fancier, then we'd all be looking our best."

"I don't know," Sullivan murmured, his hand still on her back, his long stride shortened to match hers. "The outfit you've got on seems pretty fancy."

"It's a poodle skirt," she replied, brushing her hand down the old cotton fabric. "Minnie packed it with the other things she brought over."

"Vintage?"

"Of course, so is the sweater." They were a matched

set—pale pink poodle skirt and white mock turtleneck sweater, both soft from years of wear.

"Vintage looks good on you," he said, and she blushed. Blushed!

Like a middle schooler with her first crush, a high school freshman dreaming of her first kiss. Like a woman who hadn't been hurt a dozen times before and who didn't know that she should never risk her heart.

"Vintage looks good on anyone," she responded.

"I really doubt that poodle skirt would look good on me."

"Maybe you should try it, Uncle," Twila said. "Lots of men wear skirts now. And in Ireland and Scotland, kilts are part of a long and rich cultural heritage."

She sounded like a voice-over for a documentary, and Rumer smiled, tension she hadn't even realized she was feeling seeping out. "You know a lot of history, Twila. Good for you."

"Mom says that if we don't know our history, we're doomed to repeat it," she replied, her dark eyes staring into Rumer's, distracting her from the fact that Sullivan's hand was still resting against her lower spine.

"Your mother is a very wise woman," she replied.

"*Was* a very wise woman," Heavenly cut in. "Now, she's just a vegetable."

"Mom isn't a vegetable," Moisey yelled, darting toward her sister so quickly Rumer didn't have time to catch her.

Sullivan managed it, swooping in and lifting her away seconds before her polished boot met Heavenly's shin.

"Cool it, kiddo," he said gently, still holding her as he unlocked the van and opened the back door. He set her on the threadbare carpet and looked into her face, one hand cupping her chin, one cupping her shoulder. "Do you think your mom would want you kicking and hitting people every time they said something you didn't like?"

"Heavenly says it doesn't matter what Mom would want, since she's going to die anyway."

"That's a bold-faced lie. I never said anything like that," Heavenly snapped, her face alabaster pale, her lips nearly white. She looked stricken and a little sick, and Rumer had absolutely no doubt she was telling the truth.

"You called Mom a vegetable, and that's the same thing." Moisey's voice broke and a single tear slid down her cheek.

"Well, damn. If I'd known it was going to make you cry, I wouldn't have said it." To her credit, Heavenly actually looked contrite.

"Language," Sullivan said wearily, wiping the tear off Moisey's cheek and kissing her forehead. "It's going to be okay, Moisey."

"Not if Mommy doesn't come home," she wailed.

"Is she going to?" Twila asked, her gaze on Rumer. She might be organized, she might be a great student, she might be smart, well-spoken, and polite, but there was a lot more to her than what she showed to the world. Rumer had seen little pieces of that—hints at just how savvy she was. Just how easily she could manipulate people when she wanted to.

"I don't know," she said honestly.

"Well, at least we know one adult in our lives tells the truth," Heavenly huffed, stalking around to the other side of the van and yanking open the door. "Come on, dweebs. Standing around in the cold crying isn't going to make your mother get better."

Your mother.

As if Sunday weren't hers, too, but her face and lips were still pale, her eyes deeply shadowed.

She looked like a kid who'd been through too much, had finally come through it, and was suddenly going through more. If Rumer could have taken her in her arms and told her that things would get better, she would have. She knew Heavenly, though. She'd *been* Heavenly, so she let her strap Oya into her car seat and climb into the bucket seat next to it.

The boys had already found their spots, and Twila plopped into the seat closest to the door. Moisey's tears had stopped, and she was perched in her booster swinging her scrawny legs to her own rhythmic beat.

Sullivan slid the door closed.

"Damn," he whispered.

"Language," she said.

She meant it as a joke, a distraction from the heartbreak they'd witnessed.

He didn't smile.

"I think at this point, those kids have heard it all." He was still holding the sketch pad, and he pulled the pencil out from behind his ear and tucked it in between the pages. "This is just as hard as I thought it was going to be," he said.

"Taking care of the kids?"

"Being a parent to them. Come on. We'd better get in the van and get on the road before all hell breaks loose again." He walked her to her door and opened it, holding it until she was settled into the cloth seat.

"I don't think Minnie will be happy if I slam this

in the door," he said, lifting the hem of her skirt and tucking it up near her thigh.

It should have been nothing—just a kind gesture between two people who were getting to know each other.

It *was* nothing, but she felt the warmth of his knuckles as they grazed her thigh and the quick rush of heat that flooded her.

God!

What was wrong with her?

She wasn't a teenager with a glamorized idea of love and relationships. She'd had her first kiss before she turned twelve, her first real relationship when she was sixteen. She'd been with guys who'd treated her well and ones who'd been bastards. She'd been in plenty of relationships with all different kinds of men. She'd heard all the pretty words and the trite phrases, the promises and the excuses for breaking them. She sure as heck wasn't a woman whose head could be turned by a handsome face or charming manners.

So why the heck couldn't she stop reacting to Sullivan?

Why did every accidental touch feel like the beginning of something wonderful?

And, why was she still here? Still working for the Bradshaws? Still tempting herself to get more involved than she should? Not just with him. With the kids and with Sunday.

She could already feel it happening. She was getting drawn into the drama and the heartbreak, because that's the way she was. She felt too deeply and loved too much. Jake had told her that repeatedly, and it hadn't been a compliment. It had been his way of making her understand that her expectations were too high, that her needs were too many, that her clinginess was annoying.

She frowned.

She didn't give a crap what Jake had said, but there'd been some truth to his words. If she had a fatal flaw, an Achilles' heel, it was her need to make connections, to find commonality, to belong. A therapist friend had once told her it stemmed from her childhood. That she'd felt rejected by her mother and that had caused her to feel unloved and unlovable. She'd been searching for validation ever since then, trying to prove to herself that she was worthy of all the things her mother had denied her. It was a neat theory that tied all her romantic problems into a tidy little package, but Rumer wasn't a child anymore. She'd stopped looking for validation more than a decade ago. She didn't need love to feel fulfilled and she'd stopped wanting it right around the time she'd realized Jake was cheating.

"It's the Truehart blood," she muttered. "It's tainted."

"What's that?" Sullivan said as he climbed into the driver's seat.

"Just talking to myself," she replied.

"Do you do that often?"

"Only when I'm trying to work out a problem."

"What problem?" he asked.

You was on the tip of her tongue.

She refrained from saying it. "You said Sunday was out of the ICU, right?"

"Yes."

"So, I guess that means all the kids can see her at once." She went off on that tangent, because there was no way in heck she was going to admit the truth.

"That's my understanding."

"Okay. Good."

"That's the problem you were trying to work out?"

"One of them."

"Want to talk about the others?"

"No."

"I want to talk about mine," Moisey piped up from the back, her voice clear and high and sweet.

"Should we let her?" Sullivan murmured.

"According to every child psychology class I've ever taken, children should be encouraged to share their feelings and their problems," she replied.

"Do you think your professors had kids like Moisey in their lives? Because I'd say that if they did, they might not have said that."

She laughed. "I think Moisey might be one of a kind."

"My problem is one of a kind, too, and I still want to talk about it," Moisey nearly shouted.

"Shhhh," Heavenly chided. "Oya is trying to sleep."

"If I'm quiet, they won't be able to hear, and what I have to say is of utmost importance," she whispered loudly.

"Utmost?" Rumer asked, her lips twitching with amusement.

"She's been watching documentaries with me when she can't sleep," Sullivan explained. "Lots of British history and people saying things like 'utmost importance.'"

"She is a little sponge, that's for sure." She'd noticed it from the beginning. Moisey had a good imagination and a quick mind. As great an asset as that was, it could also be a challenge. Kids like her needed their minds and their bodies occupied. Rumer had been trying. God knew she had—all kinds of outside activities. No matter how cold, how wet, how muddy, she'd pick the kids up from school and take them on walks, point out things on the farm that needed doing, and then put them to work doing it.

And, still Moisey's high-powered brain was working overtime, keeping her up at night, waking her when she finally fell asleep. She had a million questions. Not just about her mother but about life: How did the robins know that spring was coming? Why did the sky look blue some mornings and purple others? Why did Tommy Fletcher say that family could only be blood relatives? And, was it okay to punch him in the nose for it?

The questions went on and on and on. As fast as Rumer and Sullivan answered one, another pressing question was there.

Smart as a whip and extremely likable. That's how Moisey's teacher described her.

They'd also called her precocious. Teacher code, Rumer knew, for *a handful*.

"Hello?!" Moisey called again. "Does no one care about my problem?"

"I care," Rumer replied, shifting in her seat so that she could face the little girl. "What do you want to discuss?"

"It's cloudy." She waved toward the horizon and the steel-gray sky.

"Are you afraid it's going to rain?"

"I'm afraid the moon will be hidden."

Uh-oh. Here they went. Her newest obsession.

"Moisey," Sullivan said as he shoved the key in the ignition and started the van. "We've talked about this."

"You talked," she corrected.

"*We* talked, and you agreed that the moon wasn't going to help your mother get better. How about we don't stir this pot anymore? Especially not in front of your siblings. They're impressionable, and they might start believing something that isn't true."

Moisey's chin jutted out and her eyes flashed, but she didn't say a word.

In Rumer's estimation that was way worse than her throwing a raging fit. When she was quiet, she was plotting. When she plotted, things happened. Like poor Tommy who'd ended up with his pants glued to his chair. Or Bessie who'd been forced into a straw hat, a bow tie strung around her nonexistent hog neck.

"Okay, Moisey?" Sullivan prodded.

"Yeah. Whatever," Moisey said, sounding almost exactly like her oldest sister.

Then, she turned and stared out the side window, shut off and silent and as unanimated as Rumer had ever seen her.

"Honey," Rumer said. "Who told you the moon would help your mother wake up?" She'd asked the question before, and she'd gotten some cockamamie story about a fairy flying in the window at night and whispering the secret in Moisey's ear.

"I already told you," Moisey said, crossing her arms over her chest, fierce in her determination to keep the secret.

"How about you tell me again?"

"A fairy—"

"How about you tell me the truth?" She cut her off, and Moisey looked straight into her eyes. She was still the little girl that Rumer had almost run over, her arms skinny, her bones tiny, but she looked wizened and old, her cheekbones gaunt, her eyes haunted.

"I dreamed it," she said, and Rumer knew it was the absolute truth.

"Dreams aren't real," Twila said, reaching for Moisey's hand. "Don't be afraid."

"I'm not afraid, and this dream *is* real. I know it is. The moon will come out and shine right on her face, and Mommy will wake up. Just like I saw." She spoke earnestly, her attention on her sister.

Their fingers were twined together, their heads bent close—smooth black hair and shiny afro touching as they whispered secrets to each other. They'd painted their nails. Rumer hadn't noticed that—pink and sparkly. There were dabs of it on Moisey's fingers and tiny lines of it on Twila's wrist, and the connection between them, the fondness and love and affection, was as real as the dark clouds, the bumpy driveway, the day that was just turning dark with evening.

"Whatever happens," she murmured as she turned around, "they have to stay together."

"I know," Sullivan said simply.

That was it.

No explanation of how he planned to make that happen or who would be responsible for taking on the six siblings. Someone would have to. Even if Sunday woke, even if she was able to return home, it could be years before she was able to care for her children alone.

"I guess you and your brothers have worked that out," she said, because she couldn't leave it alone. Just like always, she had to stick her nose in deeper than was necessary, get herself more involved than she needed to.

"We're going to discuss things this weekend." He pulled onto the main road, the van coughing black exhaust from its muffler. She could see it in the side mirror, puffing out in a cloud behind them.

"That will be good timing," she said, hanging onto

the door as the van bounced over a rut. "The kids and I will leave for the homestead around five."

"In the morning?" Heavenly asked, because of course, she was listening. They all were.

"We start chores at six. You'll want to eat before then, so we'll make pancakes and sausage first."

"Yum!" Milo said. "Did you hear that, Henry? Pancakes and sausage!"

"Stop talking to your stupid rock," Heavenly snapped.

"He's not stupid," Maddox replied, a hint of warning in his voice.

Rumer expected Heavenly to step right into that.

She was prepared to intervene and cut off the argument before it grew into a war.

"I didn't say he was stupid. I said his rock was."

"My rock isn't stupid," Milo asserted.

"Okay. Fine. It's not stupid. It's deaf, though, so it can't hear a word you're saying." Heavenly's voice had taken on the gentle tone she used with Oya. A surprise since she usually either growled or snapped her responses to the boys.

"Rocks don't need ears, Heavenly," Milo said, and then he went on a long-winded explanation of the way his pet could absorb noise.

Rumer listened with half an ear, her brain spinning off into other directions.

She was worried about what they'd find at the hospital, worried that Sunday was as unresponsive as doctors had led Sullivan to believe. She was worried about the kids' reaction to seeing their mother with nothing but stubble for hair, the wound from her surgery clearly visible.

"Whatever you're worrying about, don't," Sullivan said so quietly she almost didn't hear.

"Who says I'm worrying?"

"You're biting your lip," he responded. "And you're gouging holes in your palms."

He touched her hand, and she realized he was right. That she'd clenched her fists so tightly, her nails had dug holes in her palms.

She forced herself to relax, to unclench her fingers and let her hands lie lax in her lap.

He lifted one of them, his eyes on the road, his left hand on the steering wheel, his right thumb rubbing at the purplish marks.

And, God!

Every muscle in her body relaxed, every bit of worry fled from her head. She wasn't thinking about Sunday, about the kids, about the hospital visit or the future. She was thinking about the heat that was pulsing through her, the longing that made her want to curve her fingers through his, let their joined hands rest on the seat between them. Linked for however long it took to get to the hospital. When he set her hand down again, she told herself she was relieved.

Because, she should be, she *wanted* to be.

But, of course, she wasn't.

Which sucked, because she might be tired and frazzled, she might spend half of every day wondering what she'd gotten herself into, but she loved working with the Bradshaw kids.

There.

She'd said it.

She loved working with them. She loved listening to Moisey's crazy theories and Twila's spouted facts. She loved seeing glimpses of a sweeter and kinder version of Heavenly. She loved watching Milo take care of his pet rock and listening to Maddox defend his brother's odd choices. She loved taking long walks with Oya strapped into a carrier on her back.

She didn't want to have to give it all up because she loved being around Sullivan.

Which she did.

She could admit that.

She loved listening to him talk about his research project, she loved seeing him with Moisey, watching the way his calm approach always soothed the little girl's tears. She loved the gentle way he responded to the kids' crazy antics.

She loved how he tried, because a lot of people would have already called it quits.

But, she wasn't going to love *him*.

Ever.

Period. End of discussion.

"So there," she muttered.

"More problems?" Sullivan asked, glancing her way, a smile playing at the corners of his mouth, that damn dimple flashing in his cheek.

"Already solved," she replied, and she meant it.

She *did*.

The hospital visit wasn't the chaotic nightmare Sullivan had been preparing for. Sunday looked . . . good. Peach-fuzz hair covering her scalp, the staples partially hidden by pillows someone had piled behind her head. She'd been breathing on her own since the day after surgery. The heart monitor had been removed, the machines rolled away. She was attached to nothing but an IV pole and a pulse oximeter that measured her oxygen level and pulse rate.

Thanks to Rumer's planning, the kids were occupied. That kept them from asking hard questions and demanding truthful answers. Currently, they were hanging artwork from a corkboard near the door. Even Oya had colored a picture, her chubby fists wrapped around one of the giant crayons Rumer had pulled from her bag.

Moisey had called the bag magical.

Maybe it was. So far, Rumer had taken snacks, coloring books, sheets of construction paper, and safety scissors out of its depths.

"Is there anything you can't fit in there?" he asked as she took a container of baby food, a bib, and a spoon from the bag's front pocket.

"The kitchen sink," she responded, not meeting his eyes.

Odd. Because, Rumer was a straight shooter. She faced people head-on, looking right into their eyes and speaking her mind.

He'd noticed that about her.

He'd noticed a lot of things. Like how she'd thrown herself into the job, no holding back, no setting boundaries. No demanding space or time off.

It seemed odd that she was suddenly avoiding his eyes, pretending to be too busy to glance his way.

"What's wrong?" he asked as she spooned orange mush into Oya's mouth.

"Why would you think something was?" She sidestepped the question, which was a hell of a lot better than a lie.

"Because you're avoiding me," he responded. He

was a straight shooter too. He didn't have the time or the patience to be anything else.

"I'm sitting six inches away from you. I wouldn't exactly call that avoidance."

"You haven't said more than ten words to me since we got here, you're doing everything in your power to not look me in the eyes, and every time you get a chance you scoot that chair a little farther away. If that's not avoiding, what would you call it?"

She sighed, spooning more mush into Oya's mouth and pulling a small pack of baby wipes from her purse. "Self-preservation."

"Want to explain?"

She looked up from the wipe she was yanking from the pack, met his eyes. "No."

"Then, how about I take a guess?" he said, and she frowned.

"How about you don't?"

"I make you uncomfortable."

"No. You don't."

"Okay. I'll rephrase that. The way you feel when you're around me makes you uncomfortable."

"This subject is not open for discussion."

"I don't see why not."

"Because we're in a roomful of kids who have big ears and bigger mouths. Yesterday, one of Milo's teachers heard him tell someone that we were living together."

"We *are* living together," he pointed out, and she scowled.

"I'm your live-in help."

"And?"

"I don't want people thinking anything different."

"Funny, I didn't take you for a person who cared much about what other people thought."

"What would make you think that?"

"You're wearing a poodle skirt," he pointed out.

She eyed him for a moment, a spoonful of mush hovering an inch from Oya's mouth.

She glanced at her skirt, probably taking in the pale-pink fabric and the black poodle applique. Maybe also noticing her shoes—old-fashioned snow boots with faux fur trim and pom-pom tassels on the front zippers.

The outfit made a statement, and it sure as hell wasn't *I care what you think about my personal choices.*

Slowly the scowl fell away and her lips curved, her eyes crinkling in amusement. "You have a point, Sullivan."

"So do you," he admitted. "We'll drop the discussion." For now.

"Thanks." She fed Oya the last bite of food and tossed the empty container in a recycle bin under the sink, the baby perched on her hip. Towheaded chubby-cheeked baby. Curly haired earth mother. His fingers itched to sketch them, to capture the way Oya's fingers tangled in Rumer's hair, the curve of her chubby cheeks and dimpled knuckles. Rumer's soft smile, the lean muscles of her arms and shoulders pressing against soft ivory fabric. The hint of creamy skin between skirt and top.

His gaze lingered there, and she must have noticed.

She tugged her sweater back into place, a hint of color in her cheeks as she turned away, focused her attention on the artwork the kids were hanging.

"You guys are doing a great job," she said, her voice a little too loud and a little too bright.

He did make her nervous.

And, he should have just let that be whatever it was.

If she'd been anyone else, he probably would have. After all, she didn't have to be comfortable around him. She just had to do her job. But, there was something about her that he couldn't resist. Something that made him study her face when he should have been working. That made him want to see her smile, hear her laugh, watch as she taught Maddox how to set a fence post or Twila how to pull wild onions from the ground near the edge of the property. Every day, he'd watch from the window as she took all six kids for after-school treasure hunts. They'd come back with robin eggshells and pond fronds, tiny wildflowers and smiles.

At night, he'd sketch them from memory when he should have been sleeping, his fingers flying across the paper, the sure strokes of the pencil tracing jawlines and scuffed shoes, holey jeans and those elusive smiles.

"What time is it?" Moisey asked anxiously, probably still thinking about the moon, calculating what time she should open the curtains and try to let its light in the room.

He didn't have the heart to tell her that the window faced another building or that there was about as much chance of her seeing the moon from it as there was for a moonbeam to wake her mother up.

"Seven," he responded, and realized Rumer had turned to face him again, her silvery-blue eyes staring straight into his.

She was trying to convey a message, but he'd never been good at reading minds, so he stood, crossing the room and leaning close as he whispered, "What?"

"She's memorized a month's worth of moonrise charts," she whispered back.

"I didn't realize there was such a thing."

"There is, and she memorized it."

"And?"

"The moon rose an hour ago."

"Da . . . rn," he said, snagging the back of Moisey's dress as she darted past.

"Let me go! I've got to open the curtains."

"I have to tell you something, kiddo." He didn't release his hold, and she yanked at his arm with such futile fury, he could swear he felt his heart break.

"Moisey," he said, and maybe she heard his sadness. Maybe she understood what he was trying to say, because she stopped fighting and tugging and looked up into his face.

"You said she'd get better," she accused, every word dripping with venom. "The very first night when Daddy died and I was crying, you told me she'd come home."

He had.

"I know."

"You lied. You're just a liar. That's the whole problem! You always lie!" She was nearly shouting now, her words echoing in the suddenly silent room.

Rumer was crouching beside her, trying to pull her in for a hug, but Moisey wanted none of it. None of them, and Sullivan was helpless, the wretch of a parent he'd known he would be—answerless, motionless—as Moisey yanked back one more time, her pretty little dress tearing. He let go of the torn fabric, feeling like the failure he knew he was.

She was crying. Not just a couple of tears, harsh horrible sobs that stabbed him right in the heart that he would have sworn a few weeks ago was impervious to pain.

She ran to the curtains and dragged them open, staring out at the brick wall that blocked everything from view.

Then, she whirled around, barreling toward him fists up, arms swinging.

"Liar!" she yelled, and the next thing he knew, he was lifting her—all her scrawny-armed punches and boot-footed kicks—and she just kind of melted against him, her soft curls against his neck, her arms around his shoulders, her hands clutching his jacket.

"What are we going to do, Uncle Sully?" she sobbed. "What are we ever going to do without her?"

And, he finally understood, he finally got it. He finally knew why Matt and Sunday had taken in kids no one wanted, traveled to Africa and to China to bring home the homeless, why they'd filed paperwork and exposed their lives to social workers and strangers. He finally understood that kind of love, because he felt it. Felt the overwhelming need to slay dragons and right wrongs, to protect Moisey's tender heart and her fighting spirit.

"Whatever happens," he whispered so only she could hear, "it's going to be okay."

"Promise?" she asked, leaning back and cupping his face, staring straight into his eyes.

"Promise," he responded.

"Uncle Sullivan," Heavenly said, breaking the silence and calling him by name for the first time ever.

Surprised, he glanced her way, realized that she was standing near the bed, looking down at Sunday.

"What . . . ?" His voice trailed off as he saw what she did, realized what she had.

Sunday's eyes were open.

They weren't just open. They were focused. On him. On Moisey.

Shocked, he set Moisey down, crossed the room, bent so he was looking straight into her eyes.

"Sunday?" he said, but she wasn't looking at him anymore. She was looking at Heavenly, a frown line creasing her brow.

"Don't cry, honey," she said, the words raspy and rough and barely intelligible.

He heard them, though.

He understood them, and he was reaching for the call button to call the nurse as Heavenly turned and ran from the room.

Chapter Eight

Running in a poodle skirt and snow boots with a baby on her hip was difficult, but Rumer managed. There was no way she was going to let Heavenly out of her sight.

She rounded the corner, barreling toward the bank of elevators that the twelve-year-old had already reached.

"Hold on!" she yelled, but the doors were already sliding shut.

"Dang it!" she muttered, darting forward and slapping her hand to call for another elevator.

To her surprise, the doors to the one Heavenly was in slid open. Heavenly was in the opening, her face wet with tears, strands of hair sticking to her damp cheeks.

"Thank God," Rumer sighed, stepping onto the elevator and jabbing the button for the lobby.

"I'm not going back there," Heavenly said, crossing her arms over her skinny chest. "You can't make me."

"Who said I was going to try?" Rumer asked, keeping her tone light. No sense adding her own emotions to the mix.

"You're here."

"And?"

"Adults always think they need to chase after kids and bring them back, but sometimes they just need to leave them alone."

"Okay."

"Why do you always do that?" Heavenly snapped, lifting a handful of her hair and then letting it float back down around her shoulders. A nervous gesture from a nervous kid who didn't know the rules of the game they were playing, because she didn't understand that they weren't playing, that everyone didn't use words or fists to manipulate and maneuver. That sometimes adults were exactly who they seemed to be, and that home really could be a safe place to land.

"Do what?"

"Agree with me."

"That's a good question, Heavenly. I'm glad you asked." The doors slid open, and she hooked her arm through the tween's, Oya still bouncing happily on her hip.

"See? You're doing it again. Acting like I'm not a pain in the ass, even though I am."

"First, I'm not acting like anything. This is the way I am. Second, you *are* a pain in the ass."

Heavenly's eyes widened.

"Just like most kids your age. I don't hold it against you, because I was a much bigger pain when I was your age."

"Right," Heavenly snorted, and shrugged.

"Ask Lu."

"Lu's your grandmother. She won't say a bad word about you."

"Right." Rumer snorted, and Heavenly's lips curved in what might have been a smile.

"Will she?"

"She always tells the truth, and I always try to do the same. So, you want an answer to your question, and I'm giving it. I agree with you a lot, because you're right. Sometimes life sucks. Sometimes things happen in families—"

"They aren't my family," she cut in.

"Legally, they are. And, from what I've seen, they are in every other way that matters."

"They took me in because of Oya. We're half sisters. Our birth mom wanted us together, and Sunday really wanted a baby in the house." She shrugged as if it weren't important, but Rumer knew it was. "If it hadn't been for my mother getting pregnant, Sunday and Matt would have kicked me out a long time ago."

"They told you that?"

"They didn't have to. I just know it."

"That's your problem, Heavenly. You know a lot of things that aren't true."

"They *are* true," she argued, her eyes narrowed, her fists clenched.

"It's interesting that you think that, since I was standing next to you in the hospital room."

"So?"

"Sunday wasn't looking at Oya. She was looking at you."

Heavenly swallowed hard, her eyes wet with tears she probably wouldn't let fall.

"As a matter of fact, you and Moisey were both crying, but you were the one she was talking to."

"She was confused."

"You're confused," Rumer said gently. "And that

confusion is making you do stupid things. Like run out on a family that obviously loves you."

"Love is a stupid idea for stupid people."

"Sometimes. And, sometimes it's an answer to someone's prayer. Your mother—"

"She's not my mother," Heavenly said, but there was no heat in her voice.

"In her heart, she is. She loved you guys enough to come back from wherever she was. Now, you're going to have to love her enough to bring her the rest of the way home."

Heavenly blinked, her expression softer than Rumer had ever seen it. "She has to make it home. The other kids need her."

Not: *I need her.*

But, it was a start.

"Of course they do. They need you, too. So do I. Oya isn't a lightweight," she joked. "My arm is about ready to break off."

Heavenly reached for the baby, pulling her into a hug.

"She feels light to me," she murmured against the baby's hair.

"You know what Lu always said to me when I was a teen and causing her more trouble than any one kid had a right to?" She put her hand on Heavenly's shoulder, steering her back toward the elevators.

"What?"

"She said that love made the heaviest burden easy to bear. Coming from Lu, that was a big deal."

"Why? Is she mean?"

"No. Not mean. Strict. But, you'll figure that out when you meet her Saturday."

"Are we still doing that?" She frowned, jabbing at the elevator button impatiently.

"Of course. Lu needs the help, and you've got the right temperament for that kind of work."

"The free-labor kind?" she asked, her snarkiness returning.

Thank God!

"The *I'm not going to puke when I smell something horrible* kind."

"I've smelled way worse than horse sh . . . poop. My mother had twenty cats and two dogs. They crapped all over the place, and she never cleaned it up. I tried, but there were a lot of them, and only one of me."

"I'm sorry, sweetie. That sucks."

"Not really. It's what I was used to. I didn't know any better until they took me away and put me in foster. The house there was clean. The people stunk, though."

"Literally or figuratively?"

"If you're asking if they really smelled bad, the answer is no. They were just bad people."

"Then, I'm doubly sorry."

"Everyone is sorry. No one can change it, so how about we talk about something more interesting?"

"Like?" Rumer asked, letting the thread of conversation go. It was the first time Heavenly had opened up about her past, and Rumer filed the information away. She'd take it out and look at it later. Right now, she needed to get Rumer back up to the room.

Sunday had opened her eyes.

She had.

Rumer still couldn't quite believe it, but they'd all seen it, and then they'd all heard her speak.

She jabbed the button to call the elevator.

Seconds later, the door opened and Sullivan was there.

She wasn't sure why she was surprised, but she was sure her expression reflected her shock.

It didn't matter.

He wasn't looking at her. His focus was on Heavenly.

"Don't ever do that again," he said.

"I can do whatever I want."

"You're twelve. You can't. The end." He touched her shoulder, and she shrugged away.

"Sunday is awake now. Only she can tell me what to do, and most of the time, I don't listen."

"Bull crap." He took Oya, grabbed Heavenly's hand, and pulled her onto the elevator.

They were two opposing forces constantly pitched against each other. Rumer could have intervened, but she figured the best thing to do was let them work it out.

They were family, after all.

Whether Heavenly wanted to admit it or not.

Rumer stepped into the elevator behind them, anxious to get upstairs, to see how the other kids were doing. They shouldn't have been left unsupervised. Sunday might have opened her eyes and spoken, but that didn't mean she could keep an eye on four kids.

"You know what the problem is?" Heavenly said, hands on her hips, eyes flashing.

Don't take the bait, Rumer wanted to say, but Sullivan had already bitten.

"What?"

"Moisey was right," Heavenly muttered. "You're a liar."

"Everyone lies sometimes," he responded. "And, if you're still pissed about what you heard me say to my brothers, you need to get over it."

"I'm not pissed about anything," she replied.

"Then why do you keep giving me attitude?"

"You're not special. I give everyone attitude."

Sullivan blinked, and then he laughed. Not a little chuckle or a quiet snort. This was full-out amusement that pealed through the elevator and landed right straight in the region of Rumer's heart.

She tried to ignore it.

God knows she did!

But, Heavenly's lips quirked in a tiny little smile, and Rumer couldn't help thinking that Sullivan's response had been just exactly right.

She was as impressed by that as she'd been touched by the way he'd comforted Moisey, and no matter how many times she told herself to stop thinking about how different he was from other men she'd known, no matter how many times she reminded herself that he was just another guy who was bound to disappoint, she couldn't stop wondering if she'd been wrong all these years. If maybe her problem with men had nothing to do with the Truehart curse and everything to do with the people she'd chosen to give her heart to.

She followed Heavenly and Sullivan as they stepped off the elevator, and she would have let them get ahead of her, allowed them to walk into the room without her.

This was their family, after all. Their miracle. She planned to give them space to enjoy it as a closed unit—no outsiders cluttering the landscape and getting in the way.

But, Sullivan stopped on the threshold, gestured for her to come.

"I thought I'd give you guys some time alone," she said.

"Sunday has six kids. Alone never happens."

"You know what I mean. Time with just your family."

"You want to know the truth, Rumer? You're as much a part of it as I am. I spent most of my adult years avoiding Benevolence like the plague. I visited Matt and Sunday once a year. Less if I could find an excuse to do it. When I showed up here after the accident, I'd never even met Oya. I'd seen Heavenly once, and the other kids barely knew who I was."

"You're still family." She tried again, but she was moving toward his outstretched hand, wrapping her fingers around his, feeling the warmth of his palm against her skin.

And, God!

She knew this was a mistake. Every bit of it.

"Family," he murmured, as he pulled her close, his thumb running along the pulse point in her wrist, "is only ever exactly what you make of it. Come on. I want to hear what the nurse has to say."

He tugged her into the room, and she went, because she had to. Because that was the way she'd always been, following the sweet words and the pretty phrases all the way to another broken heart.

Sunday didn't say another word. No matter how much the kids talked to her, no matter how many times the nurse asked her name or if she knew where she was, she didn't speak. She did keep her eyes open. They were hazy cornflower blue rather than the bright vivid color he remembered.

Currently, they were half closed, the lids hiding most of the iris. He'd have thought she was out again, but when the neurosurgeon asked her to open her eyes, she did.

"That's it, Sunday. Good job," the doctor said in one of those singsong fake voices Sullivan would have hated if he'd been the one lying in the bed.

Maybe she hated it, too.

She shut her eyes as if she were trying to shut out the world.

"Mommy?" Twila said, pushing past the doctor and sticking her head close to Sunday's face. "Don't go back to sleep, okay?"

Sunday opened her eyes.

She looked . . .

Confused. As if she had no idea where she was or who was talking to her. Sullivan's heart sank.

That would be a mess. Sunday waking up and not knowing her kids. He'd thought through a lot of scenarios. He and his brothers had been planning for almost every possibility. They hadn't planned for that.

Rumer touched his shoulder, levering up so that she could whisper in his ear. "Whatever you do, don't panic. We don't want to freak the kids out."

She sensed it, too.

Which made him worry even more.

"Mommy?" Twila tried again, her little hand resting against Sunday's face, their noses so close they were almost touching. "Did you hear me?"

"I heard you, sweetie," Sunday rasped, reaching up, slowly, carefully, her fingers brushing wisps of hair from Twila's forehead. "I won't go back to sleep."

The words were there, the sweet touch, but she still looked confused. Maybe a little alarmed.

Rumer touched Twila's arm. "I think your mother is still really tired. Since this has been such a wonderful visit, how about we go on home and let her rest?"

"But, what if she rests for weeks again?" Maddox

asked. He'd been hanging back, standing near one of the walls, shy for the first time since Sullivan had arrived in town.

It was Milo who'd moved close, was eyeing Sunday with the same confusion she seemed to have.

"You're different," he said bluntly, thick locks of nearly white hair falling over his eyes as he leaned closer. "Did aliens take away our real mom? Are you an imposter?"

"Milo! That's enough," Rumer said, taking his hand and leading him away from the bed. She knew. Sullivan knew. Apparently, Milo knew, too.

Sunday's eyes were open, she was talking, but she hadn't come back to them. Not the way everyone had hoped.

"Rumer is right," he said, pulling a handful of bills from his wallet. It could have been sixty or a hundred. He had no idea. He didn't care. He wanted the kids out before they all clued in to whatever Milo had. "This has been a great visit, but we don't want to wear your mother out."

"It was a good visit, because I opened the curtains," Moisey claimed. She'd put on her coat to cover the ripped dress, but he could still see the tracks of the tears on her cheeks. "Moonlight got on Mommy's face, and that healed her. I know it did."

"There's no way moonlight got anywhere near her, Moisey," Heavenly said. She didn't call her "dweeb," and Sullivan wondered if she sensed the change in Sunday, too.

"You don't know that."

"I do."

"You don't."

"Girls," he chided, his heart galloping in his chest,

his mind racing in a million different directions. "That's enough. I'm going to give Rumer money so she can take you all out to eat. You can have whatever you want."

"Ice cream?" Milo asked.

"After dinner," Rumer responded. Thank God she was talking, because his pounding heart had moved up into his throat, and he wasn't sure he could get the words out.

Sunday remained silent, watching as he handed Rumer the money and helped the kids get on their coats. The doctor pulled a chair over next to her and said something Sullivan couldn't hear. She didn't react. Not a nod. Not a blink. She was watching the kids like they were a beam of sunlight after a long, dark night. The longing, the hunger in her face made his stomach ache and his damn heart hurt.

When the hell had this happened?

When had he gone from being a guy who didn't want or need any connections to a guy who couldn't seem to prevent them?

Rumer grabbed his hand, tugging him a few feet from the bed and from the door. "Do you want me to bring them home after dinner?" she asked.

"That's probably for the best," he managed to say. "I'll call someone to give me a ride."

"Don't worry about that. I'll have my aunt come to the house. She'll be fine with the kids for a few hours."

"Rumer—"

"This is what you're paying me to do, remember? To step in, to figure things out, to make sure the house is running smoothly while Sunday recovers."

"I'm paying you to help at the house. Not coordinate every aspect of my life."

She shrugged, her narrow shoulders jutting up

against the soft material of her sweater. "There's no limit on what a jack-of-all-trades should do."

"Yeah. There is, but right now, I can't think of what they should be." He glanced at Sunday, and then at the kids—lined up like perfect ladies and gentlemen, staring at their mother like she really was an alien creature.

"It's going to be okay, Sullivan," Rumer said softly.

"What's your definition of *okay*?" he replied, his heart still slamming against the wall of his chest, his muscles tense with the need to do something that would change the situation.

She cocked her head to the side, her eyes silvery gray in the overhead light. "The family. Together. Creating something beautiful out of the ashes of what they had."

That was it.

Just a few words, and then she levered up on her toes again, pressed a kiss to his cheek. "I'll be back in a couple of hours. You can fill me in when I get here."

"Come on, kids," she said. "Let's go get some food. I don't know about you, but I'm starving."

She walked out of the room, and the kids filed in behind her, waving to their mom and calling good-byes and I-love-yous.

He could hear them long after they'd disappeared, their voices carrying down the otherwise quiet hall. Eventually, they faded away, and he was left standing in the silent room, the money still in his hand, Rumer's kiss still on his cheek.

He touched the spot where her lips had been, feeling like every kind of fool, because that quick peck on his cheek had felt like more than any sensual caress he ever had.

"Is she your wife?" Sunday asked, breaking the silence.

Surprised, he shook his head. "She's helping with the kids while you recover."

"My kids," she said as if she were trying the words on for size.

"Yes."

"And Matt's."

He nodded. She remembered her husband. Maybe she did remember her kids.

"Is he here?"

Dear God. He was going to have to tell her.

"You and Matt were in an accident," he began, but before he could get the words out, she shook her head.

"Never mind. I don't want to know." She closed her eyes, and he walked to the bed, lifted her hand.

"Sunday—"

"Let her rest," the doctor said, standing up and putting the chair back against the wall. "There will be time enough to explain things when she's remembered a little more."

"Exactly what does she not remember?" he asked, following the doctor as she walked to the door.

"She says she has some vague memories of the kids, but . . ." She glanced at the bed and frowned. "If I had to guess, I'd say she doesn't remember anything."

"Damn," he muttered, and she sighed.

"That's the risk with these kinds of injuries. More than likely she'll get most of the memories back. Eventually. For right now, we just need to keep things calm. We can't demand more than she can give."

"I wasn't planning on it."

"No family ever does, but we want our loved ones back, and sometimes we push a little too hard. I'm going to get occupational and physical therapy in here tomorrow. She has almost no function on her right side. Very limited reflexes in her extremities, but that might be from residual swelling from the spine injury. We've also got a great memory care team that can work with her. My suggestion is that you keep the kids away for a day or two. Maybe bring them back Friday or Saturday." She walked into the hall, offered one of her rare smiles. "This is good progress, Mr Bradshaw. Even if it doesn't look like it. Try to be happy. There are a lot of people who would lasso the moon to have what your family does."

She walked into the hall, her brisk footsteps fading just like the kids' voices had.

He walked to the chair and settled into it, his hands shaking as he shoved the money back in his wallet, useless adrenaline coursing through his blood.

He wanted to fix this, damn it, but he couldn't, so he pulled out his phone and texted both his brothers, letting them know the latest. Then, he sat in the silent room, watching as Sunday slept and the moon that he'd insisted would never be seen outside the window appeared above the building next door.

If he'd believed in signs and symbols, he'd have believed that was one, but all he'd ever believed in was hard work, honesty, and integrity. Magic and myth were great for some people. He preferred cold hard facts.

Right now, the facts were that Sunday had come out of the coma. That she probably didn't remember her kids. That someone at some point was going to have to explain that her husband was dead.

He figured he'd be the one to do that, because it would be a couple of days before his brothers arrived, and he doubted she was going to stop asking. She and Matt had been the couple everyone admired in high school. They'd been prom king and queen, couple most likely to last forever. They'd been the kind of people that everyone had liked. They weren't part of any clique except their own—the two of them and then the world. That's the way it had always seemed to Sullivan.

Now, after years of being part of that, Sunday was going to have to figure out how to go it alone. He didn't know her well enough to know how she'd handle that, but he knew this: He and his brothers weren't going to let her flounder. They'd give her whatever support was necessary until it wasn't necessary anymore. Eventually, she'd be able to run the farm again, or she'd be ready to sell it.

A shame since it had been in her family for generations, but her choice to make.

He lifted her hand, and she opened her eyes, staring at him for a moment as if she were trying to reach for a memory, figure out who he was.

When she didn't speak, he did. "I'm Sullivan. Matt's brother."

"I know," she replied. "And, I want to know why you're here, and he's not, but I don't want to know today. Maybe not even tomorrow, so you can stop looking so worried." She touched her head and grimaced. "Can you turn off the light? I've got a headache."

He did what she asked, letting velvety blackness settle over them. It was too dark to see much, but he grabbed his sketch pad, found his pencil, and then he sat in the silence, the pencil moving quickly as he sketched the outline of the bed, of Sunday, of the window and the waning moon.

And somehow, the pencil added another shape—a

shadowy form, sitting on the ledge of the window, staring at the moon. At first, he thought he was sketching a child. Moisey maybe, but the figure was too large to be a child, the shoulders too broad.

He held the sketch up to the blue-gray light that seeped in from the window, and his pulse jumped. No. It wasn't a kid. It was Matt. His baseball cap on backward, because he thought it was funny, his feet bare because that was the way he preferred it, his face turned away so that Sullivan didn't have to see his sorrow or his joy.

"Knowing you, you're having a blast," he said, halfway expecting his brother to answer.

A strange thought and a stranger sketch. He tended to zone out when he was drawing, but he usually knew what direction his pencil would head. He couldn't remember ever sketching something he hadn't intended. Then again, he couldn't remember ever being as tired as he'd been the past couple of weeks.

Taking care of six kids and a farm was taking its toll, and the sketch was evidence of that. He closed the pad, laid it on the table, leaned his head back against the chair, and closed his eyes. Rumer wouldn't be back for a while. He might as well catch up on some sleep.

"Sunday," a man said, and Sullivan's eyes flew open, his gaze jumping to the window as if he might see Matt sitting there.

There was nothing, of course. Even the moon had disappeared, drifting above the buildings and out of sight.

It had been his imagination or, maybe, someone talking in the hall, discussing weekend plans. That was the easiest explanation and the one that made the most sense, so he'd stick with it and forget the strange feeling he had that he and Sunday weren't alone, that the window ledge wasn't empty and that the sketch was the exact antithesis of everything he believed in. Not just pencil on paper, black and white, clear-cut and unarguable—a secret message from a brother he loved.

Chapter Nine

Rumer couldn't sleep, and God knew she was trying. She'd sipped chamomile tea all evening, popped a couple of the herbal headache pills, recited every boring math fact she'd ever learned. She'd counted sheep, counted hogs, counted the soft tick of the grandfather clock that stood against the wall.

Somehow, she was still awake.

The problem was, she couldn't turn off her brain, or make her thoughts stop spinning from one useless worry to another. She'd close her eyes, imagine Sunday lying in the hospital bed confused and anxious, and she'd open them again. She'd finally get that image out of her head, finally start drifting off, and Moisey's face would pop into her mind. Or Heavenly's, or Milo's, Twila's, Maddox's, Oya's.

Or Sullivan's.

Maybe his more than anyone else's.

In the two days since Sunday had opened her eyes, he'd spent more time at the hospital than he'd spent at home. That was the way it should be. There were therapy sessions, caregiver meetings, evaluations, and tests. Someone had to be there to gather the information, ask the questions, demand the answers.

Sullivan was the only family around, and the task had fallen to him. He'd left before sunrise the last two mornings, grabbing the coffee that Rumer had prepared, offering a quick thank-you and a tired smile before he took off. He'd returned just in time to tuck the kids into bed and say good night to them. She'd admit that she'd stood out in the hall and listened to him tell the kids how well their mother was doing and that she'd sat at the kitchen table while he picked at warmed-up food and pretended everything was okay.

Things weren't okay.

She was certain of that, but the kids were always around and she wasn't going to push for answers when they might hear.

So, yeah, she was worried, and it was keeping her awake.

She could lie in bed waiting for morning like she had the previous night, or she could go for a walk and clear her head. Sullivan had gone to bed an hour ago, the kids had been asleep for at least two. There hadn't been a peep from anyone since she'd turned off her light and climbed in bed. If she was quiet, if she was careful, she could get down the stairs and out the door without anyone knowing.

Fresh air. Quiet. Darkness. Those were things she craved like other people craved chocolate. She'd spent too many years of her life hiding in the corner of her mother's living room, listening to the pounding pulse of too-loud music, the bright lights and raucous sound of another party keeping her awake. As an adult, she preferred lights out at a certain time. No late-night parties that stretched into the wee hours of the morning for her, no loud music. No drugs or heavy drinking or mornings spent wondering what she'd done or who she'd been with.

She'd made her mistakes as a teen.

She'd lived through them, and she'd learned from them. Thank God, because the last thing she'd ever wanted to be was like her mother.

"Enough," she muttered, shoving aside the covers and getting out of bed, the old wood floor cold under her feet. She grabbed her coat from a hook near the door and walked out onto the landing, listening for any sign that one of the kids had heard.

Nothing. Not even a whisper of sound.

She hurried down the stairs, careful to bypass steps that creaked and groaned. Her heart beat rapidly, her hands trembling a little as she buttoned her coat. She felt like the kid she'd once been, sneaking out without permission. Which was silly, because she was an adult and had every right to go outside at two in the morning.

Her boots were in the mudroom, and she shoved her feet into them, the faux fur trim brushing her calves as she unlocked the back door, grabbed the spare keys from the little cubby near the door, and stepped outside, late winter air seeping through her coat and flannel pajamas. It was cold, but she'd warm up after she walked for a while.

She headed across the yard and into the field. The river was a half mile dead ahead. She'd been there with the kids several times, talking to them about water safety as they'd navigated the rocky bank.

She decided to head in the opposite direction, moving toward the eastern edge of the property. There was a small house there—a rancher that the kids said had once been occupied. It was empty now, and she knew where the key was, knew that the electricity and water were still on.

Maybe after she walked for a while, she'd go there, grab one of the old books off a shelf, and read until she was tired enough to sleep.

Whatever she decided, this was so much better than lying in bed and listening to the house settle and her thoughts race.

"Tomorrow will be better," she murmured as she reached a narrow access road that separated one field from another.

She followed it for a few hundred yards, then stepped into what had once been an orchard. Now the trees were bare, their limbs gnarled and twisted, their branches growing together to form a canopy that showered her with dead leaves as she walked beneath it. Like the rest of the property, she'd explored this with the kids, discovering old ladders leaning against trees and empty bushel barrels stacked in a small shed. From what she'd heard from people who'd dropped off meals or waylaid her at the school or the grocery store, Pleasant Valley Organic Farm was a raging success and testimony to Matt Bradshaw's work ethic and organizational skills. A fine businessman, an outstanding father, a pillar of the community.

Maybe he had been.

Probably he had been, but Rumer had spent a lot of time at the homestead. She'd learned about farming from Lu, Minnie, and the seasonal workers who came in to plant and tend the fields. Mostly, they grew alfalfa, but there were a few fruit trees and a ten-acre parcel for corn. Things had to be done right, and right wasn't letting orchards become tangled skeletons of trees or allowing fence posts to rot in the ground. Right was keeping up on the work no matter the season. Maybe things were different, because Pleasant Valley was organic. It was possible they were rotating fields and letting certain sections go fallow. Still, there had to be a certain level of upkeep, and she wasn't seeing it.

She made her way through the orchard and stepped out into an expanse of overgrown grass. From here, there was nothing but a yard, a chicken coop, the rancher, and a one-acre garden plot that looked like it had been harvested in the summer.

She and the kids had found a few onions and potatoes there. She'd spotted watermelon and pumpkin seeds and the shriveled remains of a few cucumbers and tomatoes. Whoever had planted it had created neat rows free of weeds. It was a garden Minnie and Lu would have been proud of. Which said a heck of a lot about its quality.

Rumer crossed the grassy yard, stepping onto a gravel driveway that curved around the back of the house. According to the kids, their grandparents had lived there years and years and years ago. More recently, it had been rented by two couples. The women were nice. The men were lazy.

Or, so Heavenly had said.

Of the two women, the one named Clementine had been the favorite. She'd babysat for them on a few occasions, and she'd always smelled like gingersnaps and soap.

The last part had been Milo's observation.

Not surprising that he'd noticed. He loved to eat. Especially sweets, and he'd most definitely have noticed anything or anyone who smelled like a cookie.

Rumer smiled as she stepped onto the back porch, feeling better than she had all day. This was what she'd needed—the cold air and the quiet, the tangy scent of old grass mixed with the sweeter smell of new growth. She reached into the potted plant that hung from the porch eaves, feeling under the fake plant, expecting to find the keys.

She found a few crumbs of dirt and a dead leaf but no key.

Surprised, she lifted the planter and set it on a dust-coated Formica table that stood in the center of the porch. She lifted out the fake plant that someone had shoved into the planter, dumped the rest of the contents onto the table. A quarter cup of soil, a few pebbles, and two fake leaves. That was it.

She plopped the plant back into the empty planter and ran her hands over the pile of dirt.

Still no key.

She doubted that checking for it again and again and again was going to change anything. It was missing. Since there were no holes in the pot and no way for a key to jump out and lose itself, she had to assume someone had taken it.

Not the kids.

She'd been keeping a close eye on them, making sure they weren't plotting a trip to the hospital. Since Rumer and Sullivan refused to take them, they could be trying to find another way to get there.

Hitchhiking. Uber. Begging a free ride from some random stranger in a grocery store.

She shuddered. Parenting was scary. She hadn't realized how much so until she'd started watching the Bradshaws. No wonder Lu's hair had turned pure white two years after Rumer had moved in. She'd been more trouble than all six of Sunday's kids combined.

She walked to the sliding glass door and gave it a tug. To her surprise, it opened. She was certain she'd locked it before she and the kids had left.

Heart pounding, pulse racing, she eased it closed again.

No way in *heck* was she walking into the house.

She'd watched enough horror movies to know that was the first step to dying.

Actually, the second.

The first was wandering around in the dark in some godforsaken place in the middle of nowhere. *Or*, traipsing around before dawn on the edge of a tiny little town that sat almost in the middle of nowhere. That described Benevolence to a T, and there she was, wandering around in the darkest hours of the morning just asking for a crazed lunatic to come after her.

She stepped away from the door, her focus never leaving the shimmering glass. She expected it to fly open and some creature from her worst nightmare to rush out. She stepped off the porch with her back to the field and the velvety darkness. She was prepared to be attacked from the front. She wasn't expecting anyone to come at her from behind.

That was her fatal error, and she should have known it.

In horror movies, the monsters never jumped out from expected places. No. They snuck up on their hapless victims and pounced when they were least expected.

A twig snapped as she took another step backward.

She froze.

Grass crunched beneath someone's feet.

She started to swing around, but something slammed into her lower spine, the hard edge of it jabbing through her coat.

"Don't move," a woman growled.

The thing poking into her back felt enough like the barrel of a gun for Rumer to do what she was told.

She froze, body stiff with fear, heart hammering against her ribs.

"The police are on their way," she lied.

"Good."

"They're not going to appreciate the fact that you have a gun aimed at my back."

"They're not going to appreciate trespassers trying to break into my house, either. So, how about you explain who you are and what you're doing wandering around my property?" the woman replied.

"Your property? Unless you're Sunday Bradshaw it's about as much yours as it is mine."

"Sunday is in the hospital. I'm taking care of the place while she's there," the woman said, the weapon still jabbing into Rumer's lower back.

Only it didn't feel as much like the barrel of a gun as it had before. Now it felt more like . . .

A broom handle?

She swung around, batting the thing to the ground and coming face-to-face with a woman who looked about as intimidating as a two-day-old puppy. Waist-length curly hair, dark eyes, thick-framed glasses, and a terry-cloth robe that brushed the ground when she took a step back.

"Sunday's brothers-in-law are taking care of the property," she said, her fear melting away as she looked into the woman's pale face. She didn't look like a monster, a serial killer or a trespasser.

"They're taking care of the house and the kids. I'm taking care of the land," the woman responded, eyeing Rumer with a mixture of curiosity and irritation. "And, just so you know, I called the police, and they really are on the way. You'd probably be smart to go back to wherever you came from."

"I came from the Bradshaws' house." Rumer lifted the thing that she'd batted out of the woman's hand. A broom. For sure. The old-fashioned straw kind. Handmade from the looks of it.

"You're a girlfriend or wife to one of the brothers?" the woman asked.

"The housekeeper. Rumer Truehart."

"Rumer, huh? Nice name. Sucky job. I'm pretty damn sure you're doing a lot more than cleaning house."

"The job is multifaceted."

The woman laughed, a quick light sound that reminded Rumer of summer rain. "I figured it wouldn't be long before the men hired one. The house is huge and the kids are a handful. Sunday was in over her head, too. She was just never willing to admit it." She ran her hand over her long hair, smoothing down some of the wild curls. "I'm Clementine, by the way. Warren."

"Clementine?" As in the woman the kids had been talking about? The one who smelled like soap and gingersnaps? Rumer resisted the urge to step closer and take a whiff of cold night air. She couldn't stop staring,

though, taking in the woman's wild hair and pale face
and glasses. Her voluptuous figure beneath her threadbare robe. "You used to rent this house, right? The kids
told me about you."

"Yes, and just so you know, it's not polite to stare."
Clementine tugged at the belt of her robe.

"It's not polite to poke someone in the back with a
broomstick and pretend it's a rifle, either."

"It is when they're wandering around your house in
the middle of the night."

"Two in the morning," Rumer corrected, and Clementine offered a half smile.

"Either way, we'd both be better off sleeping."

"Insomnia sucks."

"Here's an idea for you, Rumer," Clementine said,
the sound of sirens filtering through the early morning silence. "Instead of wandering around outside
when you have insomnia, pick up an old book. I sug-
gest *The Life of Samuel Johnson.* James Boswell's writing
might bore you to tears, but it's probably not going to
kill you."

"Walking around at two in the morning usually isn't
going to, either."

"That depends on who you run into." Clementine
took a step closer to the road, moving outside the
sphere of the light.

Rumer stayed where she was.

She was still staring. She knew that. She didn't care.
She'd never been all that keen on following social
norms. She sure as heck hadn't had them demon-
strated to her by her mother, her grandmother, or her
aunt. They were an eclectic group of individualists, and
Rumer thought she might be looking at someone who
was the same. Someone who collected old books and

planted gardens in beautiful straight rows, who rented property on an organic farm and babysat a wild group of kids almost had to be one.

A squad car raced into view, lights flashing and sirens blaring. It turned onto the driveway, bouncing over a few ruts and coming to a stop a hundred yards away. The lights cut off, the sirens stopped and a tall, broad-shouldered man stepped out.

Rumer recognized him immediately.

Sheriff Kane Rainier had the same laid-back vibe he'd given off at the hospital. No rush. No hurry.

He walked toward them, speaking into his radio as he approached.

"Ladies," he acknowledged, nodding in their direction. "Pretty morning, but an odd time to be out enjoying it."

"I agree," Clementine said, striding toward him and offering a hand. "Thanks for coming so quickly, Kane. I'm afraid it was a false alarm."

"No problem," he responded, glancing in Rumer's direction. "Out for an early morning stroll, Rumer?"

"That was the plan. I got a little . . . sidetracked."

"I apologize for getting everyone riled up," Clementine said. "I heard someone walking around outside and decided law enforcement might be a good thing to have around."

"It's always better to be safe than sorry," the sheriff said. "But, I'm thinking this might have been avoided, if you'd let people know you were back in town."

"I arrived two hours ago. It didn't seem prudent to stop by the house."

"You didn't think to call ahead of time?" Kane asked.

"Call who? Sunday is in the hospital. Matt is dead."

"You know I'm not talking about either of them,"

Kane said calmly. "Matt's brothers are running things while Sunday recovers. It would have been wise to check with them before you decided to move back in."

"I have nearly two years left of a three-year lease on this property. Sunday and Matt insisted on honoring it. Despite the fact that . . ." She glanced at Rumer. "They insisted on honoring it. I've been paying rent on the place, because I didn't want to leave them in a lurch."

"It still would have been prudent to contact Matt's brothers."

"It would have been prudent for me to do a lot of things that I didn't do." She shrugged, lifting her hair, rolling it into a loose bun and securing it with a hairband she pulled from her wrist. "I can't go back and change things, Kane. Even if I could, I probably wouldn't."

"Good to know," he said without any inflection in his voice.

There was something between them.

That was for sure.

Whatever it was, Clementine wasn't apologizing for it.

"One way or another," she continued. "I have a lease on this property. I don't need permission from anyone to live here."

"No, but I'd sure as hell like to know why you suddenly decided to return," Kane said.

"I promised Sunday I'd get the farm back on its feet. I'm going to do that."

"Promised her when?"

"Before I left."

"Then, why didn't you stay?"

"You know why, Kane. There were too many reporters hanging around, and it was making your job more difficult."

Reporters? Rumer hadn't heard anything about that

from the kids, and she hadn't spent enough time in town to hear about it from anyone else. Every minute of the last five days had been spent with one or more of the Bradshaws.

"That's an interesting story," he finally said.

"It's the truth."

"Maybe. Or maybe you were afraid my office would decide to press charges."

"If that were the case, I wouldn't be back, would I?"

"Why are you?"

"I heard about the accident. I realized leaving Sunday in a lurch hadn't been the greatest thing a friend could do, so I came back. Hopefully, Sunday will survive, and when she comes home, the farm will be everything she's been hoping for." Her voice broke on the last words, and Kane frowned.

"You're still going to have to discuss this with Matt's brothers. If they want you out—"

"Why would they?" She glanced at Rumer as if she might have an answer.

"They hired me to help," Rumer offered. "I don't think they'd turn up their noses to an extra set of hands. Especially a set that isn't going to cost them anything."

Not her business, but of course, she'd been standing there listening as if it was.

The wind had picked up, the air icy with the beginning of winter. She was so cold her teeth were chattering, and she'd have been smart to head back to the farmhouse.

Apparently, she wasn't smart, because she kept standing right where she was.

"The Bradshaws will have the final say on that," Kane said, glancing at his watch. "Hopefully, they won't complain and you can go on with your plans. Otherwise, I'll be back to help sort things out."

He walked back to his cruiser, but didn't climb in.

"How bad is the farm?" he asked, and Clementine shrugged.

"Did you see any crops last year?"

"I wasn't paying attention."

"The fields produced a tenth of what they should have. Matt was a good guy, but he knew squat about farming. Another year like last year, and this place will be in the red. Sunday was concerned they'd have to mortgage it to pay bills."

"Matt didn't mention that."

"The bills were his, so why would he?" Clementine replied.

"According to Matt, the farm was doing well."

"Like I said," Clementine began.

"The farm is a mess," Rumer cut in, because she was freezing and because it was the truth.

"Does Sullivan know that?" Kane asked, turning his attention to her.

"We haven't had a lot of time to discuss it," she admitted, "but it wouldn't take a layman six minutes to figure out that this place is going down fast."

"All right." He nodded. "We'll take care of it."

"Who's we?" Clementine asked, her hands on her hips.

"The town. We look out for each other. You're the expert, so I'll send the crews to you."

"Now, hold on a minute!" Clementine protested.

"You said you wanted to help."

"I plan on it."

"This is a big place. You'll need manpower."

"What I'll need—"

Whatever she was going to say was cut off by the

sound of a car engine. Not a nice quiet purr or a soft
rumble. This was a loud chugging protest. Rumer knew
before she saw headlights, knew before they bounced
over a rut and pulled in behind the sheriff's squad car.
Knew that she was going to see the old red van.

What she didn't know, what she never would have
expected, was that the driver's-side door would fly
open, and Sullivan would hop out. That he'd scan the
area, his gaze stopping on her. That he'd move toward
her, and then stop in his tracks, turn back around,
open the sliding door, let a half dozen pajama-clad kids
spill out.

She couldn't have expected that or the way her
heart seemed to fill up and swell out as the group
moved toward her, little hands connected to little
hands, scrawny tween arms supporting chubby baby
thighs. Towheaded boys bouncing with excitement,
their pajama cuffs dragging in the dirt.

And, Sullivan. His hand on Moisey's shoulder, his
gaze on Rumer, his eyes skimming her from head to
toe. She felt it like a gentle caress, like fingers trailing
along her skin.

And, dear God!

She wanted so much more than that.

Her mouth went dry, her heart stopped, and if she
hadn't been nearly frozen from cold she'd have melted
into a puddle just from the heat of that one searing
glance.

He took off his coat, wrapped it around her shoulders, his fingers brushing her neck as he lifted her hair
from the collar.

He was looking straight in her eyes, and she could
feel that, too. Feel the way he was drinking her in,
memorizing every part of who she was.

"You," he said, his voice harsh, "just scared a dozen years off my life."

And, then he did something else that she couldn't have expected, something that she never ever could have prepared for.

He kissed her.

Right there in front of everyone, and it wasn't just a peck on the cheek like she'd given him. It was a full-out, soul-searing kiss.

And . . . holy cow!

Her toes curled in her boots, and her hands curved around his shoulders, and she was lost. Just . . . lost. Drowning in him and in that moment.

Kane cleared his throat, and Sullivan pulled back, his eyes blazing as he looked into her face.

"What the heck was that?" she asked, but Moisey wedged herself between them, tugging at Rumer's hand.

"It was a kiss. He just kissed you," she said, and that was apparently the only answer Rumer was going to get, because Sullivan was already walking away.

A metaphor for her life and a hint at the future that was bound to come. She'd be an idiot to forget it, so she pasted on a fake smile, took Moisey's hand, and pretended her entire world hadn't just been turned upside down.

Nothing good ever happened in the early hours of the morning.

Sullivan knew that.

He'd gotten the call about Sunday and Matt at one in the morning. Years before that, his mother had died just after midnight. And then, of course, there'd been his father.

Robert had been at his worst before the sun came up, yanking Sullivan and his brothers out of bed to polish shoes or scrub toilets. There'd been no rhyme nor reason to his demands, but Sullivan's childhood memories consisted mostly of those dark hours before dawn, scrub brush in hand, bending over a toilet or a sink or a tub, crawling on his hands and knees, fishing toy cars out from under sofas while his father ranted and raved and tossed expletives and insults around like grenades.

Sullivan had gotten over that a long time ago, but he hadn't forgotten it.

So, yeah. Early morning wasn't his favorite time of day. Being woken by a phone call when it was still dark? Not high on his list of things he enjoyed.

This morning had been no exception.

When his cell phone rang, he'd known it couldn't be good news. He'd been expecting to hear someone from the hospital telling him that Sunday had taken a turn for the worse.

Instead, Kane had told him that a woman had called in to report suspicious activity on the property. She'd said someone was sneaking around near the ranch house. Kane was heading over to check it out, but he'd wanted to call Sullivan first. Just to make sure he wasn't alarmed by the sirens.

Sullivan wasn't the kind of guy who sat around waiting for other people to do what he could. He'd figured he was closer to the rancher, so he might as well go check things out himself.

Which had been his first mistake.

He should have stayed in bed and let Kane handle things.

Instead, he'd pulled on his clothes and gotten ready to head out, but sometimes—all the time?—kids woke crying or screaming in the middle of the night. For the past five nights, he and Rumer had handled it together. The way his mind had been working after the phone call, the way he'd been thinking, he'd assumed that a kid *would* wake up. When that happened, Rumer would be wondering why he wasn't around to help. So, of course, he'd written a note. He'd planned to slide it under her door.

That had been his second mistake.

Instead of finding the door closed, he'd found it open, Rumer gone. He'd known right then that she was knee-deep in whatever trouble Kane had called about. There was no way he was going to sit around twiddling his thumbs hoping she was okay.

He'd woken the kids, helped them into coats, piled them into the van, and headed over to the ranch house.

Which, of course, was his third mistake.

If it had been his final mistake, things would have been just fine, but Sullivan hadn't stopped with that.

He'd pulled up in front of the house and seen Rumer standing near it, the exterior lights shining on her wild hair and her pale face, and he'd gotten out of the damn van and nearly forgotten about the kids.

But, that hadn't been his final mistake, either.

No. He'd had to one-up every mistake he'd made since Kane's call. He'd let the kids out of the van, and then crossed the space between him and Rumer. He'd meant to ask what the hell she'd been doing outside at two in the morning, but he hadn't been able to get the words out.

She'd been shivering with cold, and all the anger and fear had just drained out of him. He'd taken off his coat and put it around her shoulders, and then . . .

Yeah.

Then.

He'd kissed her.

His last and final mistake, and damn if he was going to regret it. If he'd had the moment to do over, he'd have done it again. If he'd had it to do a million times, he'd have changed nothing.

But, now they were heading back to the house, the kids and Rumer silent as church mice. Not a peep out of any of them. A surprise, because there'd been a cacophony of noise at the rancher, all the kids except for Heavenly overjoyed to see the renter that he hadn't even known existed.

Clementine Warren. She'd handed him a rental agreement and cashed checks that had proven that she'd continued to pay rent for the property even after she'd moved out. She'd honored her contractual obligation, and with nearly two years left in the lease, she expected him to honor his. She'd explained it just like that, and he hadn't seen any reason to argue. The kids adored her, and she had some good plans for getting the farm back into working order. Sullivan might not be a farmer, he might know squat about planting and harvesting, but even he'd noticed that Pleasant Valley needed help. The fields looked bedraggled, fences were falling down. The chicken coop was empty, the henhouse piled high with dirty hay. The only animal that still lived on the property was Bessie, and her pen had been the first thing he'd put to right. Since then, he'd been working through a three-page list of things that needed to be cleaned up and improved on.

Funny. The house had been immaculate the night he'd arrived. Everything neat and orderly. The garden behind the house had been the same, the soil already turned and ready for spring planting.

Close to the house, things looked good.

Farther out, they were grim—barns and outbuildings that needed to be shored up and painted. Broken paddocks and leaky irrigation systems. He'd pored through the financial books, trying to get a feel for how things had been run, but all he'd found were household accounts in Sunday's neat, precise handwriting. Matt had apparently been handling the business end of things, and from what Sullivan had seen, he'd been doing a piss-poor job and hiding it well.

Not one person in Benevolence had mentioned that the farm was struggling. No one had said anything but good things about Matt. The entire town loved him, and Sullivan understood why. Of all the Bradshaw men, Matt was the one people admired. He was kind, easygoing, eager to please. He treated everyone he met like a friend, and that wasn't lost on a community like Benevolence.

Yeah. Matt was a great guy with lots of great attributes. Sullivan had loved him dearly, but the longer he lived at Pleasant Valley Farm, the more clearly he could see his brother's weaknesses.

He sighed, pulling up in front of the house and getting out of the van. Oya had fallen asleep in her car seat, and he unhooked it from the seat belt, lifting it from the car. He'd have opened Rumer's door, but she was already heading toward the front door, a twin clutching her hand on either side. Moisey skipped along behind her. Twila was following more slowly, a book held close to her face as she read.

"Watch the step, Twila," he said at the same time Rumer called, "Careful, Twi. Don't trip."

She glanced his way, her expression hidden in shadows cast by the porch light. He thought, for a moment, she might say something. Maybe comment on the fact that great minds thought alike, or tell him that they were finally getting this parenting thing down. She'd said similar things dozens of times in the past few days, and he'd always smiled and nodded and agreed, because they *were* getting this thing down. Mostly because of her. Rumer was the calm in the chaos, the voice of reason when the kids were completely unreasonable.

Even Heavenly seemed to have warmed up to her.

If there were such things as miracles, that would be one.

This time, though, Rumer didn't say a word. She just pulled a key from her coat pocket, opened the door, and walked inside. The kids followed one right after another while he stood there with Oya watching them go.

"Shit," he muttered.

"Language," Heavenly replied, and he realized she was standing near the back corner of the van, watching him the way he'd been watching everyone else.

"Sorry."

"No, you're not."

"You're probably right about that."

"I guess an old dog *can* be taught new tricks."

"What tricks?"

"Honesty."

"For the record, I almost never lie. Also, I'm not old."

She smiled, and it caught him off guard. Not because she was smiling, but because it was the kind of sweet, easy smile he'd seen on Rumer's face dozens of times.

"I guess you're not," she admitted, tucking a loose strand of hair behind her ear. "You're not young, either. Which means you should know better."

"Than what?"

"Rumer isn't the kind of person who's going to be swayed by one piping-hot kiss."

"Geez, kid. This is not the conversation I want to have with you."

"Yeah. Well, I didn't want to have a conversation with you about the reasons why skintight clothes shouldn't be the only weapon in a sexy woman's arsenal, but I did."

True.

He'd had that conversation with her a few times. He hadn't used the word *sexy*, though. He'd said *attractive*. He also hadn't used the words *arsenal* or *weapon*.

Apparently, despite his fumbled attempts at getting the point across, Heavenly had gotten the message. "I'm sorry if that made you uncomfortable, but we're family. We have to look out for each other."

She snorted.

"Whether you like it or not, you're my niece. Your parents aren't around. It's my job to make sure you understand the way life works."

"A piece of paper signed by a judge doesn't make a person family," she replied. "You don't have any obligation to me, and I don't have one to you, but you've been really good to my sib . . . the dweebs, and I'd hate to see you fail in the romance department."

"So, you're going to school me on romance?"

She frowned. "I'm going to tell you what not to do when you're trying to let someone know you care."

She was dead serious, and he was just smart enough to not make a joke out of that. "All right. I'm listening."

"Don't say you're sorry for that kiss."

"I wasn't planning to."

"And, don't pretend it didn't happen. If you want Rumer to fall for you—"

"I didn't say that I did."

"Your kiss sure as hell did," she snapped.

"Language."

"I'll quit cussing when you do."

"Done," he said, and she snorted again.

"Whatever. Go ahead and screw things up with Rumer. I don't care." She stalked away.

Two weeks ago, he'd have let her go.

Two weeks ago, she'd been nothing more than a troubled kid his brother had adopted, a problem child whom he'd inherited.

Now, she was his niece, someone he cared about, and he'd be damned if he'd let her go without letting her know that.

"Was that it?" he asked quietly, and she stopped on the porch stairs, turning to face him again.

"What?"

"Your advice. Was that it? Just: Don't apologize for the kiss and don't pretend it didn't happen."

"Do you really want to know?" she asked.

"Yes." He moved toward her, the car seat bouncing lightly against his leg.

"That was only what you shouldn't do if you don't want to piss Rumer off."

"What about what I *should* do if I want to let someone know I care?"

She didn't speak for a second, and by the time she

did, he'd reached the stairs. He stopped at the bottom, and they were eye to eye. She had no makeup on, no weird black eyeliner or dark red lipstick. She didn't look like the teenager he always thought of her as. She looked like the little girl she was.

"Tell her she's beautiful and mean it," she said, the words just a whisper on the cold night air. "But also tell her that she's smart and fun. Tell her you love her, because you want her to know. Not because you want her to say it back. When she's sad, tell her it's okay to cry, and when she's happy, be happy with her. Mostly, just be nice to her. Bring her flowers and candy and little gifts, but also, don't blow a fuse when she makes mistakes. Don't make her feel stupid when she messes up. Listen when she talks. Like, really listen. Don't just pretend to. Women love that kind of stuff."

"Do they?" he asked, and she shrugged.

"It seems that way to me."

"Then, I'll keep it in mind."

"No, you won't," she said. "You think I'm some punk kid who doesn't know anything, and you probably didn't hear a word I just said. Give me Oya. I'll bring her to our room." She reached for the car seat, her skinny arm seeming to strain under its weight as she walked to the door.

"I heard every word," he said before she could cross the threshold, "and, I don't think you're a punk kid who doesn't know anything. I think you're a beautiful young girl who also happens to be very smart and very fun."

She froze. Just stood there for a second, clutching the car seat; then she glanced over her shoulder and met his eyes. "Just so you know, I don't need anyone to love me. I'm fine all on my own."

She trounced away before he could respond, but there was something about the way she moved, the straightness of her shoulders and the quickness of her steps, that made him think that, for once, he hadn't said the wrong thing, that maybe for the first time since he'd walked into the family, he'd acted like he was part of it.

Chapter Ten

Rumer made breakfast and thought about the kiss.

She got the kids off to school and thought about the kiss.

She did a load of laundry, took Oya for a walk, made the beds in the guest rooms because Sullivan's brothers were coming.

And, thought about that damn kiss.

Never, and she meant *never*, had she ever spent so much time thinking about something so inane. It was a kiss, for crying out loud. Not a lifetime commitment or a pledge of undying love.

"The problem," she said as she sat on the old swing with Oya in her lap, "is that I've got a bit of my mother in me."

Oya smiled and grabbed a fistful of Rumer's curls. "Momma," she said. "Momma momma momma."

"Exactly. Now you"—she tickled Oya's belly—"have nothing to worry about. You've got a great momma. I've heard all kinds of good stories about her, and I've got no doubt you're going to grow up to be as stellar

a person as she is. Me? I've got issues, and most of
them stem from my incredible ability to go after the
wrong guy."

"Momma momma momma," Oya responded, standing in Rumer's lap and bouncing happily.

"Ah, to be your age again and completely clueless
about the world." Rumer kissed her chubby cheek and
stood, the swing creaking as it swung backward. Sullivan would be home soon. He'd decided to cut his day
at the hospital in half so he could help her get ready
for his brothers.

He'd mentioned that as he'd grabbed his cup of
coffee and run out the door.

He hadn't mentioned the kiss.

Of course he hadn't!

It had probably meant about as much to him as a
grain of sand meant to the desert.

"Which is perfectly fine with me," she lied as she
walked into the mudroom.

The truth was a lot harder to acknowledge, because
the truth was, she was falling for him. Hard. And not
just because of the kiss. She'd been falling since the day
she'd seen him walking across the yard wearing that
frilly apron.

And, of course, if she was falling for him, that could
only mean one thing: He was the wrong guy, because
when you were a Truehart woman, every guy was.

Which sucked, because she wasn't just falling for
Sullivan. She liked him. She liked the way he smiled,
the way he laughed, the way he studied the kids and
Sunday and her. She liked how he listened to Moisey
prattle on endlessly about things like moonbeams and
magic flowers. She liked that he talked to the twins like
they were young men with brains in their heads, that

he brought Twila books from the library and Heavenly old vinyl albums that she could play on the record player that sat in the corner of her room.

She liked *him*, and that was the problem, because she'd dated a lot of guys, but she'd never been friends with them. Sure, there'd been admiration and respect and all the things that went into having a relationship, but she'd never wanted to spill her heart out to them. She'd never even been all that heartbroken at the thought of saying good-bye.

She frowned, setting Oya in the ExerSaucer that sat in the middle of the room and uncovering the bread dough she'd left rising on the counter. It looked light and fluffy and perfect, and it seemed sad that she could create perfect bread dough from scratch, but she couldn't figure out how to have a relationship that lasted.

She slammed her fist into the dough, letting the air escape as the sound of a car engine broke the silence. She knew it was Sullivan. She didn't have to look out the window to check for his SUV. He'd said he was coming home early, and he had. Which was another thing she liked about him. He kept his word and did what he said he would.

She did, too, but she was starting to wonder if accepting this job was a mistake.

Who was she kidding?

She'd known it was a mistake the day she'd arrived at Pleasant Valley Farm. She'd known even before she'd gotten to know Sullivan and the kids that she was asking for trouble. She'd accepted the job anyway.

"Because, apparently, I like to tempt fate," she muttered, rolling the dough out into a smooth oval.

The front door opened, and she heard Sullivan's

boots on the wood floor, heard him open the coat closet and close it.

"Anyone home?" he called, and a million tiny wings fluttered in her stomach. That's what he did to her. Every damn time.

"We're in the kitchen," she responded, pleased that she didn't sound as breathless as she felt.

He walked into the room, and she forced herself not to look at him, to keep focusing on shaping the loaf, setting it on the greased pan, covering it with a damp towel. She listened to him talk to Oya, heard her giggling, found herself turning around. Just to see what game they were playing.

He was crouched in front of the ExerSaucer, the pack he carried to the hospital on his back, a cloth doll in his hands. He wiggled it gently against Oya's cheek and she giggled again.

There was a pencil behind his ear, the sketch pad he always carried next to his feet, and when he met Rumer's eyes . . .

When he met her eyes, the world stopped just like her heart always seemed to. She could feel time stretching out in front of her, and she could imagine this same scene playing out dozens of times in a dozen different ways over dozens of years.

And, God!

She wanted to believe in that so badly it hurt.

"What's wrong?" he asked, leaving the doll on the ExerSaucer and stepping closer.

"Nothing."

"Don't lie, Rumer. It's not a good look on anyone." He said it gently, as if he could hear the thoughts racing around in her head and knew how much she didn't want to be standing there thinking them.

"You. Me. That kiss last night," she admitted.

"How are any of those things wrong?" He'd moved closer, and she could see flecks of gold in his bright green eyes, smell sunlight and winter air on his skin.

"I work for you."

"You work for Pleasant Valley Organic Farm," he replied.

"Semantics."

"Truth," he corrected. "So, tell me: What's really wrong?"

"I already did. You kissed me." That last part slipped out, and he nodded.

"Okay."

"That's it? I tell you I'm upset that you kissed me, and you say 'okay'?"

"I was told not to apologize for it."

"You were telling people we kissed? News will be all over town by sunset."

"Would you care if it was?"

"No." She answered truthfully, because she wouldn't have cared. She'd never been the kind of person who took much stock in what other people thought of her. "But, that's not the point. The point is, you were talking about us and there is no us."

"I wasn't talking about anything. I got the advice from a witness to the event." He shrugged out of the backpack and set it on the counter.

"Kane?" She couldn't imagine him saying anything about it, but she figured he was the only one who might have.

"Heavenly," he replied, unzipping the pack and reaching into it. He pulled out a small white box decorated with a gold heart sticker and set it beside the pack. "She also told me not to pretend it didn't happen, so I won't. It happened, and for about twenty seconds, my entire world was right."

"That," she said, her heart pounding heavily in her chest, "is the most beautiful thing anyone has ever said to me."

"Then, you haven't been hanging around the right people," he replied, echoing the words he'd spoken after he'd said she was beautiful.

They were such pretty little words, and they were no different than all the other words she'd heard from all the other guys she'd been with.

Except that he meant them.

She knew that the same way she knew the sun would set and rise again, that winter would turn to spring and spring to summer, that Lu would sit at her kitchen table with her false teeth in an old jelly jar cup.

Yeah. She knew he meant it, and she felt every coldly cynical piece of her heart melt. She would have placed her hand on a stack of Bibles, stood in front of a judge, a jury, and the good Lord Himself and sworn that it did.

She needed to walk away. She needed to find something to do that didn't involve standing a foot from Sullivan. But, she couldn't stop looking into his eyes, she couldn't keep her hands from sliding up his arms and across his shoulders, drifting into his hair. It was silky and thick, the strands sliding through her fingers. She knew she needed to back away.

She *knew* it, but she didn't.

He stared into her eyes as he lowered his head, his warm breath fanning her forehead, her cheeks, her lips. She wasn't sure if she moved or if he did, but there was no more space between them. She could feel the warmth of his chest, his abdomen, his thighs, and she wanted to burrow in closer, let her hands slip beneath his coat, feel the firm muscles of his back, explore the narrow width of his waist.

"Tell me to stop," he murmured, but of course, she didn't.

His lips brushed hers, the contact so light it might have been a dream. His hands drifted along the narrow line of exposed flesh between her jeans and her sweater, and he was pulling her closer, deepening the kiss, his fingers trailing fire, his lips doing the same.

And she forgot she was in Sunday's kitchen.

She forgot Oya was in her ExerSaucer a few feet away.

She forgot that Truehart women always chose the wrong man. She forgot everything but the taste of his lips, the heat of his hands, and the strange feeling that she had finally *finally* found her way home.

Somewhere, in the tiny part of her brain that was still functioning, she heard a door open, footsteps on the foyer floor.

"Sullivan?!" a man called. "You here?"

She jumped back. Or tried.

Sullivan's hands were still on her back, his fingers tracing lazy circles on her lower spine, and he was studying her face the way he always did—as if she were the most fascinating person he'd ever met.

"I don't plan on apologizing for that, either," he murmured, his voice gruff.

"Or pretending it didn't happen?" she added, her pulse racing, her stomach churning.

"That either," he agreed with a tender smile.

She wanted to smile back. She *tried* to smile back, but what she managed was probably more like a grimace.

There were no fluttering wings in her stomach now, just the sick sense that she'd made a horrible mistake. She shouldn't have taken the job. She shouldn't have gotten attached to the kids. And, God help her, she shouldn't have fallen for Sullivan.

She was going to get hurt this time.

She had no doubt about that.

It wouldn't be like it had been with Jake—a relieved good-bye and a lot of anger.

No. Her heart would be torn out and split open and there wouldn't be a thing she could do about it.

"It's going to be okay," Sullivan said quietly, cupping her face and looking in her eyes.

"It's never okay," she responded. "Every damn time, it's wrong. It's the Truehart curse, and no woman in my family has ever broken it."

"Then the odds are high you're finally going to manage it. Someone's got to, right?"

"It's not funny, Sullivan," she said, her voice breaking a little.

"I'm not laughing." He kissed her forehead the way she'd kissed his, only he let his lips linger, his fingers slide into her hair.

"Oops! I guess I'm a little early," the man said, and she realized he'd walked into the kitchen and was standing near the doorway. Black hair, green eyes, tall and muscular, he had to be one of Sullivan's brothers. He was a rougher version of the Bradshaw good looks—his hair a little longer, his skin a shade darker, his eyes gray-green rather than emerald.

"You must be Rumer," he said, moving toward her and offering a hand. "I'm Flynn Bradshaw."

"It's nice to meet you," she responded, resisting the urge to smooth her hair or straighten her shirt. She knew what she must look like—lips red and swollen, cheeks pink, hair all kinds of wild.

She also knew that he'd noticed.

His gaze shifted to his brother.

"We've got a lot to catch up on, Sullivan," he said.

"That's why you flew out this weekend," Sullivan replied. If he felt defensive, he didn't show it.

"Want to take a walk while we discuss things? It was a long flight and a long drive. I need to stretch my legs." He smiled at Rumer. "Do you mind watching Oya for a while?"

"That's what you're paying me for," she responded, and instantly regretted it. She sounded flippant and terse—an older, more obnoxious version of Heavenly. "What I mean is that I'm always happy to spend time with Oya. She's a very sweet-natured baby."

"Is she? Things were so chaotic when I was here before, I didn't have time to notice. I'm hoping to have more time to get to know the kids this time around."

"Don't count on things being any less chaotic this time," Sullivan joked. The two were walking into the mudroom, and Rumer knew she'd been forgotten, that they were already deep in whatever conversation they planned to have.

Forgotten. Like always, and she should have felt relieved by that. Instead, she just felt tired.

She lifted Oya from the saucer, smiling as the baby patted her cheek.

"Well, it's just the two of us again, sweetie. How about a little nap? I don't know about you, but I could use one." She turned around, ready to go upstairs and put the kitchen and the kiss behind her.

Sullivan stepped back into the room, and her heart

did a crazy little jig that made her breath catch and her cheeks heat.

God!

She was such a fool.

"Forget something?" she asked, lifting his sketch pad and holding it out for him, her hand shaking just enough for him to notice.

He frowned, taking the pad and setting it on the counter.

"What's wrong?" he asked.

"Nothing a nap won't fix," she lied.

He eyed her for a moment, then shook his head. "You're lying, but Porter is two minutes out, and I don't want him interrupting whatever it is you need to say."

"I don't need to say anything. I need a na—"

"We can argue the point later." He took a small box from his backpack. "This is what I forgot."

He held it out to her.

"What is it?"

"Just something to let you know I've been thinking about you."

Outside, a car horn blasted and a man shouted a greeting.

"That's Porter. I'm heading out. See you later." He kissed Oya's cheek and then Rumer's, grabbed his sketch pad and walked outside.

Rumer stood right where she was, holding Oya and the little box, wondering how she'd gotten where she was. To this place where one smile, one word, one little gift from Sullivan could make her entire world seem brighter.

She frowned, the sound of masculine voices drifting through the closed window. She waited until they faded away, waited as Oya settled against her shoulder, eyes closed, body lax.

Finally, she folded back the lid of the box and looked inside.

Chocolate.

Two gorgeous glossy hearts. Milk chocolate drizzled with dark chocolate, cushioned by pretty foil wrappers.

"Wow," she breathed, her throat tight, her eyes burning with something that felt suspiciously like tears.

"Wow," Oya repeated. "Wow, wow, wow."

"Funny girl. Come on. Time for your nap."

Rumer closed the box, because she couldn't eat the chocolates. Not yet. They were too perfect. Not just the candy but the gift, given quietly and without fanfare.

Just because.

Had Jake ever done anything as sweet? Of course, he hadn't. He'd been all about the show.

Sullivan was all about Rumer.

The thought was there. Unbidden.

She frowned, carrying the box upstairs and into Oya's room. She set it on the dresser as she settled the baby down for a nap.

She sang lullabies and stroked Oya's downy hair and pretended that she wasn't thinking about that box and those beautiful hearts.

She knew the truth, though.

The hearts were a symbol of everything that had been wrong in her relationship with Jake. They were a reminder of all the things she'd wanted from him that he'd never given—time, affection, loyalty, companionship.

And, they were a symbol of everything that was right with Sullivan, everything that she could have with him if she weren't too damn afraid to take a chance.

* * *

When Sullivan had been really young, Sunday morning had meant church. His mother had always gotten up at the crack of dawn, moving through the house like a silent wraith, trying hard not to wake Robert. She'd stirred batter for pancakes and poured it onto a hot griddle, slathering the fluffy cakes with butter and setting them in the oven to keep them warm until she woke the boys.

He'd always been awake before she'd walked in his room, lying in bed, listening to the quiet rhythm of her morning routine and praying his father wouldn't wake up to ruin it. When she'd died, the Bradshaw family had stopped attending services. Instead of pancakes and maple syrup, the boys had eaten cold cereal and sat silently while their father snored. If they were lucky, he'd sleep until noon.

Usually, they weren't lucky.

He scowled, irritated that the memories were there, frustrated with himself for dwelling on them. He had things to do. Like finish Moisey's hair—her gorgeous curly thick hair that did not want to be bound by hair ties or bands.

"Are you sure you don't want to just wear it like you usually do?" he asked as another hairband snapped.

"Puffs *is* how I usually wear it for Sundays, Uncle Sully," she said, using the nickname that she'd coined for him.

Porter snickered.

"What?" Sullivan said, meeting his eyes. Like every other Bradshaw man, he had green irises and dark hair. Unlike Sullivan and Flynn, he also seemed to have some mad skills when it came to taming little-girl hair.

He'd already managed to scrape Oya's into tiny little pigtails. He'd gotten her dressed and fed, too.

"Nothing, Sully," Porter responded as he grabbed a wet cloth and attacked a stain on the front of Maddox's blue dress shirt.

It looked like milk, but Sullivan couldn't be sure.

He wasn't going to take the time to find out, either. Maddox was Porter's Sunday-morning responsibility.

Division of labor was what they'd all been calling it. Divide and conquer was more like it. Yesterday had been easy because five of the six kids had been at the homestead with Rumer.

This morning?

Not so much.

Probably things would have been easier if they'd let the kids sleep in, watch cartoons, and do whatever kid things they wanted to.

That had been the original plan, the one Sullivan had been following every Sunday since he'd arrived.

Unfortunately for all of them, Moisey had woken screaming in the middle of the night. There'd been nothing anyone could do to calm her. She'd been crying for Sunday, shrieking for Rumer, yelling at the top of her lungs that she didn't want anyone else.

Two hours later, when every kid and every adult in the house was wide awake, she'd finally collapsed on her bed and sobbed that she just wanted everything back the way it used to be. Daddy and Mommy. Dinners at the big table in the dining room. Sunday mornings at church and library time every Saturday.

They'd missed library time, but Sullivan would be damned if they were going to miss church. The kid deserved to have some of her old life back. So, of course, he'd made promises that he was now regretting.

Promise 1: church.

Promise 2: dinner at the dining room table.

Minutes later, she'd fallen asleep, content in the knowledge that some of what she'd lost would be returned to her. Somehow, he and his brothers had managed to get the other five kids settled, and then they'd sat at the kitchen table, swigging orange juice like it was one-hundred-proof whiskey and discussing a plan for getting six kids out of bed and ready for church on time.

Flynn had suggested drawing names from a brown paper bag and taking responsibility for whichever kids they picked. It had seemed like the only fair way to choose who'd deal with which kid. They'd planned two kids each, but when Flynn drew Heavenly's name on the first round, he'd gone about three shades of pale and claimed he'd rather face down a pit of vipers than wrangle her into going to church.

Sullivan felt the same way, so he'd offered to take on three kids to ease some of Flynn's pain. He'd ended up with Moisey, Twila, and Milo. Porter had ended up with Oya and Maddox. All of it had been settled by three a.m., the plan in place for almost certain success.

Except they were dealing with kids, so success was about as likely as finding a pot of gold at the end of a rainbow.

"Try these, Uncle," Twila said, pressing two more hairbands into his hand. She, at least, was ready to go. Milo looked presentable too, his hair combed, his shirt pressed, his tie straight, an inch of white sock showing between his black shoes and pants.

Sullivan did a double take.

He was pretty certain those were the same pants

Milo had worn to Matt's funeral. The ones that had been a half inch too long.

"Hey, sport," Sullivan said as he gently parted Moisey's hair again and wrested a band around half of it. "How about some black socks?"

"I like white."

"Uncle Porter and I are wearing black," he pointed out, and Milo shrugged.

"I still like white. My black ones are too tight for Henry to fit in." He lifted his right cuff a little higher, revealing a bulge beneath the white sock.

"Then, I guess you should wear white." He also guessed that he needed to buy the kid longer pants and bring him to the animal shelter to find a dog. Preferably one he couldn't fit in his socks.

"Maybe you should, too," Milo suggested, moving in close enough for Sullivan to smell something flowery and sweet.

Perfume?

God, he hoped not! Because if it was perfume, he'd probably gotten it from the girls. Which meant he'd been in someone's room. If he'd been in the room without permission, things could go south really quickly.

"What's that smell?" Moisey asked, turning her head just as Sullivan managed to get the second band around her hair.

It stayed.

Thank God!

"Are you wearing Mommy's perfume?" she continued.

"It's Dad's cologne," Milo said proudly.

Sullivan hadn't spent a lot of time with Matt the past few years, but he was certain his brother hadn't worn cologne. If he had, it sure as heck hadn't smelled like a field of wildflowers.

"Dad doesn't wear cologne," Twila said.

"It was his. I found it in his drawer." Milo frowned, dragging his shirt up to his nose so he could sniff it.

"Don't worry." Twila patted his arm. "You smell good."

"He smells like a garden," Moisey said, her nose wrinkled. "Of dead flowers."

"Moisey Bethlehem," Sullivan said with a sigh. "That's enough."

"It's true," she responded as he finger-combed detangler into her hair. "But, don't worry, Milo. I like dead flowers. Are we done, Uncle Sully?"

"I think so," he said, stepping back and eyeing the uneven part and the cute little pom-pom-like puffs of hair that jutted out on either side of it.

"Do I look beautiful?" she asked, her hands on her hips, the bright pink dress she'd chosen sagging down her chest and bagging at her waist.

"You don't look beautiful. You *are* beautiful," he replied, and she grinned.

"Thank you, Sully."

"Uncle," he corrected, but she was bouncing across the room, shoving her feet into yellow rain boots that were sitting near the mudroom door.

It wasn't raining.

As a matter of fact, the sun was streaming in the kitchen window.

He didn't have time to fight her on the choice.

"Everyone ready?" he asked, glancing at his watch. They were running three minutes behind, but he figured they could still make it in time.

"We've been ready for twenty minutes," Porter said with more pride than was necessary considering he'd only had two kids to corral.

"What about Heavenly?" Twila asked as they filed outside, the sun, already warm and high and bright, glinting off her dark brown hair and her shiny leather shoes. He'd left his sketch pad inside, but his fingers itched to draw her, to capture the inquisitive look in her eyes and the way she cocked her head to the side as she glanced back at the house.

"That's a good question," he responded. "I'll go check."

He took a step toward the house, and then stopped, because Flynn was on his way out, dark pants and white shirt pressed and neat, tie slightly crooked, jaw set. He wore the look of a man who'd just fought a hard battle and lost.

"What's wrong?" Sullivan asked.

"You're not going to believe this," he muttered.

"What?"

"This." Flynn reached back, snagged something. Some*one.*

Because, Heavenly was suddenly in the doorway.

Dressed in black from head to toe. Long black skirt. Long-sleeved black shirt. Black shoes and fingerless black gloves. She'd painted her nails black, too.

But that wasn't what caught Sullivan's attention.

No. It was her hair he noticed. It had been chopped to within a couple inches of her scalp, the strands dyed what was probably supposed to be blue. They looked more purplish-brown than anything. There were splotches of color on her forehead and sections of mud brown near her nape.

For a split second, he could hear his father's voice in his head, feel all those words and curses and recriminations sitting on the tip of his tongue.

They were late, for God's sake!

They needed to leave now!

What the hell had she been thinking?

Why the hell would she do something so stupid?

But, she was watching him defiantly, her chin angled up, her hands fisted, and all the words fell away, all the anger died.

"You cut your hair." He stated the obvious and her chin jutted up a notch more.

"And colored it," she said. "Sunday said I could."

"When did she say that?"

"On my birthday last year. She said when I turned thirteen, we'd get my hair cut and colored any way I chose. And, we'd get another piercing in my ear."

His gaze jumped to her ear.

Sure enough, there was a silver stud in the cartilage and smeared blood on the lobe.

"I'm not sure she meant that you should do those things yourself," he said, and she shrugged as if none of it mattered.

"I guess at my age, I'm old enough to do what I want," she responded, her voice wobbling.

And, that's when it registered.

Not the hair or the ear or the sadness in her eyes.

The words:

She said when I turned thirteen . . .

I guess at my age . . .

"It's your birthday," he said, but it came out as more of a question, because he was hoping to God that he was wrong. That he hadn't somehow missed one of the most important milestones in a kid's life. Child to teenager. Young girl to young woman.

"So?" she responded, her voice still wobbling, her chin still high.

"Why didn't you tell me?"

"Because I hate birthdays," she said.

"You told me about Twila's birthday. You can't hate them that much."

"She's a kid. She deserves nice things."

"So are you," Porter said. "So do you."

"Whatever," she replied. "It's just another day. Sunday and Matt were the only ones who ever remembered it."

Her voice broke, then. Just broke, and he broke, too, because she was the toughest kid he'd ever met, and she was standing on the back stoop with home-dyed hair and a self-pierced ear crying.

"It's okay," he said, moving past Flynn and pulling her into his arms. She didn't lean against him, but she didn't pull away. Just stood stiff and straight, her skinny frame shaking with sobs.

"No, it's not. It's horrible. Everyone at school is going to laugh at me. Just like they always do. My damn mother was right. I'm a freak!" she wailed.

"If she really said that, she was the freak. Not you," Flynn said, his voice gruff.

"Who cares?! This is the biggest stupidest mistake I've ever made!" she sobbed, tears rolling down her cheeks and carrying black eyeliner with them.

"Everyone makes mistakes," Sullivan responded, her words dancing around his head. The ones she'd spoken when she'd given him advice about Rumer: *If she messes up, don't make her feel stupid.*

How many times had she messed up and been made to feel that way?

"No, they don't. Not like this. Not when they have to go to school and see all the people who hate them." She swiped at the tears, took a quick step back.

"You're wrong. Plenty of people cut their hair and

regret it," he said, not touching on the school thing. As far as he'd known, she'd been doing just fine. Apparently, he hadn't known anything. He'd call the school in the morning and arrange a meeting with the principal. For now, though, he'd just deal with what was in front of him.

"They do?"

"Sure."

"I've never seen anyone with hair messed up this bad."

"That's because they fix it before they go out in public."

"Even if you're right, it doesn't matter. I don't know how to fix it. I've been trying all morning." She touched the ends.

"Then it's a good thing you have us around," he said, glancing at his brothers and hoping against hope that one of them had a clue.

He could tell from their expressions that they didn't.

"Hair salon?" Porter finally suggested.

"This is Benevolence. Not LA. Nothing is open on Sunday."

"Right. I forgot."

"See? I told you," Heavenly spat, all her tears replaced by anger. "I'm going to have to go to school like this."

"No, you're not!" Moisey nearly shouted. "I know what to do!"

"You're not touching my hair!" Heavenly shouted back, but Moisey was running inside, and Sullivan doubted she heard.

"She's not touching my hair," Heavenly muttered meeting his eyes.

"Of course she's not."

"So . . . what's the plan?" Flynn asked as they walked into the mudroom, the kids trailing along behind them.

"I guess we rinse and wash it first. Then, we color it again." He'd think about the uneven jagged butcher job after that.

"Don't you think she's got enough color in it?" Porter was still holding Oya, but he reached past, turning on the faucet in the mudroom sink.

"She needs the right color," he responded, offering Heavenly a smile that he hoped made him seem confident.

He was confident all right.

Confident that failure was right around the corner.

Poor kid.

"I vote for purple," Maddox said.

"No! Green!" Milo argued.

"I think her regular color is pretty," Twila cut in.

"Since I'm the artist," he said, "I'll decide. One of you grab a towel. Someone else bring shampoo. Maddox, get a chair."

For once, everyone did exactly what they were told.

Minutes later, he had Heavenly settled in the chair, a towel wrapped around her shoulders and chest.

The rest of the family stood nearby, watching with mixtures of fascination and horror.

He thought about waiting, just letting it be until he could find a hair salon that could fix it, but he imagined some damn bully seeing her and snapping a photo that could be posted to social media and used to torture her for years.

"Uncle Sullivan?" she said, and he realized he was standing there with a shampoo bottle in his hand, staring at her poor messed-up hair, doing absolutely nothing about it, because he had no idea where to start or how to help and he was scared . . .

Yes, s*cared* . . .

That he was going to fail her.

"Yeah?"

"It's okay. I trust you," she replied, and then she leaned her head back into the sink and waited for him to begin.

Chapter Eleven

She was driving like a bat out of hell, speeding along at twenty miles an hour above the posted limit, probably breaking every conceivable traffic law that existed.

And, she didn't care.

All she cared about was getting to Heavenly.

It's an emergency. She's blue. We don't know what to do.

That's what Moisey had said, her call an unexpected interruption in an otherwise quiet morning. A very quiet morning. Rumer had been alone, mucking the stalls, listening to her own thoughts. Most of which had to do with Sullivan or the Bradshaw kids. She had no idea what she was going to do about them, and that was weighing on her.

Quitting the job seemed like the easiest and least painful solution. She'd just have to come up with an excuse, give her resignation, walk away before Sullivan had the chance to walk away from her. She would have already made the call and given her notice, except for the kids. They needed her. Even if they hadn't, she wasn't sure she would have been able to do it.

She'd grown up a lot the last few years.

She'd matured.

She didn't want to let herself be the person she'd been when she'd met Jake—a little childish, a little nervous, content to have a mediocre relationship because she hadn't wanted to be alone.

She enjoyed being alone now.

She liked her own company.

But, it had been nice to have Sullivan enter that empty space in her heart, the one that no other man had ever been able to fill.

It had been nice, but it wouldn't last. If she didn't walk away from him, he'd walk away from her.

She believed that with every fiber of her being, and she still hadn't made the call.

So, maybe she didn't believe it.

Not the way she'd believed in sunrises or second chances.

That's what she'd been thinking about while she mucked stalls.

She'd been so deep in her head, she'd nearly jumped out of her skin when her cell phone rang. She'd pulled it out, seen the Bradshaws' number, and answered immediately, certain there was something wrong.

She'd been right.

She'd made all the kids memorize her cell phone number. Just in case. Now, she wished she'd had them practice emergency protocol. The information Moisey had given had been limited. Something about Heavenly being blue and crying and the uncles not knowing what to do. When Rumer had asked if anyone had called 911, Moisey had insisted that the uncles were taking care of things, but that they needed her help. *Now.*

That had been Moisey's last word before she'd disconnected.

Rumer had called back, letting the phone ring a dozen times before she'd given up. Obviously, something was going on, and obviously, she needed to be there.

Now.

Not when Minnie's sluggish vintage Cadillac decided to get her there.

"Dang it!" she growled, stomping on the accelerator and getting a lukewarm response from the transmission. "This car is slow as molasses."

"Not quite," Lu said calmly, her purple dress tucked neatly around her legs, her black leather purse in her lap. She'd been getting ready for church when Rumer had barreled into the house, and she'd insisted on coming along.

So had Minnie. She was sitting in the back seat, going through her medical kit. Just in case she needed it.

Rumer was hoping and praying she wouldn't. But a blue kid? That didn't sound good.

"Better floor it," Lu said conversationally, her gaze on the side mirror. "The cops are on our tail."

"What?" She glanced in the rearview mirror, saw lights flashing and a squad car closing in. She was on the country road that led to Pleasant Valley Farm. There was no one else around, so she had to be their target.

She'd be happy to stop and give them her information. She'd be happy to accept a ticket and own up to her mistakes.

After she reached the house.

"He's getting close. Hopefully, he's called in our location and blocked the road leading in and out of here. I'd hate for anyone to get in the middle of this. At these speeds, someone could get hurt," Lu said, a note of warning in her voice.

"This isn't *Cops*, Ma. We're not involved in a high-speed chase," Minnie responded. "Rumer's going fifty."

"The speed limit is thirty," Lu reminded her. "And, she's got a cop behind her, so it's a chase. Things could get dicey if we don't pull over. Then again, if we do, we'll probably get arrested for fleeing an officer of the law."

"We're not going to get arrested, so don't get yourself all excited. Your heart can't take it."

"My heart checked out just fine when I went to the doctor last week. All the blockages are gone, so I'll get as excited as I want."

"Suit yourself, but we're not going to get arrested." Rumer put on the hazard lights, acknowledging the officer and hoping that would satisfy him until they reached the house.

She glanced in the rearview mirror again. The officer was right on her tail, edging in close enough that he could have rammed her if he'd wanted to.

He?

The driver had shoulder-length blond hair, so a woman seemed more likely. Maybe she'd be more sympathetic. Or not.

"Here," Lu said, digging into her purse and pulling out a white cotton cloth. "Let's hang handkerchiefs out the window, so he knows we're friendly."

She had her window unrolled, the cloth waving like a surrender flag before Rumer could tell her not to.

"You do the same, Minnie." She tossed another cloth in the back, and Minnie—right-brained, analytical, book-smart, people-savvy Minnie—did the same.

So, now they were speeding down the middle of a country road, cops chasing them, surrender flags waving from the windows, plumes of dirt and exhaust streaming out from behind them.

Dear God!

Could things get any crazier?

Could her life be any more nuts?

Maybe. Probably. But Rumer didn't know how.

She turned onto the gravel driveway, tires spitting out dirt and pebble, Cadillac bouncing over ruts and into divots.

The house was just ahead, the yellow siding cheerful in the sunlight. No ambulance in view. No emergency crews. The place looked quiet.

Maybe too quiet.

Usually something was happening there—kid running around in the yard, someone sitting on the porch swing.

She parked the car and jumped out, waving at the cop as she ran up the stairs. The door was locked, so she fished the spare key out from under a loose floorboard, shoving it into the lock as the officer pounded up the stairs behind her.

"Ma'am," she said. "I'm really going to need you to stop."

"I will. I just have to check on the kids. There's been an emergency."

"We haven't had one called in," the officer said, stepping into the house behind Rumer.

"Rumer!" Moisey cried from the top of the stairs. "I knew you'd come."

She ran down as fast as her legs could carry her, throwing herself into Rumer's arms with so much force she almost knocked her off her feet.

"Honey! What's wrong? Where's Heavenly?"

"She's in the mudroom. The uncles are scrubbing her down."

"Scrubbing her down? What does that mean, doll?" The officer frowned. She looked to be in her mid-forties, blond hair a little brassy, blue eyes a little tired.

"Well, we were going to church, and she had blue on her, and the uncles weren't happy about it, so they're trying to get her back to her normal color, Deputy Reynolds."

"You can call me Deputy Susan," the officer said.

Obviously, they knew each other.

That was good. Great, even. Deputy Susan could try to get the information out of Moisey. Rumer was going to the mudroom.

She ran down the hall, ignoring Lu and Minnie, who'd just walked in the front door. The kitchen was empty, but she could hear water running and see Maddox and Milo standing in the mudroom doorway.

They must have heard her approaching. They turned, relief and pleasure washing over their faces.

"Rumer!" Maddox said, rushing toward her. "Wait until you see this!?" He sounded both intrigued and horrified.

"See what?"

"Heavenly cut off all her hair, and she put colors in it, and now they can't get it out. Uncle Sullivan's already washed it like a bazillion times, and it's still poop brown," he whispered, his gaze darting to the mudroom doorway.

"No, it's not," Milo argued. "It's poop green."

"Her hair?" Rumer asked, hurrying across the room, desperately hoping they were exaggerating.

The mudroom was filled with kids and men. Porter over near the back door, Oya in his arms, his gaze focused on the sink. Twila was beside him, nervously raveling and unraveling her braid. Flynn stood closest to the kitchen, his broad shoulders partially blocking Rumer's view.

She could see enough to know the boys hadn't been exaggerating. As a matter of fact, they might have understated the gravity of the situation.

A chair had been pulled over to the sink, and Heavenly was sitting in it, her head tilted back, a bottle of water in her hand. Sullivan was bent over her, his back to Rumer, squirting a few drops of shampoo onto her hair.

Or, what was left of it.

She had chopped it off and dyed it, the color a mixture of puce and purple and blue. Her scalp had stains from whatever she'd used. So did her cheek, which was also smeared with mascara and eyeliner.

She'd been crying.

There was no doubt about that.

"I don't suppose someone wants to explain what's going on," she said, and Heavenly jerked upright, water dripping down her pale face.

"Why are you here?" she asked. "It's your day off."

"Moisey called me," she responded.

"I was wondering what she was up to. If I'd known what she was doing, I'd have stopped her," Sullivan said, turning to face her. So, of course, her heart did its funny little pause, her mouth went dry, and, for about two seconds, all she could think of was the way his lips had felt against hers.

"I don't mind," she finally managed to say. "I was mucking stalls. This looks like a lot more fun."

"That depends on what side of the shampoo bottle you're on. I don't think Heavenly is having all that much fun. Which is a shame since it's her birthday." He emphasized the last part, and she didn't miss that. She also didn't miss the two red splotches on Heavenly's normally pale cheeks.

Was she embarrassed that he'd mentioned her birthday, or that she'd chopped off her hair?

Butchered her hair?

It looked like she might have taken a hacksaw to it, but far be it from Rumer to point that out. She'd done her own stupid things when she was that age.

"Your birthday, Heavenly? Why didn't you tell me?" she asked, keeping her voice light and cheerful.

"I hate birthdays," the teen responded, her cheeks still pink.

"Happy birthday anyway," she said, sidling past Flynn and moving closer to the sink. The floor and walls were splattered with grayish water and cut hair. His shirt was splattered, too, the white button-up dress shirt now multicolored. He'd rolled his sleeves up, and she could see the muscles beneath his tan skin.

He looked way too good, and she was noticing way too much, so she turned her attention to Heavenly. "So, was this a birthday hairdo gone wrong?" she asked.

"Kind of," Heavenly responded, closing her eyes as Sullivan rinsed soap and color from her hair.

"Sunday said she could have it done on her thirteenth birthday. But, Sunday wasn't around today." Sullivan took a towel from a stack someone had set on a chair nearby and rubbed Heavenly's hair.

"Did I hear it's someone's birthday?" Lu squeezed

into the room, forcing everyone to shift position to accommodate her.

When Rumer shifted, she bumped into Sullivan.

"Careful," he said, his breath tickling the hair at her temple. His arm wrapped around her waist, holding her steady even though she hadn't been falling. She could have stepped away, but his arm was warm, his muscles firm against her abdomen. His hand splayed against her upper lip, and her heart started to beat a happy rhythm that she really wanted to ignore but couldn't.

Lu's gaze dropped to Sullivan's hand, lifted to Rumer's face, and then shifted to Heavenly. To her credit, she didn't blink an eye at any of it.

"I see you got your hair done for your birthday," she said.

"I did it myself."

"You don't say?" Lu responded, and Heavenly grinned, obviously catching on to the sarcasm and appreciating it. Not surprising since sarcasm seemed to be her second language.

"I do say, and I'd be saying a lot more, but Uncle Sullivan hasn't cussed in a couple of days, and I told him I'd quit when he did. So, I've got to keep things clean."

"Rumer?" Susan called. "Did you figure out what the emergency was? Because, I'm not getting much info from Moisey."

She peered into the room, her eyes widening as she caught sight of Heavenly. Unlike Lu, she didn't hold back on her judgment. "Heavenly Melody Bradshaw, what in God's name did you do to yourself?"

"My middle name isn't Melody," Heavenly retorted, her fingers inching up to touch her hair, then dropping away again.

"Well, what is it? Because if I'm going to lecture you like I do my daughters, I'll need to know." She strode in, squeezing between the Bradshaw men, stopping an inch from where Heavenly was sitting.

"I don't have a middle name."

"Well you do now. Just like I said: Melody, and not because it sounds catchy with the first name. Because, my daughter said you have a beautiful voice. You know Tess Reynolds?"

"Maybe."

"What do you mean maybe? She's in the school choir. Sings soprano. Stands right next to you?"

"I guess I do."

"Right. You guess. Typical teenager response." Susan stepped closer, running her hands through the wet strands.

"This," she announced, "can be fixed."

"It can?" Heavenly said at the same time Sullivan responded with, "I've been telling her that for a half hour."

"To answer your question, Heavenly—yes, it can. But, not by you, Mr. Bradshaw."

"Really? You're really sure you can fix it?" Heavenly touched her hair, this time letting her fingers linger on the jagged edges near her nape.

"Hun, my older daughter, Micah, bleached her hair when she was your age. With real bleach. She let it soak in for so long, her hair burned off. If I can fix that, I can fix this. But, not with shampoo. What'd you use to color it?"

"Some dye I found in Sunday's closet."

"You were snooping through your mother's things?"

"I was packing clothes for her to have at the hospital,

and I saw the dye while I was doing it," Heavenly huffed, her arms crossing over her chest.

"Funny," Sullivan murmured. "I can't see Sunday using blue hair dye."

"It wasn't hair dye. It was fabric dye."

"Geez," Susan muttered. "This is going to take a while. I'm going to call in and let the sheriff know what I'm up to, Heavenly, and then I'm going to put this mess to right. On one condition."

"What condition?" She scowled, but she looked more relieved than angry.

"You sing in the festival this Friday."

Heavenly's scowl deepened, and if she'd had room to do it, she probably would have stomped away. "I can't."

"Of course you can. Not only can you, but you have to. The choir is counting on you."

"I missed five rehearsals. If you miss three, you're out."

"You had extenuating circumstances," Sullivan cut in, offering the same argument he and Rumer had been using for the past few days. They'd both spoken to the choir director. They'd cleared everything with her, but for some reason, Heavenly still refused to participate. "Mrs. Myers understands that, and she's more than happy to let you come to rehearsal tomorrow. She'll even schedule some extra practice just for you."

"I said, I can't," Heavenly snapped.

"Right," Sullivan responded. "You keep saying that, but you're not telling any of us why."

"Because I don't have a dress, okay? Sunday promised to take me out to buy one. We were going to the bridal boutique in Spokane, because she wanted it to be really special. She said it was a big deal, and she wanted my dress to be as beautiful as my voice is." Her chin wobbled, her lower lip trembled, but she didn't cry, she just glared at them all like they'd caused the problem.

"You need a dress? That's the reason you won't go to rehearsals?" Sullivan shook his head, raked a hand through his hair, looked like a guy who had no clue why someone would worry about having the right outfit for the occasion. "I'll take you to get one tomorrow after school."

"Have you seen the way you dress?" Heavenly asked.

Porter chuckled.

Sullivan didn't seem amused. "I dress like a guy who's been hanging around six kids for a few weeks. That doesn't mean I don't know a pretty dress when I see it."

"Hold on," Minnie said as she poked her head in the room. "Just hold on one minute."

"No," Rumer said.

"You don't even know what I'm going to say."

"You're going to offer one of your outfits."

"So what if I do? She'd look lovely in anything, and I have more than enough clothes to share."

"Really, Minnie, I know you mean well—" Rumer began.

"That suit Rumer was wearing when we met, the one with flowers on the buttons? That was yours, right?" Heavenly interrupted, leaning forward and looking more excited than Rumer had ever seen her.

"Right."

"Do you have something else cool like that?"

"Honey, I have more cool clothes than any one person needs. You get your hair fixed, and I'll go pick out a few things and bring them back here. I guarantee, you'll have something stunning for the festival,

and I guarantee it'll be one of a kind. Just like you."
She flounced away, and Susan nodded.

"That's settled then. You're singing in the festival,
and I'm fixing this mess. Sullivan, you'd better call
April and let her know. She might want to stop by and
do a little extra coaching today."

"It's Sunday. I'm sure she's busy."

"Have you not heard a word I've said? Heavenly is the
star of the show, the reason the Benevolence Middle
School choir is going to win the regional trophy and go
on to the state championship. April is going to be
thrilled to hear that she's going to participate."

April might be thrilled, but Heavenly didn't look it.
She'd sunk back into the chair, her expression closed,
her fists clenched.

"Is everything okay?" Rumer asked, touching her
bony shoulder.

"Dandy," she replied.

"You'll be even better once you get that damn stud
out of your ear," Susan said, shoving in next to Rumer
and poking at Heavenly's ear.

"Ouch!"

"Exactly. You can't do cartilage piercings at home.
You'll get an infection. Can someone get me alcohol
and cotton balls? Scissors. We'll need hair dye, too.
Let's go with honey blond. That'll be closest to her natural color."

"I want it blue," Heavenly muttered.

Susan ignored her.

"I'll get the dye and bring back the clothes," Minnie
offered.

"I'll make a cake, because it's her birthday," Lu added,
and then everyone was moving, walking out of the
room, going off to do whatever it was they needed to.

Except for Sullivan. He stayed where he was, watching as Susan removed the stud.

"It looks like you've got things under control," he said, and Susan nodded. "I've got some errands to run. I shouldn't be long."

He walked past, and Rumer was telling her just how relieved she was that he was going, when he grabbed her hand, dragged her along with him.

"Hey!" she said as they stepped into the kitchen. "What're you doing?"

"I need help," he said, clutching her hand like it was a life preserver and he was a drowning man. "I need to buy her a present, and I have no idea what to get her."

"Nothing is going to be open, Sullivan. It's Sunday."

"Things will be open in Spokane, and that's where I'm going, because I'm not going to be *that* parent— the one who always has an excuse for not making his kid feel special."

That parent . . .

His kid.

She wondered if he'd realized the way he'd phrased it; if he realized how attached he was getting, how quickly his nieces and nephews were becoming more than just a job he had to do.

She sure as heck knew how attached she was getting to the kids.

And, to him.

She knew it, and she seemed helpless to change it, to put on the brakes and stop herself from slamming full-speed into disaster.

"You didn't know it was her birthday, Sullivan," she began, because she needed to stop. Just *stop*.

"How does that matter? She's a child. She's got no present. Her hair looks like she stuck her finger in a light socket, her mother's in the hospital, and she's living with a bunch of kids and three men she barely knows. It's her thirteenth birthday. Thirteen. That's a big deal for a kid, right? It's the difference between being a child and being a teen, and that little girl deserves something to commemorate it," he whispered.

"I'm sure—" *You can find something.* That's what she planned to say. It's what she should have said. But, he looked desperate, and she was staring into his beautiful eyes, thinking about how it would feel to be a thirty-something guy buying a gift for a teenage girl he barely knew.

"We can find something," she finished.

Just one word of difference, but it was every difference that mattered; the difference between going and staying, spending time together or alone, building more connections or breaking the ones that had already formed.

She knew she'd made the wrong choice. Again. Said the wrong thing by one damn word, but when he smiled, when he leaned down and whispered "thank you" against her lips, it felt like the rightest thing she'd ever done.

They found the gift in a tiny antique shop in the seediest area of downtown Spokane. Sullivan had planned to go to an electronic store, hoping that he'd gain inspiration once he'd arrived. Rumer had had other ideas. She'd given him directions to the shop, one she'd said she visited every summer during school break.

She'd led him through the narrow aisles, stopping at a dusty display case filled with broken jewelry and broken beaded handbags, and then she'd told him to choose something that he thought Heavenly would like.

The challenge had scared the crap out of him. He'd brought Rumer so he wouldn't have to make a wild guess about what a newly thirteen-year-old would like.

He stood there staring at what looked like old junk, thinking that there was nothing a goth-ish girl like Heavenly would like. And then he'd noticed a small box filled with what looked like tiny charms. He'd asked to see it, and had been surprised when the clerk pulled out an old charm bracelet. A cat, a bird, a flower, a heart, two musical notes, a grand piano, a book, and a feather all dangled from a tarnished silver bracelet.

He'd bought it, because it reminded him of Heavenly— scraped and wounded and tarnished from years of neglect, but somehow still unique and lovely.

Rumer had chosen a small beaded handbag and a stack of old sheet music that had been lying in a heap next to a bookshelf filled with old books. She was standing there now, thumbing through an old version of *Dick and Jane*, her hair deep brown in the dim light, her skin flawless. She wore faded overalls that were three sizes too big, the cuffs dragging the floor and nearly hiding the old leather work boots she wore. A thermal shirt clung to her chest and rode up her waist. He could see hints of creamy skin between it and faded denim, hidden and then revealed as her old wool coat flapped open and closed again. He didn't think she'd brushed her hair that morning, and he was pretty damn sure she had a couple of pieces of straw lost in the wild curls. There were shadows beneath her eyes, a smudge of dirt on her left cheek, and she was still the most stunning woman he'd ever seen.

She met his eyes. "You're staring."

"Am I?"

"You know you are," she said, setting the book back on the shelf and grabbing a small stack of old Nancy Drew and Hardy Boys mysteries.

"Sorry, it's a bad habit. Something I do when I want to memorize something," he said, but he wasn't sorry at all.

"Why in the world would you want to memorize me?" she asked with a shaky laugh. She was nervous. He'd noticed that on the car ride into Spokane, and it had surprised him. The first day they'd met—when she'd been heading into the unknown, applying for a job she'd seen advertised in a small-town newspaper— she'd been confident and self-assured and hadn't shown even a hint of caution or anxiety.

Now, she seemed jumpy and skittish, her muscles taut and tense.

"I like to get the details right when I sketch some- thing," he responded.

"I don't think I gave you permission to sketch me."

"Do you want me to stop?"

"If I say yes, will you?" She paid for the books, drop- ping them into her purse.

"No," he answered honestly. "Probably not."

That made her smile. "Sullivan, what are we doing?"

"Shopping for gifts for Heavenly," he replied, open- ing the door and holding it so she could step outside. He caught a whiff of fresh hay and sunshine, of wild- flowers and soap, and he thought that if he spent the rest of his life walking beside her, it wouldn't be enough.

"That's not what I'm talking about, and you know it."

"Are we back to discussing the kiss?" He thought they probably were.

"There was more than one," she reminded him as if he might have forgotten, as if that would ever be possible.

"If there were more than a million, I don't think it would be enough," he said, and she stopped in the middle of the sidewalk, turning so she could face him.

"Don't say things like that, okay?"

"I always tell the truth, Rumer. It's a habit I've cultivated for years. I'm not going to stop now because the truth makes you uncomfortable."

She frowned. "I'm not asking you to be dishonest."

"Sure you are. You want me to hide the way I feel and pretend something that isn't true. If that's not dishonest, I don't know what is."

"I'm not asking you to pretend, either. I just . . ." She shrugged and started walking again.

"Just what?"

"Truehart women can do a lot of things, Sullivan. They can run businesses and corral kids and organize chaos, but there are a couple of things none of them have ever been able to figure out." She raked a hand through her hair, tugged a small piece of straw from the curls, and scowled, watching as it floated to the ground.

"Are you going to tell me what they are?" he finally asked, because it seemed like she was done talking, but he wasn't done listening.

He thought she planned to ignore the question, to keep her silence, but they'd reached his SUV, and she stopped there, lifting the cuff of her overalls. "We can't sew a straight hem. Not one of us."

"Sounds like a fatal flaw," he said solemnly, and she offered a quick, sad smile.

"That's not the real problem. The real problem is that we also can't figure out how to choose a good man."

"What?" he asked, certain he must have heard her wrong.

"Haven't you noticed that there are three generations of Truehart women, and not one of them has a man in her life?" They'd reached his SUV, and she'd turned to face him again, her eyes the color of summer skies and silvery rivers. If he'd had his sketch pad, he would have drawn just that part of her. The windows to the soul, but hers were shuttered, whatever she was feeling hidden beneath a veil of indifference that he found both annoying and frustrating.

He believed in honesty. He gave it without holding back.

He expected the same from the people in his life.

"One of them does," he pointed out, and she scowled.

"You know what I mean."

"No. I don't, because what you're saying is that three obviously intelligent women can't figure out the difference between a decent human being and an asshole."

"That's not what I'm saying."

"Yeah. You are." He opened her door, and she scrambled in, her eyes flashing with annoyance.

"We know the difference. We just tend to attract—"

"Stop," he said, more irritated then he should be. Maybe more offended, too. "Because the more you talk, the more I'm hearing that because you're attracted to me, I must be one of the assholes the women in your family are trying to avoid."

"Who said I'm attracted?" she asked, and then sighed. "That was probably the stupidest question I've asked in a while."

"Probably." He closed her door. Gently. Because he'd never be the man his father was, rounded the SUV and climbed into the driver's seat.

"You're angry," she said.

"And?"

"I didn't mean to insult you, Sullivan. Or to imply that you're the one with the problem. You aren't. I am. I've got baggage. Sometimes it weighs me down."

"So, stop carrying it."

"That's an easy thing to say when you're not the one who's been carting it from place to place and relationship to relationship your entire life." There was no heat in her voice. She sounded more resigned than angry.

"So, you're just going to quit traveling because you've filled up your suitcases with other people's junk?" he asked, pulling onto the road, the soft hum of the engine drowning out her sudden silence.

He waited, not speaking into the moment, because he didn't want to fill it with useless platitudes. He had his baggage, too. He knew what a burden it could be.

"It's not other people's junk. It's mine. I don't want to be hurt, Sullivan. I'd rather have nothing than have everything and lose it."

"That's a piss-poor reason to walk away every time you have a chance at something good."

"You wanted honesty. I gave it to you."

"Here's a little honesty for you, Rumer. My father was a bastard. When I was a kid, I watched him beat my mother. I listened to him torture her verbally. She didn't leave him, and she didn't live long enough for me to ask why not. I spent the next few years planning my escape. I left when I was eighteen, and I had no intention of ever returning. I sure as hell didn't plan on returning and becoming a surrogate parent to six kids, because I was damn certain I was going to be as shitty of a father as my dad was. But, here I am, out on a

Sunday morning buying old jewelry for a little girl, because I want her to be happy."

"Heavenly is lucky to—"

"I wasn't fishing for compliments." He cut her off. "I was stating facts. I wanted to walk away, because I didn't want to hurt the kids any more than they'd already been hurt. I stayed because I was all they had. Somewhere in between those two things, I realized the kids didn't care about my baggage or my bastard father or my inability to make a damn birthday cake. All they cared about was having someone around."

"You're making it really hard for me to keep my distance," she whispered, her face turned away, her eyes focused on the landscape that was zipping by.

"Maybe you need to figure out why you want to."

"I already told you why."

"You gave me an excuse," he said gently. "You don't want to be hurt, and I'm not planning to hurt you, but the truth is, relationships are about risks, they're about wanting something so badly you're willing to get your heart broken to have it."

That was it. All he was going to say, because he was a straight shooter, he didn't believe in games, and he sure as hell wasn't going to beg for something she didn't want to give.

"I know," she finally said so quietly he almost didn't hear the brokenness in her voice.

Almost.

But, he did, and he couldn't ignore it any more than he would ever be able to ignore her.

"Do you think Heavenly will like the bracelet?" he asked, giving her an easy out, a change in subject, letting her have the space she obviously wanted.

"I think she'll love it," she responded.

"I hope so."

"I know so. Did you notice how excited she got when Minnie offered to bring her a vintage dress?"

"It was the first time I'd ever seen her really excited about something."

"I was thinking the same," she said.

"Great minds?"

She glanced at him then, offering a quick smile. "We're definitely getting the hang of this parenting thing."

"Getting the hang of it? I'd say we make a damn fine parenting team, Rumer Truehart."

She laughed, and he reached for her hand, planning to give it a friendly squeeze, but she held on, her fingers weaving through his as he merged onto the highway and headed back toward home.

Chapter Twelve

So, she'd messed things up.

Which, she'd been bound to do.

She was, after all, a Truehart. When it came to things like love, she was an absolute expert at ruining them.

She'd known that her whole life. Why it was suddenly pissing her off, she couldn't say.

Wouldn't say?

Yeah. That was more the case, because she actually *did* know why she was pissed off about it.

She'd spent the past week cleaning house, chauffeuring kids, going to teacher meetings, and cooking meals. Nothing different than the prior week, except that Sullivan had been making himself scarce. Instead of eating with the family, he took a plate to his room, claiming research paper deadlines or bookkeeping for the farm.

Which, by the way, was beginning to shape up.

Kane had made good on his promise, sending out dozens of volunteers to get the land ready for planting season. Clementine had been good to her word, too. She knew how to get things done. Even the orchard was being renewed, the trees trimmed back, the dead ones removed.

Pleasant Valley Organic Farm was running like a well-oiled machine, everyone doing his or her part. All of them working together to keep things going until Sunday recovered enough to take over. She'd been moved to a rehab facility Monday. Rumer and the kids had visited her twice since then. She always seemed a little confused and a little sad, her speech slightly slurred, her movements sluggish. She had her right arm in a brace and braces on both legs, but she'd managed to take a few steps to show the kids that she could.

As far as recoveries went, hers was going about as well as could be expected. Rumer told the kids that all the time. She explained things like head injuries and brain damage and memory dysfunction, but she hadn't out and out told them that Sunday remembered very little of their lives together.

She suspected they knew.

They were always quiet when they visited and silent after, but Rumer and Sullivan had agreed to let things play out for a while longer. There'd been some improvements in Sunday's memory, and the doctors were hopeful for more.

Time was what was needed, and she and Sullivan had agreed to wait a little longer before they explained the truth to the kids.

They'd agreed and then they'd moved on. Sullivan doing his thing. Rumer doing hers. No more great minds thinking alike. No more co-parenting. She was the housekeeper doing her job, and he was the uncle doing his best for his brother's kids.

She was supposed to be happy about that.

He'd obviously listened to what she'd said about not

wanting to be hurt. He'd obviously decided to respect her boundaries.

And that was what she was pissed about.

Not at him.

At herself for being too scared to tell him the truth—she didn't want the boundaries, she didn't want the distance. She wanted him.

"You really need to stop being such a chicken," she muttered, opening her closet and pulling out the soft sweater dress she'd borrowed from Minnie. Tonight was the music festival. Flynn and Porter had flown back for the night just to hear Heavenly sing. The choir was scheduled to perform at seven. Heavenly would perform at eight. She had to be at the school at five, and the rest of the family was dropping her off and then going to dinner.

The family.

Which Rumer was not.

She'd helped the crew get ready—clean clothes, brushed hair, shiny shoes, lectures on respectful behavior.

The whole nine yards.

She'd helped Heavenly into the seventies prom dress she'd chosen from Minnie's collection. Pale lavender eyelet with Swiss dot sleeves and a high neckline, it worked perfectly with her wispy pixie haircut and gamine features. Her choir robe had been pressed and hung, and Rumer had handed it to Sullivan as the entire clan walked outside. He'd looked as nervous as Heavenly. Maybe a little more, his tie crooked, his hair mussed.

She'd wanted to straighten the one and smooth the other. She'd wanted to stand on her tiptoes and kiss his lips, and tell him that everything was going to be just fine.

But . . .

He was respecting her boundaries, and so she'd just stood at the door and waved and promised that she'd be there before the choir sang.

"Dummy," she growled, wrestling herself into the dress, smoothing it down over her hips, and eyeing herself in the mirror above the dresser.

Good enough.

That was her verdict, and since she didn't need to be any better than that, she figured she was ready to go. She grabbed a blazer from the closet, shrugging into it, and snagging her purse from the hook. It was heavy with books and toys and crayons; heavy with the feel of kids and family and love. She'd miss that when this gig was over.

She walked downstairs, moving through the empty house, listening to the creak of old wood and the settling of century-old beams. Did Sunday remember any of this? Did she miss it? Or had home become the place she was? Had the hospital and staff, nurses and doctors become her place of refuge?

One way or another, it would be a difficult adjustment when she returned. The kids would struggle. She'd struggle.

And, Rumer would be in Seattle, back at work, back in her neat and orderly apartment with no one knocking on her door before dawn or screaming in the middle of the night.

"God, I'm going to miss that," she said as she stepped outside.

"Miss what?" a woman responded, and Rumer nearly jumped out of her skin.

She whirled around, saw that Clementine was sitting on the old porch swing, legs crossed and hidden by a long cotton skirt, her hair pulled back into a perfect braid.

"Holy cow, Clementine! You nearly scared the tar out of me!"

"Sorry about that. If it makes you feel any better, you scared me, too. I thought everyone had gone to the festival."

"Then, why are you sitting on the porch?"

"I like the view, and Sunday never minded." She smiled, but there was something dark in her eyes, something sad and secretive. "Are you heading to the school?"

"Yes."

"Can I ask why you didn't just go with the rest of the family?"

"I'm not family."

She snorted.

"I'm not."

"Tell that to the kids. See what they have to say about it."

"They know that I'm working for their uncles."

"What they know and what they feel are two different things, Rumer. Love happens quickly for children."

"I know."

"Then, don't plan on walking away with your heart free and your soul unattached."

"Who says I was?"

"No one. I'm just making a statement. I've always liked Sunday and the kids. I want what's best for them."

"Sunday and the kids? Not Matt?"

"I liked Matt, too, but, then, everyone did."

"I get the feeling there's a story in that."

"Maybe, but it's not mine to tell." She smoothed her hair and glanced at her watch. "What time does the festival start?"

"About an hour from now, but Heavenly's group isn't performing until seven."

"It's only five-thirty. You're leaving early."

"I want to get a good seat." She also wanted to check on Heavenly. The teen had been quieter than usual the past few days. Rumer had chalked it up to nerves about the upcoming performance, but Heavenly had refused to talk about it.

She'd also refused to talk about her mother, her siblings, her feelings about any of them.

"Do you mind if I come along?" Clementine asked.

Surprised, Rumer met her eyes. "Of course I don't. I'm in my grandmother's pickup, though. It's not all that comfortable."

"I guarantee you I've ridden in worse." Clementine followed her down the porch stairs and across the yard, her long skirt swooshing through the grass, her boots clomping on the gravel drive. Combat boots and cotton skirts, and a butter-yellow sweater that fell nearly to her knees. On anyone else, the look would have been more street person than haute couture, but on Clementine it worked.

"Any news about when Sunday will be returning?" she asked as Rumer unlocked the truck.

"No. She's in rehab until she regains more function. Right now, she needs help with everything."

"That's a shame, and I'm sure very frustrating for her."

"I'm sure. She's not saying much, though."

"Does she know that Matt's gone?"

"Sullivan and his brothers told her last weekend.

Sullivan said she took it pretty well." He'd also said that she'd cried. No loud, gasping sobs, silent tears that had rolled down her cheeks, soaked the collar of her T-shirt, and broken his heart.

He hadn't said the part about the broken heart.

She'd seen it in his eyes and heard it in his voice, and if she hadn't already drawn her line in the sand, if he hadn't proven that he wouldn't step over it without an invitation, she'd have massaged the tension from his shoulders, whispered in his ear that things were going to be okay.

"It's a sad situation any way you look at it." Clementine sighed, tucking her skirt a little tighter around her legs. "Hopefully, me going to this shindig isn't going to cause problems. It suddenly occurred to me that it might."

"Why would it?"

"Just a little trouble I got into. Or, maybe, it would be more accurate to say, trouble I didn't report to the police."

"That's vague."

"It's old news, Rumer. The young couple that were living in the rancher with me and my . . . *ex* abandoned their newborn. She had a heart condition, and her mother wanted to get her medical attention. The father thought God would heal her. I tried to convince them both that the hospital was the only place for a heart baby. The next thing I knew, the baby was found by a shop owner in Benevolence, and all hell had broken loose."

"How does that have anything to do with you?" Rumer pulled onto the road, the old truck bouncing along like it had the very first day she'd arrived at the farm.

"I knew who'd abandoned the baby. I didn't go to the police."

"Oh."

"Yeah. Exactly. The people in Benevolence didn't trust me to begin with. Now, they really don't, but I know how to bring the farm back from the brink. I'm going to do it before I leave again."

"Leave and go where?"

"Good question. Pleasant Valley Farm was supposed to be my new beginning. I'm going to have to come up with another one. Eventually."

Rumer planned to ask what she meant, but her cell phone rang, and she pulled it out of her pocket, answering without glancing at the caller ID.

"Hello?"

"I need you to come get me," someone sobbed, the words so garbled, she could barely understand them.

"Okay. How about you tell me who you are and where you are, so I can do that?"

"It's Heavenly."

Her stomach dropped, her mind racing through a million possibilities, none of them good. "What's going on?"

"I just need you to come," the girl cried.

"I'm almost at the school. Tell me what part of the building you're in. I'll be there in two shakes of a stick."

"I'm not at the school." She was still crying, her voice muffled by what sounded like wind or traffic.

"Then, where the heck are you?!" she nearly shouted, squealing into the school parking lot and braking hard.

"I don't know."

"What do you mean—?" She stopped herself. Just stopped. Made herself take a breath and focus. Heavenly wasn't at the school. Which was bad. She was crying.

That wasn't good, either. But, she was obviously alive and okay enough to make a phone call.

"Okay," she said more calmly. "Where do you *think* you are?"

"I don't know!" Heavenly wailed, sobbing wildly into the phone.

Clementine touched Rumer's arm, met her eyes. "What's going on?" she mouthed.

"Call Sullivan," she replied, and Heavenly sobbed even more loudly.

"Don't call him! He'll freak," she gasped.

"*I'm* freaking! You're supposed to be in the school. With your choir director. Getting ready to sing. How did you end up lost?" she asked as Clementine jumped out of the truck and made the call.

"I was trying to get to Mom." She sniffed, the sobs seeming to die down. Maybe just talking to someone she trusted was calming her fear. Whatever the case, Rumer was going to take advantage of it, because the sun was already going down, the temperature was dropping, and Heavenly was wandering around somewhere in a cotton eyelet dress and platform heels.

"Where does your mom live?" she asked. "And how did you plan to get to her?"

"Not my birth mom. Sunday. I . . . wanted to talk to her before I sang. I wanted her to hear the song, because she's the only person I really ever sing for, and she's the only one who can tell me if my voice sounds good."

She was crying again, and, God help her! Rumer wanted to cry, too.

"Honey, listen to me," she said instead. "We'll work all that out after we figure out where the heck you are. Did you try to walk from the school?"

Heavenly hesitated, and Rumer went cold with fear. "Heavenly! Did you walk or did you get a ride with someone?"

"A guy I know from choir offered to give me a ride, but then I didn't know how to get to the rehab facility, and he brought me to the hospital instead."

"You're in middle school. Which guy in your choir has a license?"

"Dominque Samuel's brother, Tanner, does. I know him because he works the sound system for performances."

"Oh. My. Gosh. Heavenly, what were you thinking?"

"I was thinking I didn't want to sing in the damn choir without Sunday hearing the song," she said, sniffing back more tears.

"Okay. That's fine," she said, not wanting to upset the teen more than she already was. They both needed to be clear-headed and focused. "We'll talk about your choices later. Right now, just please tell me that you're still at the hospital."

"I already told you that I don't know where I am. I asked for directions to the rehab place, and a lady at the hospital told me it was only a couple of miles away, so I thought I could walk, but I guess I got turned around, and I can't even find the hospital anymore."

"Do you see any street signs?"

"Not on this street, but I saw one a minute ago. You want me to walk back and look for it?"

"Yes, but stay on the phone while you do it." She leaned across the seat and motioned for Clementine to move closer. "Can you go find the choir director for the middle school? Her name is April Myers. Tell her there's been a mix-up and Heavenly is on her way."

"You're asking me to be the bearer of bad news?" she responded.

"Would you rather go hunt down a distraught teenager?"

"Not in a million years. I'll find the director. You find the kid." She raced off, cotton skirt billowing as she sprinted toward the door.

Rumer yanked the door closed, put the truck into gear, would have pulled out of the parking lot, but she heard a car horn, then saw the van rolling toward her.

The back door slid open, and she caught a glimpse of Twila's worried face and Moisey's excited one before Sullivan hopped out and closed it again.

He jumped into the truck, his muscles taut, his expression grim as he eyed the phone. "Is that her?"

"Yes."

"I need to talk to her."

"She's a little worried about you freaking out."

"She should be," he muttered as she passed him the phone.

"Heavenly? It's Sullivan. We're on the way. Stay where you are until we get there. Yeah. I do know where you are. I've got an app to track you using your phone." He paused. "You're darn right I invaded your privacy. I worry about you. I want you safe. I don't ever not want to be able to find you. But, don't get your britches in a bunch about it, because I won't have any need to track you after tonight. Your butt is going to be grounded from now until you turn fifty!"

He didn't return the phone.

Which was fine. Rumer was driving, going a little too fast, watching the sun dip lower in the sky, worrying as it disappeared below the Spokane skyline.

"Yeah. I'm still here," Sullivan said, breaking the

silence, "and you're still there, and the sun is about to go down. Maybe you should have thought this through a little more before you went running off on a fool's errand." He paused, apparently listening to Heavenly's side of the story.

"That's a great excuse, kid. Really great. Except for one thing, you could have told me you wanted to see her. You could have explained everything before you had some bonehead teenager drive you into the city. I'd have let you skip school. We could have done it this morning, had Starbucks and one of those cheese pastries you like." He squeezed the bridge of his nose, and God! His hands were shaking.

Shaking!

"She's just a kid, Sullivan. She made a mistake. Getting angry about it—"

"This," he said through gritted teeth, "is not anger. This is godawful, gut-wrenching, holy-freaking terror. She's thirteen! Alone on the street looking like a fashion icon from the seventies. Do you know how many perverts are out there?"

"One is too many."

"Exactly!" he nearly shouted. "Damn it," he muttered. "I'm sorry. This isn't your fault."

"You don't have to apologize. You didn't do anything wrong."

"I damn near took your head off for making a comment." He still had her phone, and he pulled his out, too.

"We're ten minutes away, Heavenly. So help me, if you move from that spot, every hair on my head will turn white, and you'll be the one I blame for it."

Heavenly must have been talking, because he fell silent.

His hands were still trembling, and she lifted the one closest to her, crossing that line, the one she'd drawn, the one that was a clear demarcation of the roles they should play.

And, it didn't feel wrong.

It felt natural and right and good.

"She's going to be okay," she said, and he nodded, his hand tightening on hers as she exited the freeway and entered the city limits.

She was standing on the street corner, just where the GPS tracking app indicated she would be. Lavender dress glowing in the dusky light. Pale arms and upper chest visible through the Swiss dot mesh that covered them. Long neck and narrow shoulders making her look delicate and vulnerable and so young his heart hurt looking at her.

He should have made her wear a coat. He should have insisted on boots instead of the open-toed platforms she was wearing. He should have done a dozen things he hadn't. Including and not limited to handcuffing her to her choir director when he'd dropped her off at the school.

He was out of the truck almost before Rumer stopped it, a dozen words on the tip of his tongue. He didn't say any of them, because she was moving toward him, the dress hiked up around her scrawny calves, her eyes red-rimmed from crying.

"I'm sorry, Uncle Sullivan."

"Me too," he said. Just that, because he wasn't sure

what else he could say without sounding harsh and
angry.

"I guess I won't be able to sing tonight," she murmured as she climbed into the center of the bucket seat,
moved her skirt so that he could climb in next to her.

"There's still time to make it there," Rumer said,
already pulling away from the curb.

Heavenly didn't respond, and he thought there was
more to the story about how she'd ended up in Spokane
than what she'd been saying, more than some desperate need to see her mother.

"Do you not want to sing?" he guessed.

She shrugged.

"How about words?" he suggested. "They're usually
a lot more helpful than a shrug."

"I'm . . . scared," she whispered, playing with one of
the charms that hung from the bracelet he'd given her.

"To sing in front of so many people?"

"To fail. To show everyone that they're right, and
I'm just a stupid loser who can't do anything well."

"First of all," he said. "You're not stupid or a loser—"

"I guess you forgot the reason why we're sitting in
this truck," she replied, and he smiled. Just a little. Just
a hint, because he couldn't help being amused by that.

"What you did was stupid. That doesn't make *you*
stupid. So, let's move on to something else. Like being
afraid to fail. You can't ever succeed if you're not willing
to do that."

"That's what Sunday always said."

"Sunday was right."

"Sunday isn't getting up in front of judges and
singing some dumb song for them. I am."

"The song is haunting and beautiful," he responded,
because he'd listened to her sing it the night she'd

agreed to participate in the festival. Mrs. Myers had asked if he could drive her to the church and let her practice there. He'd agreed. He'd also agreed—at Heavenly's insistence—to stay outside the sanctuary.

He hadn't agreed not to listen.

He'd stood in the vestibule for an hour while she'd practiced a Scottish folk song. Not in English. No. She'd sung it in Gaelic, her voice pure and as haunting as the melody.

It still gave him goose bumps to think about.

"You haven't heard it," she responded. "You'll probably hate it."

"I heard it when Mrs. Myers coached you."

"You told me you wouldn't listen," she grumbled.

"I said I wouldn't sit in the sanctuary when you practiced. I didn't. I stood in the vestibule for an hour straight wondering how a thirteen-year-old kid could sing a song with that much heart in it."

"Sunday taught it to me. Her mother taught it to her. It's about a maiden who sings under the trees while she waits for her love to come home from the sea," she said wistfully. "Even Mrs. Myers doesn't know if I'm singing all the lyrics right. Only Sunday does, and I wanted to be sure I had it right before I sang tonight."

"It's too late to check in with her now. Next time, tell me what you need ahead of time. I'll help you get it if I can, okay?"

"Okay," she responded, leaning her head back against the seat. "I wish she could be there, though. I only picked the song because she loves it. Otherwise, I'd have sung Adele. Everyone knows her lyrics."

"Adele's got nothing on you, kid," he said, and meant it.

"No one can top Adele, and I'm not trying to. I just

don't want the kids to laugh at me because I'm singing some weird song in another language."

"Do you think it's weird?" Rumer asked.

"Well . . . no, but—"

"Then own it the way you own that dress and that bracelet and that awesome haircut."

"Tess loves my hair. She's trying to get her mother to give her the same cut." She touched short strands, and Sullivan pictured her in a few years, a little more confident, a lot more grown up.

He didn't think he'd want to be all the way in Portland when she went from being a gawky young teen to a beautiful young woman. No, he thought he'd rather be close to the farm with a locker full of shotguns and a list of questions to ask any guy who happened to show any interest in her.

"You and Tess have been talking?" Rumer asked, obviously not at all concerned about the fact that Heavenly was going to be dating one day.

"We ate lunch together this week. I thought she was a snob, because she's one of those pretty girls that always acts perfect, but she's really nice. I was going to ask if she could spend the night next Friday, but I guess I messed that up."

"I never said you couldn't have someone over. I just said you were grounded," Sullivan reminded her. "So, I might be willing to let your friend stay over."

"Really?" Heavenly asked excitedly.

"Yeah. You just have to agree to one thing."

"I won't be mean to the dweebs," she vowed.

"Not that."

"I'll clean the whole house so Rumer doesn't have extra work to do."

"Not that, either."

"Well, it's not like I smoke or do drugs or any of that crap. What else is there?"

"No boys. Ever," he responded.

Her eyes widened, and her lips quirked, and then she was giggling, the charms on the bracelet jingling as she threw her arm around his shoulder and hugged him.

Hugged him!

"I guess I won't be having her over then," she said, and Rumer joined her laughter, the two of them sniggering nearly all the way to the school.

They made it just in time for Heavenly to throw on her robe and march out with the choir. As far as Sullivan could tell, the performance was flawless. An hour later, Heavenly walked out onstage again. This time, in her lavender dress, her hair feathering around her face and nape. She looked cool as a cucumber.

Sullivan was a nervous wreck.

He sat in the audience, Oya in his lap, Maddox leaning against his arm, his mouth so dry, he thought he could gulp a bottle of water and still feel parched.

The music began, the intro played on an Irish tin whistle, the notes drifting into the soft rumble of voices in the audience, of papers and cloth rustling as people looked at programs or shifted in their seats.

Sullivan didn't move. His palms were sweating, damn it. As if *he* were the one standing up on the stage waiting to sing the first note.

Rumer leaned toward him, her lips tickling his ear.

"She's going to be fine," she whispered.

"What if she forgets the words?" he whispered back. "Or gets so scared, she can't sing? What's that going to do to her? I should have told Mrs. Myers she couldn't do it. I should have—"

Heavenly began singing, the first stanza so perfectly

pitched, so lovely, the audience stilled. No murmurs now. No rustling.

"Holy crap," Rumer breathed, her fingers curving around his. He could feel the goose bumps on her forearm, the wild slushing of blood through her veins.

He knew how she felt. Amazed. Awed. Surprised.

He felt the same. He'd bet every person in the audience did.

Because, no kid Heavenly's age should be able to sing like that—face to the heavens and arms opened as if she were waiting for her lover to walk into them. No inhibitions. No self-consciousness. She was singing to a phantom audience in some faraway place in her mind, singing perfectly, displaying her soul for the entire room to see.

And, God!

All he could think was that she needed someone standing behind her, holding a shotgun, a baseball bat, a bowie knife, making sure every damn loser in the world stayed away.

When she finished, no one moved.

Other participants had gotten applause and catcalls and shouts of encouragement. She got silence as the last note faded, as the tin whistle played the coda.

He watched as she came back to herself, her focus shifting from the song to the audience. She scanned the crowd, and he thought she might be looking for her family.

He'd be damned if she didn't see it.

He stood, tugging Rumer up with him. She was already clapping, the sound breaking whatever spell had fallen over the audience. One by one, people stood, Rumer's applause turning into the thunderous sound of the audience's approval.

He knew from watching the other participants that Heavenly was supposed to bow to the audience, to the judges, and then to the musician.

He knew she was supposed to walk off stage to the left, and disappear into the wings.

Instead, her face crumbled, all the coolness disappearing, her eyes flooding with tears. She lifted the dress up to her knobby knees and ran down the stage stairs, barreling past Mrs. Myers and out the auditorium's side exit.

The audience was silent again, and Sullivan was moving, handing Oya off to Flynn and running up the aisle, slamming open the exit door, Rumer right behind him.

Chapter Thirteen

They found her in the school playground, sitting on a swing, the hem of the dress dragging in the dirt. She wasn't crying anymore, but she looked so sad, so lost, that Rumer wanted to bundle her in the truck and take her back home, let her hide out from the world like she seemed to want to.

"Sunday was supposed to be here," she said before either of them could speak. "She promised me she would be. Matt did, too, but he wasn't the one who taught me the song. He wasn't the one who was going to buy me a dress." She shrugged as if it didn't matter.

"She would have been here if she could have," Sullivan said, taking the swing beside hers, his long legs stretched out, his heels pressed into the soft earth.

"I know." She pushed off, swinging back and then forward, the dress kicking up clouds of dust, her hair and face silvery in the moonlight.

She sang like an angel, or, like an old soul. Like someone who had seen everything there was to see and still found reason to dream. But, she was still just a child, one who was trying to figure out the world and her place in it.

"We can tell her about it tomorrow," Rumer suggested, settling into the swing on Heavenly's right. "I have it on good authority that one of your siblings made a secret recording of the performance. We'll go to the rehab center and play it for your mom."

"You have the day off tomorrow. Besides, it'll be too late by then." She leaned back in the swing, arms outstretched, fists tight on the ropes as she stared up at the sky.

"Too late for what?" Sullivan asked, his hair inky black in the darkness. It had grown longer in the past two weeks, the dark ends brushing his nape. He still hadn't shaved, and she wondered if he planned to.

And, if he'd still be around when he did.

His life was in Portland, after all.

Eventually, he'd go back to his job and his home there.

A strange thought, because she couldn't envision the farm without him on it. She couldn't picture the kids without imagining him beside them. She couldn't think of the future without wondering where he'd be.

"The photo." Heavenly pushed off again, her head nearly brushing the ground as she leaned even farther back.

"What photo?" Sullivan asked.

"Everyone who participated in the festival gets to have their picture taken with the judges. You stand in the middle of the stage and hold your certificate or your award. Then, the judge gets off the stage, and the parents come on, and the photographer takes a photo of that. Mrs. Myers said everyone who sings gets one picture free with their entry fee. We were going to hang it in my room." She'd stopped swinging and was just hanging there again. "But, I don't have a father, and Sunday can't be here, so . . . no picture with family. I'll just hang the one of me and the judge up, I guess."

"Your dad may not be around anymore," Sullivan said, standing up and offering Heavenly his hand, "but, you've got three uncles who will stand on that stage with you."

"I think they only let parents," she said, but she'd accepted his hand, was allowing him to pull her to her feet.

"I don't plan to ask who they allow. I plan to walk up there and take my spot," he responded, putting his hand on her shoulder and looking in her eyes. "If anyone complains, I'll tell them to take a hike."

"No, you won't."

"Yeah. I will. We're going to get the picture together, and then we'll make copies so you can have one on your wall, and I can have one on mine."

"Thanks, Uncle Sullivan."

"You may not be thanking me when you have my ugly mug hanging on your wall."

She smiled, and he chucked her under the chin.

"That's it, Heavenly. That's the way you're going to face the world, okay?"

"What way?"

"With a smile and a mean right hook. I'm going to make sure I teach you that skill. Just in case you ever need it."

They'd started walking back toward the school, and Rumer was still in the swing, watching them go, seeing the way Sullivan's hand rested protectively on his niece's shoulder, the way she seemed to lean just a little into him.

She knew what she was seeing.

She'd seen it before, felt it before.

It was the beginning of family—two disparate paths coming together to create one single journey. Strange how that worked. How one minute you were alone, trying to find your place, and how the next, you were walking beside someone who was doing the same exact thing. How suddenly, in that moment, you became part of something bigger than yourself.

They stopped at the edge of the playground and turned toward her.

"Aren't you coming, Rumer?" Heavenly called.

"It's a beautiful night. I thought I'd sit out here and enjoy it."

"Then we will, too," the teen said, heading back in her direction, Sullivan right beside her. His hand was still on her shoulder, but his gaze was on Rumer. She felt the weight of his stare, the warmth of it.

He smiled, and her heart tripped, her breath caught, and her soul stirred, whispering something that she'd never heard before. Not anytime. Not with any man.

Home, it seemed to say.

And, suddenly, she knew the truth of the way things were. She understood what she hadn't before. She wasn't falling for Sullivan. She was falling in love with him.

And, God help her, that intrigued her as much as it terrified her.

"You okay?" he asked, pulling her to her feet. They

were just inches away, and if she'd wanted to, she could have taken half a step forward and been in his arms.

"I . . . think so."

He frowned, pressing his palm against her forehead. "No fever. Do you have a headache?"

"It's a heart problem, Sullivan. Not a head problem," she admitted.

"Yeah?" He tugged her that half step into his arms. "Maybe I can help with that."

"Geez," Heavenly said with an exaggerated sigh. "Are you going to kiss her again?"

"Is there some reason why I shouldn't?" he asked, staring into Rumer's eyes, waiting for her to tell him to stop.

Or not.

They were just a breath away from each other, and then they weren't. He tasted like coffee and mints and sunrise and hope. He tasted like all the dreams she'd given up on because she'd been certain they could never come true.

"Heavenly!" a woman shouted, an edge of panic in her voice. "Heavenly Bradshaw! Where are you?!"

"Over here, Mrs. Myers," Heavenly called. "At the playground."

"Thank God!" The choir director raced around the corner of the building, her hand on her chest, her lungs heaving. "You have to get back inside. Now!"

"Why?" Heavenly responded, but she ran toward her, her dress wafting out behind her.

Sullivan took Rumer's hand and dragged her in the same direction.

Dragged because her legs barely seemed to be working.

Her brain didn't seem to be working, either.

Or, maybe it was working overtime, because she could swear she saw the Bradshaw bunch coming at her from all different directions. Flynn, Maddox, and Milo sprinting across the parking lot. Porter, Moisey, and Twila jogging out of the building. Clementine hurrying along the edge of the playground, Oya in her arms.

"You found her!" Moisey shrieked, breaking away from Porter and running to her sister's side. "This is the best thing ever. Isn't it the best thing, Heavenly?"

"I don't know what you're talking about, dwe . . . Sis," Heavenly responded as they ran to the front of the building.

"You won!" Mrs. Myers responded, grabbing her hand and sprinting back toward the building. "Not just for your age group, either. They're giving you the Exceptional Promise Award. That's a ten-thousand-dollar college scholarship and free tuition to attend vocal training summer camp at the Peabody Institute this summer." She was panting and wheezing, but she wasn't slowing down. The group hit the front doors at a full-out run. "I've been doing this for seven years, and I've never seen them give out the Promise Award."

"Is that why we're running?" Heavenly asked as they bolted into the school lobby.

"We're running because of some archaic rule about being there when they present the prize. You don't show up, you don't get it. Fortunately, the adjudicators saw how upset you were, and they're taking their time awarding fourth, third, and second place," Porter explained, yanking open the auditorium door and nearly lifting Heavenly off her feet to get her inside.

They made it with three minutes to spare, and when Heavenly walked up to accept her award, Rumer thought her heart would burst with pride. It didn't matter that Heavenly's hem was dusty or that she had tear tracks on her cheeks. It didn't matter that she didn't offer a hint of a smile as she shook the adjudicator's hand. It didn't matter that she was bound to cause more trouble before her growing up was finished. All that mattered was the way she scanned the audience, the way her gaze landed on her family.

That's when she smiled, a soft, sweet curve of the lips that seemed to encompass them all.

"She's quite a kid," Sullivan said, still holding her hand. Such a simple thing, something that she'd done with every guy she'd ever been with. It felt different with Sullivan, though. It felt like today and tomorrow and yesterday, all of it rolled into one perfect moment of connection.

"You're quite an uncle."

"I haven't done anything but be here for the kids," he responded.

"Like I said," she responded. "You're quite an uncle."

"We'll see how that works out in a year or two or ten," he muttered.

"What's that supposed to mean?" she asked, studying his face the way he always studied her, wishing she had the talent to pick up a sketch pad and pencil and re-create the lines and angles and emotions she saw there.

"Forever is a long time to not turn into my father," he replied, rubbing the back of his neck and watching as the adjudicator stepped to the podium.

"Forever isn't any time at all. Not when you love someone, and you love these kids," she replied. "So, it'll go in the blink of an eye. One minute, we'll be here watching Heavenly accept her award, the next we'll be walking her down the aisle."

She realized what she'd said a moment too late, realized that she'd plunked herself right down in the middle of a story that wasn't hers.

She might be falling in love with Sullivan. Heck, she might even already love him. That didn't mean he had any obligation to love her. It sure didn't mean that they'd be together for any longer than it took for tomorrow to come.

"We?" he asked, but the adjudicator was giving a speech about the Promise Award and the moment was lost.

She was happy to let it go.

She didn't want to have deep conversations with Sullivan about their future. She didn't want to hash out rules of engagement or try to figure out what the next few minutes or years would mean for them.

She just wanted to be there right now and not think about anything but the moment, because if she thought too hard, if she let her brain go too far into the future, she'd start seeing the end instead of the beginning.

They drove to Spokane and found an ice cream place that was still open, because that's what Heavenly wanted to do. Sullivan had braced for the worst. Six kids in a tiny ice cream joint an hour past their bedtime was bound to be a disaster, right?

To his surprise, the kids had all been on their best behavior. Even the twins had seemed determined to act angelic.

That was Sullivan's only excuse for what happened next.

First, Heavenly had suggested going to the rehab facility so that she could tell Sunday her good news. Second, he'd agreed.

After that?

Things had gone downhill rapidly.

Sunday had been sound asleep when they'd arrived. She'd woken when the nurse had opened the door and announced them. Her confusion had seemed worse than usual, her focus vague, her smiles forced. The kids' joy had gone from epic Christmas-morning proportions to trying-to-be-happy-for-the-sake-of-the-adults.

Rumer had been the one to cut the visit short, because Sullivan hadn't been able to do it. The kids had just been so desperate to make it work, talking and laughing too loudly and too much. Sunday, on the other hand, had seemed content to lie in bed and watch them, her smiles forced, her words few. He hadn't wanted that to be the last memory of the night. He hadn't wanted the kids to fall asleep with that image of their mother in their heads. So, yeah, he'd stayed longer than he should have. Apparently, he could present lectures to auditoriums filled with students, write research papers that were going to be peer-reviewed by men and women a hell of a lot smarter than he was, but he couldn't take control of a situational failure and figure out how to make it a success. Not when it came to the kids.

That didn't bode well for his future with them.

He frowned, staring up at the living room ceiling and listening to the house settle. Flynn and Porter had left at midnight, both of them heading to the airport to red-eye it home. They'd be back in a month, or when Sunday was released from rehab. Whichever came first.

And, Sullivan? He should have been sleeping, because mornings came quickly when there was a baby in the house. Instead, he was lying on the living room couch, watching through the window as the moon drifted lazily toward the horizon and thinking about all the ways he might fail his brother's kids.

A floorboard creaked in the upstairs hall, and he tensed, expecting to hear Moisey screaming or Twila sneaking to her parents' room to grab a book from one of the shelves. She'd been doing that weekly, picking one of the ancient tomes that either Sunday or Matt had collected. He'd looked through the leather-bound first editions of books that were published in the eighteenth and nineteenth century. Some of them had hand-colored illustrations. Some had old maps folded up in their pages. They weren't cheap yard sale finds. These were masterpieces, works of art from a bygone era in the book publishing world. He didn't think a kid Twila's age should be rifling through them, but he hadn't had the heart to tell her to stop.

Which seemed to be a theme with him.

He didn't want them hurt any more than they already had been, but if he wasn't careful he would hurt them more. There had to be boundaries. There had to be rules. There had to be structure without anger, discipline without rage. He wasn't sure he'd be able to give those things consistently. Hell! He'd already lost his cool with Heavenly *and* with Rumer, and maybe that was why he was still awake. He was replaying those moments in the truck when he'd been frantic to get to

Heavenly, when he'd been so terrified that words had
spilled and he'd had absolutely no control over them.

The floorboards creaked again, the soft rustle of
fabric drifting down the stairs. Seconds later, the loose
board on the landing groaned. Someone was coming
down, and that was unusual enough to bring Sullivan
to his feet.

He waited, expecting a towheaded boy to appear
and maybe sneak to the kitchen for an early morning
snack.

Instead, Rumer was there, hurrying into the kitchen
without even a glance in his direction. He heard her
pad across the floor, knew she was slipping her feet
into the old galoshes that were sitting near the sink in
the mudroom. He imagined she was grabbing her coat,
too, sliding her arms into it. Imagined her hair caught
in its collar and the way it would feel to pull it out, let
the silky strands slide through his fingers.

The back door opened, a cold breeze wafting from
the hall that led into the kitchen. The door shut again,
the quiet click fading into silence.

He should have let her be. She had a right to her
time, and he had the obligation to give it to her. He'd
been trying to give it to her all week—keeping his distance, letting their relationship be the professional one
she seemed to want.

And, then today had happened and it had all flown
out the window—every good intention, every vow that
he'd respect the no-trespassing sign she wore on her
heart. Gone. Just as quickly as sunlight at dusk. He
didn't want to try to recapture it. The truth was,
there'd been a dozen times during the week when he'd
wanted to walk outside with her, sit on the old swing,

ask her about her day. There'd been more than a dozen times when he'd heard her voice or her laughter and thought about how easy it would be to love her.

Love?

That was a new one. It sure as heck wasn't something he'd ever wanted or needed in his life, but he could feel it there. Just on the other side of where he stood, and if he let himself, he knew he could reach out and grab hold of it.

"Geez," he whispered, walking to the window and staring out into the yard. His life had become a colossal mess of emotional crap that he had absolutely no experience dealing with, and he could only blame one person for that.

"Thanks a hell of a lot, Matt," he whispered, and he could swear he heard his brother laugh.

The landing creaked again, and he whirled around not sure what he expected to see—maybe Matthias's ghost drifting toward him.

Heavenly stood at the bottom of the stairs, bare toes peeking out from a too-long nightgown, the medallion around her neck.

"Rumer's outside," she said as if that explained her presence.

"I know."

"So, why are you inside?"

"I'm giving her space?"

"To decide she's going to leave us?" she asked, sitting on the bottom step and tapping her toes on the wood floor.

"She always leaves on Saturday," he reminded her, taking a seat beside her.

"That's not what I mean."

"Want to explain what you *do* mean?"

"The kids have already lost a lot of things. They lost Matt. They lost Sunday."

"Sunday isn't lost."

"Yeah. She is. Who knows if she'll ever find her way back?" She picked at a thread on her sleeve and didn't meet his eyes. "So, that's the thing. She's lost, and the kids don't need to lose someone else. They like Rumer, and if she suddenly decides not to work here anymore, they're going to be really upset."

The kids? Or you? he almost asked.

"Okay," he said instead, and she finally looked up, her face a pale oval in the moonlight that seeped through the window.

"What's that supposed to mean?"

"Just that I understand what you're saying to me."

"I'd rather you understand that Rumer can't walk off and leave and not come back. The kids would be heartbroken."

"I know, but I can't control what other people do. I can only control what *I* do. I can't make promises that someone else will stick around, but I can promise that I will."

"Right," she snorted, pulling her knees up to her chest, and resting her chin on them. "In all my life, I've never known one person who hasn't left. I've never known one person who's kept a promise, either."

"You've only been alive for thirteen years, so maybe your experience is limited."

"From where I'm sitting, thirteen years seems like a very long time." She sighed. "I wish you'd go out and talk to her."

"Rumer?"

"Who else?"

"I think she wants to be alone."

"That's the problem with the world. People think they know things when they don't, and they act stupid because of it. Like today when I thought I knew how to get to the rehab center. I could have died out there all because I thought I knew something that I didn't."

"I'm glad you learned from the experience, but I doubt I'm going to die if I don't walk outside and talk to Rumer," he said wryly.

"Do you really want to take the chance?" she responded, and he laughed.

"No. I guess I don't. So, how about you go up to bed, and I'll go outside?" Because, why not? He'd been thinking about following Rumer anyway. Thinking about walking through the field with her as the moon set, thinking about the way the darkness would cast shadows on her curly hair, cut deep grooves beneath her cheekbones, contour the angle of her jaw and highlight the softness of her lips.

"Go outside? Or go outside and talk to Rumer?"

"Both."

"Humph," she responded.

"What does that mean?"

"It means I think you're a chicken, and that you'll probably go outside and stand there hoping something wonderful will happen."

"I'm a lot of things, but I'm not a chicken." He pulled her to her feet. "Go on to bed before the other kids wake up. It'll be a heck of a lot harder to talk to Rumer if they're all running around in the yard."

She retreated up the stairs, and he walked into the kitchen, grabbing his jacket from the hook near the back door.

He slid into it as he stepped outside, then stood on

the back stoop and scanned the yard, the field, the gravel driveway. He didn't see Rumer, and he wasn't going to call for her and risk waking the other kids.

He also wasn't going to stand there waiting for something wonderful to happen. Life didn't work like that. It didn't plop success and happiness in a person's lap. You went after things or you didn't. You waited for opportunities or you created them. He lectured his students about that all the time, because they were artists with big dreams and, often, not a lot of follow-through.

He was an artist, too. A dreamer.

And, a realist.

Waiting around had never been in his nature.

He stepped into the yard and was walking toward the back field when he heard the quiet groan of old metal and the dry rustle of dead leaves. He knew the sound. He heard it every day when the boys played on the old tree swing.

He switched directions, rounding the side of the house, the old elm tree coming into view.

Rumer was there, sitting on the swing, her face hidden by the shadows of the tree. She looked lonely, dwarfed by the ancient elm, sitting in the darkness with filtered moonlight dappling the ground near her feet.

She must have seen him coming, because she stood, took a step toward him, and stopped. As if she were afraid to move any closer and just as afraid to move away.

"Sullivan," she said. Just that. Just his name, but he heard fear and worry and hope in her voice. "What are you doing out here?"

"I guess the same thing as you. Thinking."

"About?"

"Us." He moved closer, and he could see the details of her face—the sharp angle of her jaw, the soft curve of her ear, the dark sweep of her lashes as she blinked.

"I didn't realize there was an us."

"Liar." He touched her cheek, traced a line from there to the corner of her mouth, his blood heating, everything in him wanting to pull her into his arms.

"Maybe," she admitted.

"What are you afraid will happen if there is?" he asked, sitting down on the old wood swing, letting cold air cool the fire that was racing through his blood.

"The same thing that has happened to every relationship I've ever been in. It will end."

"It could end," he responded honestly, because he'd never let himself get this deep. He'd never allowed himself to feel what he felt when he was with her. "But, maybe it won't."

"I'm not big into maybes," she said.

"And, I'm not big into farms and kids and teenage angst, but here I am."

"You didn't have a choice."

"Of course I did. There were people who would have taken the kids while Sunday recovered. This is that kind of town, and they're those kinds of people. But, the kids would have been parceled out in groups of two, living apart for however long things stretched on. That's not what my brother or Sunday would have wanted, so I made my choice. I guess you'll have to make yours."

"Make it? I'm here, aren't I?"

"That's not what I mean, and you know it."

"What I know is that yesterday was a long day. Today will be too. I need to get some sleep."

"You weren't worrying about that while you were sitting on this swing looking like the woman from that song Heavenly sang."

"A woman singing under a tree?" She laughed, but there was no humor in it. "If I'd been doing that, you'd have thought a cat was yowling at the moon. My singing voice is that good."

"Not a woman singing," he responded, ignoring the joke. "A woman waiting for her dreams to come true."

"What dreams?" she scoffed. "That my knight in shining armor will come running to my rescue? That he'll slay the beasts and kill the monsters and protect me from the wicked queen?"

"You don't need a knight in shining armor. You know damn well how to rescue yourself from the monster and the beasts and wicked queens."

"What else is there to dream about, Sullivan?" she asked wearily, crossing the space between them and settling on the swing's bench seat. It was small, but she managed not to touch him.

Not a brush of the arm or shoulder or thigh, the distance as purposeful as the stiff, tense way she held herself.

"Quiet walks through yellow fields of wheatgrass?" he suggested. "Dances in the moonlight when no one is watching? A million moments of silence and a million more of laughter?"

"Just stop, okay?" she whispered, and he could hear the brokenness in her voice.

"I didn't want this, either," he replied. "I wasn't looking for it, but it's here, and I'm not going to walk away from it. Not unless you ask me to."

She didn't respond to that, didn't tell him to go and

didn't ask him to stay. He thought that was it. The end before they'd even had a beginning.

And, then she sagged toward him, her shoulder bumping his as she swiped a hand across her face.

He saw the tears then, silvery lines on her pale skin.

"Don't cry," he murmured, sliding his arm around her waist, pulling her into his side, sitting there with her as a gentle breeze rustled the dead leaves and whistled under the eaves of the old farmhouse.

Chapter Fourteen

She didn't know how long she sat there sniffing back tears.

Maybe a minute. Maybe twenty.

She only knew that Sullivan was beside her.

Not a knight in shining armor. Not a hero from olden days. Not a guy who thought she needed him beside her. A man who wanted to dance in the moonlight and sit on swings and walk in fields of grass. One who wanted silence and laughter and a million moments of time.

And, God!

Those were all the dreams she'd ever had, all the things she'd wanted that she'd never found. She didn't know what to do with that or with him, because she could already feel her heart breaking, but she couldn't make herself walk away.

"What's wrong?" he asked, shifting so that he could look into her face.

"Nothing," she answered honestly, her throat raw, her chest tight.

"Then, why the tears?" He touched her cheek, his fingers skimming across the damp flesh.

"I just . . ." She shook her head.

"Don't want to be hurt again?"

"Don't want to miss out because I'm too afraid to try," she replied.

He smiled that easy, sweet smile that made her heart stop. Only this time, it didn't stop. This time it leaped, and she could swear it was leaping right toward him.

"Then, how about you try and I try, and we see what happens?"

"How about we do?" she said, her throat tight, her pulse thrumming.

And when he stood, when he offered his hand, she took it, because what else could she do? Where else would she go but into his arms as he swayed beneath a blue-black sky dusted with silvery stars?

"You are so damn addicting," he murmured, his lips brushing hers so tenderly she could have cried with the beauty of it. "I could spend every minute of every day with you and it would never be enough."

"Sullivan," she began, because she wanted to tell him all the things she'd never said to another man: that she found her best self when she looked into his eyes. That when she was with him, she was finally home. But, her throat was too tight, and the tears were falling again, slipping down her cheeks and splattering onto the grass.

"Did I upset you?" he asked, and she shook her head, because he hadn't, and because she finally knew the truth: This was the real deal, the happy-forever. This was the thing everyone wanted and few people ever found.

She wasn't going to screw it up.

She wasn't going to turn it away.

"It's okay," she said. "I'm okay."

Her hands rested on his shoulders, the cool breeze wrapping them in its velvety embrace, the grass brushing her calves as they swayed to a rhythm only he could hear. She kissed the hollow of his throat, felt his quick, sharp breath, let her lips skim up the side of his neck. When she kissed him, it felt like the first time and the last and every damn time in between.

She could swear the heavens opened, light shone down from above, and angels sang, their voices faint but beautiful.

"What the hell?" Sullivan asked, his voice gruff as he pulled back, bright light splashing across his cheeks.

And, Rumer realized she really was seeing light and hearing angels.

No. Not angels. One voice. Pure and high and haunting. One song, drifting through the quiet morning.

She turned, Sullivan's arms still around her, saw Heavenly standing near the house, her face lifted toward the heavens, her eyes closed. Light spilled out of the kitchen window and the open back door.

"Heavenly, what are you doing out here?" Sullivan asked, and the teen opened her eyes.

"The dweebs are up. All of them. But, I didn't want to disturb you, so I told them they had to wait."

"You didn't want to disturb us so you turned on the lights and sang until we noticed you?" Sullivan asked dryly, and she grinned.

"I didn't want to disturb you, but I didn't want to deal with the dweebs, either."

"Are they in their rooms?" Rumer asked, imagining all the trouble unsupervised kids could get into.

"No, they're waiting in the mudroom, because Moisey wants to go for a walk."

"It isn't even dawn, yet," Sullivan muttered, his arms still around Rumer.

"You don't have to tell me that. She's the one who's all desperate and crying."

"I'm not crying," Moisey called from somewhere inside the house.

"You are, too!" Heavenly yelled back.

"She thinks starlight can straighten hair, and she wants her hair to be like mine," she continued more quietly. "I told her I'd trade her. I love her curls."

"I love you!" Moisey shouted, and then the horde spilled out of the house, four pint-sized bodies running down the back stairs and into the yard.

"I told them not to come out," Twila gasped as she carted Oya across the yard. "But, no one would listen to me."

"Because you're an old fuddy-duddy," Maddox said, but then he took her hand as they continued across the yard, and the light from the house spilled out onto blond heads and dark ones, curly hair and straight, smiles and scowls and chubby cheeks, and Rumer knew she'd never seen anything as beautiful as that wild, crazy bunch.

"Guess that's it. Our moonlit dance is over," Sullivan muttered.

"The moon set before I came out here."

"Then, I guess we'll have to try again another night. We might have to try for that silence thing, too, because I don't think I'm going to get much of that anytime soon," Sullivan responded, his breath tickling her temple, his hands still warm on her waist.

"If you can't beat them, join them. That's what Lu

always says. Or, make them join you. How about we
take that walk in the field? They can burn off some
energy," she suggested.

"And, we can hold hands and watch the sun rise
while they run around like little lunatics exhausting
themselves before the day has even begun? Sounds like
the perfect recipe for some of the silent moments I was
talking about."

"Exactly," she said, and he smiled.

"Great minds."

"You know, Sullivan," she replied, leaning in to kiss
him again. Because he was there and she was, and these
moments were the things all her dreams were made of.
"I think we're getting pretty good at this co-parenting
thing."

He laughed and took her hand, calling for the kids.

"Yes!" Moisey squealed when she heard they were
going for a walk. "The stars are even still out!"

"Are they?" Sullivan frowned, stripping off his jacket
and tossing it around her shoulders.

"I'm not cold, Sully," she claimed as he pulled the
hood over her hair.

"I don't care about the cold. I care about those darn
stars shining on your beautiful hair." He touched one
of the curls that had escaped the hood, tucking it beneath the fabric.

"What do you mean?" Moisey asked, scowling up
at him.

"You said the stars will straighten your curls."

"They will. Just like the moon woke Mom up."

"I like your hair, Moisey, the same way I like you—
just the way it is."

"Really?"

"Yep. That's why I want you to keep it covered. I

mean, if you *really* want straight hair, that's fine, but I think you need to know that every time I see your curls, I smile."

"You must not see them very much, because you almost never smile," Maddox said, and Heavenly snickered.

"I also always want to sketch them, because they remind me of how fun and happy you are," Sullivan continued, ignoring the other kids, his focus on Moisey.

"Did you sketch my curls? Did you sketch *me*?"

"Yep. A dozen times. One day, I'm going to hang the pictures in my office at school."

"Can I see them when you do?"

"Sure," he said.

"At the college?"

"Yep."

"For real? Or are you just saying that so I'll go away?"

"Moisey Bethlehem Bradshaw, enough," he said with a sigh that reminded Rumer of the day they'd met, of his tired eyes and his frilly apron and the way he'd struggled to connect with the kids.

They'd all been strangers then. Now, they were family.

"Wow," she said as Moisey skipped away. "You really are getting the hang of this parenting thing, Sullivan."

"*We* are," he corrected.

And, she smiled, holding his hand as they walked across the yard together, the kids squealing and chattering behind them as the new day dawned, bright and sweet and beautiful.

Connect with U s

Visit us online at
KensingtonBooks.com
to read more from your favorite authors, see books
by series, view reading group guides, and more.

Join us on social media

for sneak peeks, chances to win books and prize packs,
and to share your thoughts with other readers.

facebook.com/kensingtonpublishing
twitter.com/kensingtonbooks

Tell us what you think!

To share your thoughts, submit a review,
or sign up for our eNewsletters, please visit:
KensingtonBooks.com/TellUs.